ALSO BY ARLENE HUNT

For Antonia, *para siempre*.

Jessie Conway fanned herself ineffectually with her hand and wished for the umpteenth time the relentless heat would let up a little. She was thirty-eight years old, tall but evenly proportioned, with shoulder-length hair, the shade of which was the envy of every bottle-redheaded woman in Rockville.

'Miss Conway?'

'What can I do for you, Riley?'

'It's really hot. I'm really hot. It's really hot today.'

'Would you like me to open the window, Riley?'

He nodded.

'Use your words please.'

'Open the window.'

'What else should you say?'

Riley scrunched his face, thinking. Jessie waited while he figured it out. Riley was fourteen and one of the smarter pupils in her class. Certainly he had the potential to live some kind of productive life when he left school behind. Manners were crucial in this. Jessie hoped the universe treated him a little better in the future than it had thus far.

'*Please?*'

'Very good, Riley.'

Jessie rose from her desk, crossed the room and grappled with the sash window. Despite being pretty strong, she could barely raise it an inch. This section of Rockville High was old and in need of care and attention. Something it rarely received.

'That child is never happy unless he's complaining about something,' Tracy Flowers, her teaching assistant muttered, sliding in beside Jessie to help wrestle the window.

'He's right though, it is hot.'

'Don't see how this will help; it's as hot out there as it is in here.'

Tracy was twenty-four years old. She had joined Rockville High the September previous and was without doubt the best teaching assistant Jessie had ever worked with. She liked to grumble, but she was tough, kind and most importantly, she was scrupulously fair with the children. That day she wore a yellow sundress the colour of buttercups. Jessie thought it looked very pretty and would have liked to have said so, but Tracy did not take a compliment well and she did not enjoy people drawing attention to her.

Between them, they managed to force the window up about a foot. Jessie leaned her hands on the ledge, savouring the slight breeze and the comforting drone of a lawnmower somewhere in the distance. It truly was a beautiful June day.

Only one more week until the holidays, she thought, smiling. She wondered if Mike, her husband, had called the broker on the rental cabin like he had said he would that morning. Knowing Mike, he had most likely forgotten. She decided she'd call him during recess to remind him.

As she turned back towards the class, Jessie caught a glimpse of a dark green Toyota cruising slowly along the ring road that encircled the campus. The windows were tinted and closed tight. Air conditioning, Jessie thought, something else the school board claimed they could not afford to repair. The car slowed, turned into the main car park normally reserved for staff and disappeared from view.

Jessie moved away from the window and went to help a sweet-natured girl named Martha Fisk affix glue to the card she working on. Martha's tongue jutted out to the side as she concentrated on her task. There was glitter just about everywhere.

'This is very pretty, Martha.'

'Uh-huh.'

'Who are you making this for, your Mom?'

Martha shook her head.

'Your sister?'

She nodded.

'Well it's very–'

'Uh-oh.'

Jessie leaned over the child's shoulder. Martha had glued six tinfoil stars to her card and one to the desk.

'Uh-oh. *Uh-oh.*'

'That's okay Martha. We can peel it off. It's okay. Look.' Jessie lifted the star and wiped the tiny smudge of glue with her thumb. 'See, all gone.'

Martha offered Jessie a painful, pathetic grin. Her gratitude broke Jessie's heart. Martha was missing her front teeth. No one had ever received a satisfactory answer from her about what had happened to them, only that they had been gone a long time and she didn't like talking about it. Questions put to Martha's mother, the only time she had bothered to show up to a parent teacher meeting, had been met with a bored shrug. 'Probably she banged 'em. You see how she is, that damn kid's always fallin' and floppin' all over the place.'

'Miss Conway?'

'What can I help you with, Austin?'

'I need to go pee, Miss Conway.'

Jessie pointed to the big plastic clock hanging behind her desk.

'See the big hand, Austin? Remember we talked about this? When that big hand reaches the number six you can go.'

'I need to go *real* bad, Miss Conway.'

'Tracy, would you show Austin to the bathroom?'

'Sure. Come on, Austin.'

'I don't want her to go,' Austin said, shrinking back from Tracy. 'I don't want *her*.'

Tracy's expression remained neutral; she was used to this reaction, but Jessie felt a flash of anger and shame. Austin's father disliked and mistrusted 'coloureds' and was more than happy to say so to anyone who might listen. He spent much of his limited time outside prison terrifying his youngest son with stories about what the 'coloureds' might like to do with soft, small-boned boys like Austin, should they get the chance.

'Austin,' Jessie said, 'remember we spoke about this? You do not shout in class – if you shout in class you will lose your yard privileges.'

'I *heard* you.'

'Do you still want to go to the bathroom?'

Austin looked at her sulkily and shook his head. He bent to his work, pink with temper and Tracy went on about her business, stoical.

Jessie glanced at the clock again. She would be glad when this day was over. On paper, Jessie's pupils were described as 'marginalised', which was nothing more than politically correct claptrap for 'extremely messed up'. Most of the children in Jessie's class were the product of appalling neglect, both mental and physical, and abuse, also both mental and physical. They were the children of alcoholics and drug-addicted parents, of parents who spent half their lives in jail, the rest of the time trying to spend their welfare on booze, weed and crystal meth. That was if they even *had* parents to speak of. Many of Jessie's pupils were being reared by their grandparents; sad, tired, ill-equipped people whose hearts were in the right place, even if they did not have the wherewithal to help their grandchildren in ways other than feed and house them.

Jessie lifted a pop-up picture book from under a desk and slotted it into what they romantically called 'the library', though it was little more than two shelves of tattered books bought and paid for by fundraisers and raffles. The bell finally rang. Her pupils collected their belongings and hustled their way to the door. Some said goodbye; most did not.

'What a day,' Tracy said, when the last child left. 'I swear, I don't think I can face another week of this.'

'Nobody ever said Special Ed. was easy,' Jessie said, tying her dark red hair into a ponytail.

'No, I guess they didn't.'

Jessie rested her hand on Tracy's shoulder. 'You're doing great.'

Tracy offered her a wry smile that said she thought differently. 'I'm going to go get some strong coffee. You coming?'

'Be with you in a few minutes. Save me a dessert if there is any. I think I heard talk of key lime pie earlier.'

'Aw man, how can you eat that stuff and never put on a single pound! I even look at pie and my hips expand.'

'It's a secret; if I told you I'd have to kill you.'

Tracy laughed and left.

Jessie wiped the board clean and began to write up the assignments for the following class. When she finished, she picked up her handbag and was about to exit the class when she heard popping sounds. They were loud and they were close.

Jessie opened the door and stepped out. Children milled about the hall, a number of them looked curious.

'What's going on?' Jessie asked a heavily built boy she recognised from year eight.

'Dunno.'

The freckle-faced girl with him looked scared. 'Sounds to me like gunfire.'

'Nah, no way,' the boy said. 'Probably a cherry bomb or some shit.'

Then the fire alarm came on, filling the halls with deafening wails.

'Okay, okay,' Jessie clapped her hands to get attention. 'You know the drill, everybody make their way outside to the basketball courts. No running, no shoving please. Nice and easy now. Use the nearest exit please.'

Jessie pushed her way through the children and followed the corridor until she reached the main foyer. Rockville High was a single-storey building, built around this double height space, off which ran four 'wings'. To Jessie's immediate left was the staff room and to her right the cafeteria. Children spilled into the space from three separate hallways. Some of them laughed and hooted; others seemed more anxious. There were a number of students by the lockers opposite the cafeteria doors, changing books and emptying contents into backpacks as though the alarms were not going off at all.

Jessie caught sight of Adam Edwards, the Vice-Principal, striding to the foyer from the B wing. He was trying to get people to make their way to the A wing, pleading with them to remain calm and to move quickly but without running. Jessie was puzzled as to why he was not shepherding them towards the main doors. She turned her head and saw that there was a chain strung through both doors, with a heavy padlock hanging from it. She immediately made her way towards the Vice-Principal.

'What's going on?'

'I don't know. I was in the science lab. Someone said there was shooting. When I got down here the front doors were chained.' He leaned in closer and whispered, 'So is the fire exit by the bike shed.'

'Do you think this is real?'

'I don't know.'

'Are all the doors locked?'

'I don't know. Principal Carmichael is checking the C wing. I think we should get everyone outside.'

'What can I do?'

'You can help me get everyone outside and accounted for.'

She could see he was struggling to keep his voice calm. This alarmed her. Edwards was a tall man, good-natured but serious at the best of times and not one for panicking. More children were streaming in to the foyer. Jessie noticed the group she had spoken to outside her classroom.

'I thought I told you to go outside,' she said to the girl with the freckles.

'The doors are locked. Someone locked them with a chain.'

Edwards raised his hands over his head.

'Everyone, listen to me now. Stop pushing and slow down. Make your way to the rear emergency exit in a calm and orderly fashion. Come on now. I want everybody to move outside please. Everyone make their way to the basketball courts, nice and slowly. Miss Conway, can you make sure the cafeteria is empty?'

'Sure.' Jessie began to walk towards the cafeteria, but as she did, one of the swing doors opened and a tall youth she recognised as Kyle Saunders stepped out. He carried a semi-automatic weapon dangling from a long strap across his chest. Adam Edwards saw him; his eyes widened in surprise. He reacted fast. He grabbed the nearest child to him and shoved her towards a hallway.

'Go.'

Kyle Saunders raised the gun. His face was shiny and his lips were peeled back over his teeth. His eyes roamed over the teeming foyer.

'Hey maggots! Yo! Maggots, remember me?'

'Kyle–' Edwards put out his hands out before him, chest height. 'Put the gun down, Kyle. Put it down now, we can talk about this.'

Kyle's stared at Edwards for a moment, smiling a weird smile. Jessie could see some doubt come into Edwards' eyes.

'Kyle, listen to me now–'

Kyle opened fire.

The first spray of bullets took out the glass bricks that ran the length of the wall above the lockers. Children ran screaming in every direction. Some fell and were trampled; others flattened themselves against walls, covering their heads with their hands as though this might save them. One or two stood and stared, rooted to the spot in disbelief.

The second burst of gunfire was lower. A piercing scream was cut short. A round hit Edwards directly in the chest, spinning him where he stood. He took a step and dropped to the floor.

Jessie stared at Alan Edwards' body, her face frozen, unable to comprehend what had happened.

'*Alan.*'

She took a step forward but blood was beginning to pool under him and his fingers were scrabbling for purchase on the tiled floor. Behind him, another boy lay twisted and broken, his backpack still on his shoulder.

Kyle Saunders threw back his head and whooped. He was still howling when Jessie Conway slammed into him at speed. The force of the impact sent Kyle crashing through the swing doors of the cafeteria, with Jessie practically on top of him. They smashed into a table, toppled over it and hit the ground hard.

Jessie recovered first. She slammed her knees into Kyle's stomach and ripped the strap over his head. Before he knew what had happened, she grabbed for the gun. She felt the heat of the muzzle blister the skin on her fingers, smelled cordite and sweat from Kyle's body. She threw all her weight backwards, bracing hard against his gut, screaming as she leaned away.

Kyle was too strong and managed to reclaim his grip on the gun. He wrenched it free and snapped the stock up towards the side of Jessie's head. He clouted her with it, but she twisted her body to one side just before he could land a full force blow. Kyle scrambled to get his feet under him. Jessie rose first; she shouldered him and forced her body between him and the gun. Spittle sprayed the side of Jessie's face as Kyle tried to ram the gun up under her chin. She held on doggedly, keeping the weapon as close to her body as she could, the muzzle pointed up and away from her.

They tussled back and forth. Kyle loosened one hand and punched her in the back, above her kidney. In desperation, Jessie stamped down on Kyle's foot and tried to get her shoulder into his chest and force his grip to break over her shoulder.

Nothing worked.

She kicked and kicked, aiming her heel for any spot she could reach. She landed a bone-crunching snap to his shin but Kyle punched her again, and this time it hurt, bad. Jessie's grip began to fail. She tried one last desperate swing. As she twisted, she saw another boy standing up on a table at the far side of the cafeteria near the drinks machine. He was slender and young, with a thin wispy moustache he had not yet grown into. He was dressed head to toe in black. All these things Jessie registered in the blink of an eye. There was one more detail.

He had a shotgun trained on them.

'Shoot her!' Kyle Saunders screamed. 'Shoot the fucking bitch!'

There was a deafening blast. Jessie felt pain along the left side of her face seconds before she collapsed under Kyle Saunders' full weight.

The gun was now in her hands and she blindly raised it and fired towards where she thought the other boy might be. Through the smoke, she saw him fall backwards off the table and drop out of sight.

Jessie lay still, dazed. Kyle Saunders' lower body was twisted across her hips. She turned her head and saw that he was dead. There was nothing left of his head but a mass of bloody scalp and glistening bone fragments. Jessie's ears fizzed and rang. She lowered the gun to the floor, crawled out from under Kyle and sat up. Blood spilled onto her chest and lap. She blinked at it uncomprehendingly. By the time she got to her feet and staggered across the floor her shirt was saturated. She fell down and landed close to two terrified girls huddled beneath an overturned table. She recognised their faces but could not remember their names.

'Get out of here.'

The girls cringed against each other. One of them mouthed something but Jessie could not decipher the words.

'*Go.*'

They fled.

Jessie crawled across the floor to where the boy had fallen.

He lay on his back, panting. The shotgun was off to his right, out of range. One arm rested across his chest; by his side curled the other. The front of his shirt was slick with blood. His eyes were open and as she moved closer they clicked around to her.

'Oh,' Jessie whispered when she saw the damage she had inflicted.

He smiled, in reality a terrible grimace. A bubble of frothy blood appeared at the corner of his mouth, popped, and was replaced by another. Jessie leaned all her weight on her right hand and took his left with hers.

'Why did you do this?'

But he did not answer and after a moment his eyes lost their focus, his chest stopped moving and he was gone.

Jessie stared at him. She tried to stay upright, but could not summon the strength. She sank to the floor beside the dead boy and wiped the blood from her eyes. She saw Tracy Flowers lying by the drinks machine. She had lost a shoe and the back of her sunny yellow dress was drenched in blood.

Jessie wanted to go to her but could not. She vomited, closed her eyes and finally darkness took her.

His given name was Caleb Switch, although it had been so long since he had used it he scarcely thought of himself as such.

Caleb unpacked his few things and laid them out carefully on the table. He opened a plastic box and from it ate a light protein-rich meal he had prepared the night before at the apartment. While he waited for his food to digest, he flicked through the latest magazine on traditional hunting, scoffing at the wilder stories printed within. The magazine was a luxury. It was delivered to his apartment in the city once a month. The name on the mailing list was Arthur Weils. The same name was on the deeds of the apartment and all the utility bills. Arthur Weils was who he was now, Arthur Samuel Weils. His friends might call him Art, had he had any friends of whom to speak.

The real Arthur S. Weils was buried in the scrub behind the cabin in which Caleb was seated, free at last from the self-loathing and disgust he had passively endured during his miserable thirty-six years on the planet. Whenever Caleb thought of the real Arthur Weils – which was seldom – he reasoned he had done the man a favour. Certainly, Arthur had not put up much of a struggle once Caleb's intention became clear. Caleb had not expected him to do so; Category B types did not have the will to survive. They were beta, weak, content to wander through life following the herd blindly, stoically accepting of their fates. Hell, they were hardly much more than meat shells. But they had their uses, and indeed Art had provided.

When he was finished reading, Caleb removed his clothing and stood naked before a full-length mirror. He studied his reflection in the speckled glass. He was twenty-eight years old. He wore his dark hair just so, not too short or too long. He had a beard, closely cropped against his skin. People said it looked distinguished. Conveniently, it disguised a large scar that ran from the left side of his lip to below his jaw line, one of many childhood presents he had received from his old man. He was six foot two inches tall and at one hundred and ninety pounds was lean and muscular, preferring to eschew showy gym muscles for actual physical strength. He carried no traces of excess fat and shared none of the softness many men his age carried. People who did not look after themselves disgusted him. Soft, doughy, pasty-faced men, with their paunches and sagging tits, women with swollen bellies and thunderous thighs, all were repugnant. His body would never be like that. He would not allow it. His body was a machine, a tool. To that end he maintained it perfectly.

He warmed up slowly, taking time to stretch his hamstrings and loosen his calf muscles with a series of timed stretches and twists. As he moved he felt the blood course through his body and savoured the tension in his limbs.

Once warm, he belted a weight around his waist, grabbed the chin-up bar he had built into the ceiling and executed a set of twenty perfect fully extended chin-ups. He dropped to the ground, undid the weight and performed the same number of push-ups. The muscles in his back rippled, the veins popped in his biceps. He repeated the combination three more times.

He finished the final set and stood before the mirror again. He scrutinised his body for a full minute, searching for flaws. He found none.

He walked, naked, to a metal shelf fastened to the opposite wall by brackets. He had built the workbench himself and it was meticulously organised. Every tool had its place; every surface was clean and free of dirt. On it sat a heavy-duty canvas bag and beside that a slim metal case.

Caleb pulled out a stool and sat down. He unzipped the bag and removed from it a custom-made take-down longbow. He assembled it with practised ease, snapped the rubber hand guard over the hinge and restrung it in one fluid motion. He waxed the strings and ran his thumb over the cedar limbs, checking for nicks or scratches. The bow was a thing of rare beauty. He had purchased it over a decade before from a master craftsman who lived in Marshall, North Carolina. It weighed less than two pounds, had a twenty-eight-inch draw and was as silent as the grave. His accuracy with it was beyond question. Any fool could fire a gun or a crossbow from a distance, and these days most any fool surely did, but only the true hunter could place himself within the perfect strike zone using a stick bow.

Satisfied, he removed an arrow from the quiver. The arrows were a speciality of his and he made dozens of them every year. They were made from light wooden shafts finished with both eagle and buzzard fletching. The fletching was wrapped with muskrat sinew. The tip of each shaft held a single broadhead arrow with a four ridges. He made the arrowheads from obsidian, using a knapping design his old man had taught him. Each arrowhead was then heated, allowed to cool, and honed so fine they could slice through dense rubber like it was butter. Caleb held one up to the light. He looked down the line, visualising it as it left his bow. It would fly straight and true, of that he had no doubt.

As well as his bow, he carried an old army knife that had once belonged to his grandfather, and a 30/30 Winchester rifle with open sights he had inherited from his father. The rifle was an annoyance.

Although this particular model was relatively light to carry, it did slow him down some. He had never needed to use it, but experience had taught him to be prepared for the unexpected.

He put the rifle down and unwrapped the knife. The handle was cherry wood. There had once been a pattern on it – he vaguely remembered it – but it had long been worn smooth. He thumbed the blade and a bead of blood rose immediately to the surface of his skin.

Caleb rewrapped the knife and walked to the gas-powered shower to the rear of the cabin. He turned on the water and when it was almost too hot to bear, he stepped under it and washed using a special soap. He removed all traces of sweat from his body, lathered again and rinsed a second time. Scent carried on the air and it was easy to reveal a position that way. He finished off with an ice-cold blast to close his pores and then shut off the water. He stepped out of the shower and returned to the main room of the cabin, allowing the air to dry his skin.

He studied the map pinned against the wall opposite the workbench, running through a mental checklist of the terrain, memorising the route. There were natural predators in the woods, bears and coyotes both. The bears round his way were skittish and more interested in feeding and staying as far as possible from humankind. The males tended to bluster, but a sow with cubs would charge without hesitation and it did not do to forget that.

He tapped the map with his index finger. The area he hunted lay deep in the woods that straddled North Carolina and Tennessee. His cabin was situated in a remote and unpopulated valley, many miles from popular hiking trails and camps. There had been a small town in his valley many years before but it had long been abandoned to nature. And nature had reclaimed it.

When he was dry, Caleb unlocked a metal trunk and lifted out the individual zip-locked bags which contained his hunting clothes. After a hunt, each item was carefully washed, dried and sealed in the plastic with a number of leaves and fresh pine cones. Hunter magazines spoke of high-tech carbon suits that could reduce scent and the like, but his way was the old way and it did not fail him.

Caleb dressed quickly and smeared dark green non-reflective grease across the paleness of his cheeks and the back of his hands. He covered his head with a freshly washed black cap. It never ceased to amaze him how many hunters took care over scented clothes but wore the same cap day in, day out, forgetting how rancid a sweat-soaked brim became.

He strapped the knife to his left thigh and carried the rifle, quiver and bow out to the truck. He laid them on the floor behind the driver's seat and covered them with tarp. A flurry of excitement ran through him. This was the best part of the hunt. All the work, all the painstaking preparation led towards the coming hour. He leaned against the truck and tilted his face to the cloudless dawn sky above and thought himself a fortunate man.

Caleb drove off his property and turned right onto a small dirt road so little used that grass grew almost knee high down the centre line. Caleb drove with the lights dimmed, though he did not meet a single vehicle, nor did he expect to. This deep into the valleys there was hardly a soul to be found. He drove on for a number of miles, climbing steadily as he did so. He crossed an old wooden bridge, barely wide enough for his truck, and after another half mile turned into a rutted track leading up the side of the mountain. He dropped down into second gear, then into first, as he progressed higher and higher. In some sections the trees and bushes on either side were so overgrown the track was hardly passable.

It was another twenty-five minutes before the pathway flattened out and he bounced over a rutted culvert into a small clearing. He backed the truck between rocks and switched off the engine.

The clearing was almost two thirds of the way to the summit of a mountain known to him as The Devil's Ridge and the last place he could safely drive. He sat for a few moments, staring across the expanse of trees, listening to the engine tick as it cooled. He watched the first traces of light illuminate the highest limbs. He became aware of his breathing, felt his chest rise and fall, slow and regular.

He was ready.

He stepped from the Jeep, walked to the rear and vaulted onto the bed in one smooth movement. He hoisted the spare wheel up and opened the door to a hatch he had built in under the flatbed.

Within the confined space lay a bound and gagged girl. She wore sprayed-on jeans and a dark red leather jacket. Her hair was dyed a harsh, flat peroxide blonde, with a couple of inches of roots visible.

She screamed behind her gag as he dragged her out. The sound irritated him.

'Quit it. No one can hear you out here anyways.'

He threw her over the side of the truck where she fell to the ground with all the grace of a sack of grain. He jumped down, hauled her to her feet and removed the gag. Immediately she started babbling at him.

'Please … oh please mister … please don't hurt me. Please, I won't tell no one about you, I swear mister, I won't say–'

He pulled the knife free from its sheath and pressed it against her cheek.

'I said quit making noise.'

She shook violently but quietened. He traced the knife down her skin and sliced through the binds on her wrists. He pointed across the clearing with the blade.

'D'you hear the bridge a while back?'

She blinked at him and licked her lips a number of times.

'Well, did you or not?'

She nodded.

'Yonder through those trees is a path of sorts. If you can find it you can follow it along 'til you reach a creek. Follow that, you might make it back to the bridge. You make it that far you might make it further and hit on a road.'

She blinked, turned her head towards the trees, then back to him, disbelieving. Her throat glowed white in the gathering light.

'Mister?'

'I'm giving you a head start of five minutes. I suggest you make the most of it.'

She shrank back against the truck. 'You'll hurt me if I run.'

'I'll hurt you if you don't.'

'I don't want to die. Please mister, I don't want to die.'

'Then you best get moving.'

She hesitated. He waited. They always hesitated.

She looked this way and that, sizing up the situation, such as it was. He wondered what she thought was going to happen? Did she think it would be like the movies? The good guys would land in a helicopter and whisk her to safety? How come they never got it until the last second?

Finally she moved off, walking first, keeping one eye on him. Caleb stood perfectly still. At ten feet she began to run awkwardly over the rocky ground. She had not gone forty feet when she tripped and fell over. He watched her pick herself up and stumble on again.

Category B, he thought, no doubt about it.

When she finally reached the trees at the other side of the clearing, Caleb turned his face to the rising sun and counted down the minutes. This was why he rarely bothered hunting street trash. They had no real fight in them, no gumption. No will to survive.

When the correct time had elapsed, he fetched the rifle and the bow from behind his seat and set off after the girl.

It was time to hunt.

Darla Levine was prodding a broccoli and grated carrot salad with complete disinterest when the cell phone set on the dash of the Escalade trilled to life. She checked the number and groaned. It was the boss of the local 'schutzhund' association returning her call to arrange a photo shoot and short interview for the weekend edition of *The Rockville Gazette*, the local newspaper for which Darla worked.

Darla let the phone ring. She was supposed to be a busy reporter and busy reporters didn't hover over their phones praying for a story to come to them.

'You gonna answer that?' Chippy Gomez reached for it with his grease-smeared hands.

'Don't touch that!' Darla slapped his hand away and snatched up the phone.

'Ow.'

'What did I tell you about the phone?'

'Let it ring.'

'And?'

'Don't touch it.'

'Right.'

Chippy shook his hand and returned to his burger. The ringing stopped.

'Shit,' Darla said, staring at the message indicating a missed call.

'You shoulda answered.'

'Why don't you mind your–'

The phone began to ring again, this time Darla didn't wait.

'Darla Levine.'

'This is Andrea Wilson.'

'Mrs Wilson, great to hear from you!' Darla sang in her professional phone voice.

They exchanged pleasantries and got down to business. Darla forced herself to at least sound interested in what she hearing, but it was hard work. Darla considered dumb men training dumb dogs as weapons to be spectacularly stupid, but her boss liked mutts and – inexplicably – schutzhund was becoming a popular pastime in Rockville. On any given Saturday, a person could find groups of grown men standing in fields, beating their padded arms, shrieking and threatening each other with sticks while German shepherds, Rottweilers and Belgian Malinois strangled themselves into a foaming frenzy until their release, upon which they would sprint across the open ground and launch themselves at their padded assailant. If the dog took a man down the spectators whooped and hollered and clinked their beers together. Man's best friend, the greatest penis extension ever invented, Darla thought sourly as she hung up.

'That the dog woman?' Chippy asked around his burger. Darla tried not to look at the congealed mass in his mouth. She tolerated Chippy's brain-dead conversations, his casual attitude to work, his rudeness and his inability to use deodorant, but she hated that he talked with his mouth full and had lost count of the number of times she had told him to stop doing so. Had she her way, she would have opened the Escalade and booted him out there and then. Unfortunately, her boss,

Popeye, paid Chippy cheaply and off the books, and he could at least operate a camera.

'Yes.'

'She say when we need to go see her?'

'Tomorrow at noon.'

Chippy looked worried.

'What?'

'I don't like dogs. Especially those big ones.'

'Too bad, it's a two-page spread in the supplement. We need the photos of them in action.'

'Those dogs, man, I seen them. They're real mean.'

'They're *supposed* to be mean. They're attack dogs.'

'Shit man, what if they attack us?'

'Then we'll have a different slant on the story.' Darla shot him a sneaky glance. 'But seriously, if I were you Chippy I'd wear good running shoes.'

'*Me?*'

'Sure, I like dogs, so I'm okay, but you … they can smell fear you know. Smell it like a shark smells blood in the water.'

'Oh Jesus, really?'

'Trained for it. You'll be like a big piñata to them.'

Chippy grew pale under his tan. Darla glanced out the window and thought about how much she really hated her life.

She had worked at *The Gazette* for four years. Four years of covering stupid drunks who crashed their cars into trees on payday, stupid cats trapped behind walls and stupid hick families who swore they saw '*something*' in the wood while camping. But this, this stupid *dog* crap, seemed like a new low.

It was a joke assignment; she had become a joke.

Darla sighed. It hadn't started out like this. True, her father, Ted Levine, had been the one to get her through the door at *The Gazette*, but nepotism did not prevent her from working hard. It was just that nothing really ever happened in Rockville. Hell, even Denton, the next city over, had a decent football team whose players were constantly in the news for various stupid but entertaining pranks, and provided not one but two politicians caught with their pants down in bathrooms, swearing blind they had no idea foot tapping could be so suggestive, while their wives stood, stone faced, behind them.

'Hey, ain't that the guy?' Chippy said.

'That's him.'

Darla watched Sam Villiers stroll down the street. His massive gut was cinched tight beneath a pink and green checked shirt, which was tucked into gaudy mint-green pants that would not have looked out of place on a '70s pop singer, assuming the pop singer was a small obese auctioneer with a brand spanking new addition to his police record which he hoped and prayed no one knew about.

'Let's try to get a shot of him with the bank in the background,' Darla said. She grabbed her recorder and fluffed her hair in the rear-view mirror.

'Aw, look, he's turned around.'

They watched Villiers pat his pockets and do an about turn.

'Musta forgot something.'

'You don't say.'

'Prob'ly his wallet.'

'Mm.'

'Funny how he always eats in the same place.'

'What's funny about it?'

'How come he don't get bored, man?'

'How come you don't get bored asking stupid, unanswerable questions?'

'Me, I get bored eating the same shit. Gotta change it up.'

'You've eaten tacos and burgers every single day we worked together.'

'Different shit in 'em though, it ain't the same if the shit's different.'

The phone rang again. Darla offered a silent thank you to whatever saint it was that covered mindless conversations.

'Darla Levine!'

'Where are you?'

It was Pip Lowe from the newsroom.

'Opposite Bunny's on Chadwell Street.'

'We're getting calls about an incident at Rockville High. Something's going on over there right now.'

'What kind of incident?'

'I don't rightly know. But it's big enough that the Sheriff has despatched two cars. They're en route.'

Darla sat up a little bit straighter. 'That all you got, Pip?'

'Hold on.'

Darla heard muffled sounds in the background before Pip came back on line. 'We're getting news that one of the kids might have been shot. But I don't have confirmation on that.'

'I'm on it.' Darla hung up. 'We need to get to Rockville High *now*.'

'What's up?'

'Shooting.'

Chippy gunned the engine while Darla dialled from memory the number of Vonda Kelp, a money-hungry shrew who had been 'temping' at the Sheriff's department for as long as Darla could remember.

'Vonda, it's Darla. What going on?'

'Oh my gosh,' Vonda's voice dropped to whisper. 'We've had a ton of calls in the last few minutes. Someone is shooting over at Rockville High.'

'What do you know?'

'Nuthin' 'cept that shots have been reported.'

'Shots? More that one?'

'I can't say for certain. Sheriff Dubray's gone over there himself to see what the heck is going on.' Incredibly Vonda's voice dropped another octave. 'He looked real worried when he left here.'

'Anyone hurt?'

'I don't know,' Vonda said, 'but it sure can't be good if there's shooting though, can it?'

By the time his brother showed up for work, Mike Conway was sweating up a storm and in as foul a mood as it was possible for any man to be. Earlier that morning, he'd sliced his palm open removing the shattered windscreen from a Honda Accord. Now his hand was throbbing and he was behind his day's work by an uncatchable rate.

'Nice of you to bother making an appearance.'

'I'm here ain't I?'

Ace Conway ambled across the courtyard at a leisurely pace. He removed his cap and ran water from an outdoor hose over the back of his neck. He shook his head, straightened up and put his cap back on. He wore a thin cotton t-shirt under his overalls and work boots that had once been tan but were now the colour of sludge. Beneath the faded trucker cap, a piece of red leather tied his long hair in a low ponytail at the base of his neck. Prison tats defaced almost every inch of his scrawny arms.

'We open at seven. It's gone eleven.'

Ace stuck a cigarette between his lips and lit it with a match. Mike watched the flame and saw the tremble in his brother's hand. He figured Ace was hung over and probably had more than just alcohol in his system. This was nothing new. Ever since Jessie had insisted he take his brother on, Ace had rewarded her faith and Mike's loyalty by arriving to work late – if he showed at all – stinking of hooch and stale smoke, usually wearing the same clothes he'd left wearing the day before.

Mike tried to keep a lid on the bulk of his emotions. It did no good to nag his brother. Ace would do what Ace would do. Nagging made no real difference and only served to aggravate them both. His brother was a grown man and at forty-four was senior to Mike by five years.

'Whatcha do to yer hand?'

'Windscreen on the Accord split.'

Ace's pale eyes drifted towards the main building. 'Well, what's on the agenda for today, *Boss?*'

Mike bristled at the title. He knew Ace was rattling his chain. Hell, neither of them wanted this situation. A condition of Ace's parole was that he involve himself in gainful employment, and there wasn't any sucker left in Rockville that was going to give Ace Conway a job, except for blood.

'Going to strip out the engine on the Datsun. Can you finish this off while I make a few calls?'

Ace shrugged, managing to look more tired and disinterested by the second. Mike took that as a yes and went inside to the back office, happy to be out of the sun and away from a man he had once idolised with ever fibre of his being.

Later they worked on the Datsun. Ace passed his brother whatever tool he needed, whistling tunelessly between his teeth.

'Wrench.'

Ace slapped the wrench into this hand and took up whistling again. Mike attached and leaned his weight onto his wrench. He tightened the bolt briefly before changing direction. The bolt gave. He did another, then another, passing each one back to Ace until he was done. When he had removed them all, Mike straightened and rubbed the small of his back with his hand. Lately he noticed he'd been getting a lot more twinges and aches. It bothered him, made him feel a little bit old and a little more mortal.

'You okay?' Ace asked.

'It's nothing.'

'Got something in the truck for pain, you need it.'

'No thank you.'

'Suit yourself.'

'We're gonna need the winch.'

'It's ready already.'

'Got the reconditioned–'

'Set up, all it's doin' is waitin' on you,' Ace said, pausing to spit to one side, a habit Mike detested.

The exterior phone bells jangled. Mike took the bolts from his brother and dropped them into the top pocket of his overalls. The bell rang on. He squinted towards the window of the wooden porch that served as their front office. From where he stood he could see through to the counter. Emma, the surly receptionist he had hired three months before as a favour to his mother, was nowhere to be seen.

'Where's she got to now?

The bell stopped and then began again almost immediately.

'Can you get that, Ace?'

Ace strolled inside without a hint of hurry to his heels. Mike pulled a bandana from his left pocket and wiped his hands. It was swelteringly hot and the sky overhead was cloudless and so deeply blue that it looked strangely unnatural. He removed his baseball cap and dabbed the sweat from his brow as he glanced at his watch. Just after one. He wished it that was closer to quitting time. He could really use a cold one or two.

Mike returned his attention to the busted engine. He heard the screen door slap open.

'Mike! You need to come in here.'

'What is it?'

'Trouble.'

Mike dropped what he was doing and hurried across the yard. As soon as he stepped inside Ace thrust the remote control for the customer television into his hand.

'What's going on? Where's Emma?'

'She took off out.' Ace jerked his jaw towards the street. 'Saw her car kicking up dirt out front. That was Lou-Ann Granger on the phone. She says she was at home getting lunch ready when she heard word there's been a shooting at the school. Says it's on the TV.'

Mike switched on the small, wall-mounted set and flicked to the local news station. He immediately recognised Rockville High, the school where Jessie worked. Standing before the main gates was Lucy Francis, a local reporter more famed for her public romances than her journalistic skills. Lucy gripped her microphone tightly; her voice was high with barely contained excitement.

'Sources tell us the shooters entered the building sometime after twelve and opened fire. Though there has been no official confirmation yet, a witness told this reporter that she recognised one of the shooters and believes him to be a pupil expelled from the school a month ago. Witnesses say many of the exits were barricaded, causing pupils to panic in the crush to get free. It is not known if the shooters have been apprehended, or if they have made any particular demands...'

'What the hell?' Mike stared at the screen in disbelief as the camera panned left and came to rest on a spotty youth wearing a Rockville Bears cap.

'Now obviously–' Lucy jammed the microphone under his wispy-haired chin, '–you cannot name the shooters, but did you personally recognise them?'

'Yeah, I like, know 'em to see.'

'Can you tell me if they are pupils here?'

'One of 'em is, for sure.'

'And the other?'

'Dunno,' the youth shrugged. 'I guess.'

The phone began to ring again.

Ace picked up and listened. 'Yep,' he said after a long silence, 'he knows, he's lookin' at it.'

Lucy Francis now faced the camera. 'A spokesman for the Sheriff's department has issued a brief statement saying a SWAT team is on its way, but that until then no one can enter the school as it is unclear if the shooters are still at the location or whether or not they may have bombs or other incendiary devices…'

Mike grabbed the keys for his truck from a rack behind the desk and raced out the door.

Caleb Switch was restless. It was late on Saturday evening and he was back in the apartment in Charlotte. He had arrived home in the afternoon and gone to bed for a nap. Sleep had eluded him and now he was trying to put his finger on why he was so unsettled.

The long drive back to the city had been slow and irritating. His shoulders felt tense and he had a faint headache behind his eyes. Caleb switched on the light in the bathroom, swallowed a painkiller and studied his reflection. Normally after a successful hunt he felt calm for weeks, subdued even. But this time was different, this time he felt no such release. He felt no sense of accomplishment.

The girl had been too easy. It was as simple as that. He should have known better than to run a Category B target. They were only useful for two things: money or a cover story. That was it.

He ran water over his hands and dried them on a pink frilly towel.

She hadn't even made it to the creek. He had scarcely believed it when he had discovered her hiding crouched behind a tree less than two miles from the release site. She was covered in scratches from where she had fallen and was sobbing loud enough to hear from thirty-five feet away.

Caleb shook his head. It had been like shooting fish in a barrel.

Certainly no great demands had been made on his skills. He hadn't even bothered to quench his urges with her before he despatched her.

Despondent, he switched off the light and went to the kitchen. Though he had little appetite, he made a grilled cheese sandwich and carried it through to the dining nook. He sat at the mahogany table, surrounded by photos of Arthur Weils and his deceased aunt, the original owner of the apartment, Maryanne Weils. There were still a few hours to kill before he walked the four blocks to the nondescript office building where twice a week he volunteered on the Voice of Hope switchboard.

Thinking of the evening ahead cheered him up some. The job was a goldmine and was his fourth such stint as an operator. Caleb had long discovered the rich seam of rubes and targets that help lines like the Voice of Hope church provided. True, there was no end to the sad sacks of shit who made self-pitying phone calls, seeking solace, seeking redemption, seeking to be heard and absolved. Throughout their tearful litanies they offered Caleb all manner of information about themselves. Information he took great care to sift though, searching the useless sands of their misery for the nuggets he desired. So far it had been most productive. He had found what he hoped was a perfect Category A target and was in the process of selection. The process could not be rushed. Slow and steady was the way. It was a matter of stalking the game, learning what makes it tick, its habitats, strengths and weakness. In this type of pursuit Caleb excelled.

The Voice of Hope church itself was a small Pentecostal church and the late Maryanne had been a member until she could no longer look after herself and the state had shipped her off into a wretched home where she had eventually died from boredom. Fortunately, long before she shuffled off the mortal coil, Maryanne had repeatedly told her church friends of her beloved nephew Art, who she claimed visited her often. So when 'Art' turned up in Charlotte to attend to his dead aunt's estate, Caleb suddenly found himself a shining star in a tiny community grateful for young bucks who could quote the bible chapter and verse (a gift from his mother this time). Caleb's background check had been minimal. Pastor T. Creedy claimed that, by default, a believer in Christ had to be a decent person. It had taken Caleb less than three weeks to wiggle his way into the inner sanctum and become a valued and trusted member of the congregation.

Landing on his feet was nothing new to Caleb. He did not believe in luck, he believed in the law of nature. Animals did not ascribe to luck. They lived and died by their instincts. They made split-second decisions based on the information they had before them.

The night Caleb had met Arthur Weils he had been sitting on a bar stool in a town called Hickory. Caleb had been minding his own business; bored mostly, bored and watchful. Arthur had already sunk a skinful before he arrived and plonked down beside Caleb. He was drunk and morose and in need of a friend. Caleb might have finished his beer and left, if only Arthur had kept his mouth shut. But Arthur Weils was full of gin and regret; he began to complain about the hand life had dealt him, swirling his gin clockwise and leaning towards Caleb with watery, red-rimmed eyes.

Within minutes, Caleb had decided Arthur was a perfectly useful Category B candidate, and from that instant, poor, dumb Arthur might as well have had a bullseye painted on his chest.

Caleb bought him a drink, listening as his new buddy sobbed and gibbered and spoke of being dumped by a woman, how he hated his job. He wept when he said his only remaining relative, a kindly aged aunt from Charlotte, had upped and died and he, Arthur, was returning there to pack up her home and join her in the great hereafter. The more Arthur rambled on about his grief, his wasted life, his fear of rejection, his lack of a sex life, his anger at the outside world and its rejection of him, the more Caleb's instincts kicked in.

When the time came to act it had been ridiculously easy. Arthur, so trusting of his new friend, had invited him back to his tiny apartment to partake of some drinks. Caleb offered to drive them.

That was the last anyone ever saw of the real Arthur Weils.

After that, it had simply been a matter of Caleb shedding his identity – or rather the identity he had been using – and adopting Arthur's. It helped enormously that Arthur was an unlikeable idiot and that his only living relation had conveniently died.

Free from restraints, Caleb made his way to Charlotte and began to avail of his new identity with impunity, starting with Arthur's inheritance and now mining the life of Aunt Maryanne for useful progression.

Caleb sat at the table in the dining nook and picked up his long bow. He unstrung it and checked it for signs of damage. He pulled out a tin of wax from a leather bag and began to smooth his strings. As he worked, he became dimly aware of the news running softly on the television in the living room. He reached for the remote and turned up the volume.

'America stunned as another high school shooting rips a community apart.'

Caleb watched the story unfold with little interest. He thought the anchorman fake and his tone risible. Then the red print speeding across the bottom of the screen attracted his attention.

'Jessie Conway, a remarkable hero who saved so many lives…'

Hero.

Caleb curled his lip. Hero was a junk word much bandied about by the media. Footballers were heroes when they scored a touchdown; fire-fighters doing their damned jobs were heroes; nurses were heroes, no wait … they were *angels*. Heroes: the word had been diluted down to nothing by lazy rhetoric.

A photo of a smiling redhead appeared on screen. Caleb leaned forwards, resting his elbows on his knees. She was pretty: shy smile, pale skin and wide, expressive eyes.

'Tonight Jessie Conway remains in hospital, although her condition is said to be no longer critical. Reports say the Special Education teacher and Coach was operated on earlier and is recovering well from her ordeal. Mrs Conway was injured during a struggle with one of the shooters during the Rockville High attack resulting in the deaths of three innocent people. Among the dead are Vice-Principal Alan Edwards and teaching assistant Tracy Flowers, as well as pupil, James Aldershot. A number of other pupils remain in hospital, though their injuries are not thought to be life threatening.'

The clip then changed to a roving reporter giving an overview of the shooting. Footage taken on the day in question popped up on screen. Caleb watched a grainy video of Jessie Conway being wheeled out of the school on a stretcher, surrounded by SWAT officers.

Caleb turned back to his weapons. Hero. People didn't even know the meaning of the word. He glanced at the screen once more. They were now talking to another woman, a larger lady a caption identified as Principal Carmichael. Caleb switched off the television and returned to his work.

Jessie opened her eyes and blinked at the brightness of the overhead lights. She was thirsty and her mouth felt dry and sticky. Her head hurt; she raised her hand to it and felt bandages under her fingers.

'How are you feeling?'

Jessie turned her head slightly. Fay Conway, Mike's mother, sat by the side of the bed on a plastic chair. Fay was a sprightly, rather glamorous sixty-four year old. She had ash-blonde hair cut in a chic bob, lived in pastel linen pantsuits and wore glasses about her neck on a fine gold chain. Jessie could not recall a time she had ever seen her mother-in-law without make-up.

'Would you like me call the Doctor?' Fay rose from the chair and reached for a red button.

'No. No, thank you.'

Jessie closed her eyes again. She was in pain and confused. She tried to remember where she was. She had no recollection of being moved into the room in which she found herself. She tried to focus, but could only picture a yellow sundress. She saw the red stain spreading across it. She saw Tracy Flowers lying on her side by the soda dispenser.

She opened her eyes and looked at Fay.

'Is Tracy dead?'

Fay lifted Jessie's right hand from the bed cover and held it in between her own. Jessie searched her mother-in-law's face. She and Fay had never been close, but she knew Fay to be a woman of integrity. The expression on her face was almost more than Jessie could bear. More memories came now, rushing in like raging waters. Edwards' fingers scrabbling on the floor, children screaming, the boy looking up at her, the blood staining his teeth.

Jessie began to shake.

'Oh!' Fay looked alarmed. She jabbed the buzzer by the bed with her thumb.

'Now Jessie, you listen to me. Everything is going to be okay. Mike will be back shortly. He was here earlier. He would have been here, but I sent him home to grab a shower and a change of clothes. We weren't sure when you might wake up.'

'Is Tracy dead?'

'We can talk about this later honey, I think I should go find—'

'Fay, please.'

Jessie tightened her grip on Fay's hand. Fay glanced towards the door; then her shoulders slumped.

'She didn't make it. I'm sorry ... but she's gone.'

'How ... many others?'

'Three dead, five wounded.'

Jessie squeezed her eyes shut tight.

'Would have been a whole lot more too if it hadn't been for you. What you did ... what you did was incredibly brave. Jessie Conway, you saved them.'

'Those boys ... why did they do this?'

'I do not know. I heard they left some kind of tape, but I don't know what was on it. Karen will know more. She'll be here shortly.'

Jessie choked back a sob. 'I saw her. I saw Tracy in her dress. I couldn't reach her.'

'Oh no, Jessie, no, there was nothing you could have done. I am sorry for your friend but I believe she died instantly.'

Jessie could no longer contain her emotions. She wept. Fay tried to comfort her, but nothing could stem her grief. A blonde nurse came in. She spoke awhile with Fay and left. When she returned, she carried a needle filled with liquid, which she injected into the drip by Jessie's bed. Jessie closed her eyes, her body stopped trembling and she returned to the darkness.

When she woke again it was dark outside. Fay was gone and Mike had taken her place. He sat twisted sideways, his head resting on the thumbs of each hand, one leg hooked under her bed. She watched him for a moment, letting her eyes roam over his weathered skin, his tousled brown hair. He wore a clean denim shirt open at the neck, blue jeans and, she knew without looking, tan boots, laced but one from the top.

'Mike.'

Mike turned his head. Jessie was shocked to see how exhausted and worn he looked.

'Hey.'

He bent over her and kissed her forehead. She smelled soap and diesel on his skin and a faint trace of jasmine.

'Is it true? Three dead?'

'She had no business talking about that to you.'

'I asked her. Is it true?'

'Yes.'

'They were children, the shooters, Mike. They were just children.'

Mike's expression tightened. 'There was a detective here earlier; he wants to talk to you, get your statement.'

'I scarcely know what to tell him.'

They sat in silence for a while.

'How do you feel?'

'Fuzzy. My head hurts.'

Jessie studied her husband's eyes. They were cool green, like the still water in the lake behind their house.

'What is it?'

'I can't believe this happened.' Mike took her hand in his. He pressed his finger down on the soft spot between her thumb and her index finger. Jessie eased her way closer to him.

'How are you feeling?'

'I don't know, numb I guess. I can't … there are gaps.'

'I'm not surprised; you took a fair amount of shot to your head.'

'The boy … Saunders, he started shooting at people, like we were animals or something. Like we were nothing.' She swallowed. 'He was laughing, Mike, he laughed the whole time.'

'Sh, Jessie, don't upset yourself.'

'The other boy, the one I shot …' She closed her eyes and waited until her voice was steady enough to ask the question she needed to ask. She pulled back and looked at her husband. 'Who is he?'

Mike smiled, but only with his mouth; his eyes remained troubled. 'We don't need to talk about that right now. What we need to concentrate on is getting you better and getting you home. I swear, that dog of yours is more work than one man can handle.'

'Do they know why they did this? Fay mentioned a tape or –'

'Jess.'

'I want to know. I *need* to know.'

Mike's grip grew uncomfortably tight, but she gave no outward sign. After a prolonged silence he sighed and began to tell her what he had learned. When he was done talking she no longer cared that her head ached. She no longer cared about her hair or her ear.

'He was fourteen?'

'He was fourteen with a loaded gun. Jessie, he tried to blow your head off.'

'But he was *fourteen* – a child.'

'Three people are dead because of Kyle Saunders and Hector Diaz. Don't you go feeling bad about the hand *they* forced. They had the school on lockdown; they meant business. From what I'm told, Saunders left some kind of video bragging about what he was planning to do. He would have slaughtered anyone who crossed his path.'

Jessie thought of the boy – no, she knew his name now – she thought of Hector Diaz on his back, with his fingers curled by his side, the bubbles popping between his bloodstained teeth. She began to cry, silently at first, then harder, as sobs wracked her body.

'Jessie, listen to me,' Mike held her, his voice firm. 'Everyone knows what you did. You prevented a massacre and that's the fact of it. What you did was unbelievable, I don't –'

The door to Jessie's room opened and a large shape in a powder-blue suit filled the gap.

'Knock knock! May I enter?'

Jessie wiped her eyes and blinked. She recognised Zachary Williams, pastor from the Church of the Risen Lord. Pastor Williams was something of a celebrity in Rockville. He had a weekly radio show and was as media friendly as he was spiritually connected to the Lord. Fay was one of his most ardent admirers and attended his services weekly.

'Pastor,' Mike nodded, smiling.

Pastor Williams set a large garish bunch of flowers on Jessie's bed.

'My dear,' he said, taking Jessie's free hand in his massive, freckled paws. 'It is truly a miracle to see you with us this day. The Lord in his infinite wisdom has watched over you.'

Jessie attempted a smile but could not quite pull it off. She did not much care for Pastor Williams and had endured a number of run-ins with him over the years. He was on the board of Rockville High; she thought him to be a bully and a bigot behind his pious façade. Not that it mattered what she thought. He was a local, born and bred; adored by many from the tips of his expensive python skin boots to his barley-coloured locks and whiskers, the cultivation of which Jessie believed was another calculated act.

'Everyone asks after you and I *mean* everyone. They want you to know that you are in their prayers, young lady.'

'Thank you.'

'How *are* you?'

'Tired.'

'That is understandable.' He sighed deeply, rolling his shoulders back as though the weight of the world rested upon them. 'This is an exacting time. I have this moment come from the grieving family of poor James Aldershot. Seventeen years old. Those poor people, the light has gone from their lives.'

Jessie did not know how to respond. Her head ached so badly it was all she could do to focus on his face.

'They ask for answers, but what answer can I give that will comfort them now? We are becoming what God warned us about in Isaiah 5:20. These evils, these trials. God warned us, for he said, "Woe to those who call evil good and good evil, who put darkness for light and light for darkness, who put bitter for sweet and sweet for bitter."'

Pastor Williams paused in a theatrical fashion, as though he stood in the ornately carved pulpit of his church. 'We have put everything before our God. We leave our children to fend for themselves, to seek solace and understanding in video games and violent programmes. Then we ask, "*Who* is to blame?" Who can we point the finger of recrimination at next? God's revelations, his very words are being ignored. His love is constantly rebuked. We are staring into the abyss and we–'

Jessie could stand it no longer. 'I'm sorry, Pastor Williams. But please … I am very tired. Perhaps we can talk another time.'

'Of course.' He placed his hand on her forehead. His skin felt smooth and dry, like that of a snake. 'I will stop by tomorrow when

43

you are feeling more up to company. May the Lord keep and protect you.'

As he moved away to the door, he paused, as though something had occurred to him.

'Where is my head today, I almost forgot. Jessie, Mike, I have a small favour to ask.'

'What is it?'

'Darla Levine, you know, our own local girl from *The Gazette*. Well Darla wondered if perhaps you might give her a moment of your time. When you feel up to it of course.'

Jessie's chest tightened. 'I don't really feel up to speaking to the media.'

'Of course, I completely understand.' Pastor Williams smiled. 'Darla though, well, she is not really media as such; she's one of us. She would be highly respectful of your sensibilities.'

'Then let her start now,' Jessie said, feeling a wave of exhaustion she could barely fight. She glanced at her husband. 'Mike.'

'I think Jessie needs her rest, Pastor. We can speak on this tomorrow.'

'Of course,' Pastor William said again. He turned to the door, but not before Jessie caught the glint in his eye and knew he had placed another black mark against her name.

Darla Levine stalked down the corridor and stopped outside a frosted glass door. The letters on the door read: 'Lee Petro'.

Darla forced herself to square her shoulders and take a number of deep breaths. 'You are a professional', she told herself. 'Don't take any shit and don't let him run all over you.'

She tugged at her skirt and smoothed her hair. Ever since she'd received the message that Popeye wanted to see her she had been filled with anxiety. She loathed her boss with the fire of a thousand suns, although she made sure to hide her feelings well. Not that it made any difference. Her charms, though prodigious, made not the slightest dint on Popeye. She knew he thought of her as nothing more than fluff in a skirt.

She knocked.

'Get in here!'

Lee 'Popeye' Petro was an old-school newsman, the type who had clawed his way from cub reporter to the position of Editor-in-Chief and made sure every one knew about it. He was demanding, egotistical, difficult and brutish. Since he had taken over *The Gazette*, advertising revenue was up 24 per cent and production costs down 31 per cent, mostly due to a reshuffle, a pay freeze and a rigid firing policy. The newspaper owners loved the ground Popeye walked on; everyone below him on the totem pole hated his miserable guts.

'Good morning Lee, you wanted to see me?'

'Did you get a message saying I wanted to see you?'

'Yes.'

'Then why the hell are you asking me?'

'I, um–'

'Let's hear it. Conway situation, go.'

Popeye looked up from his desk; an unlit, well-chewed cigar jutted from his mouth.

Darla felt herself wilt slightly under the intensity of his gaze. Everything about Popeye was horribly intimidating. He was a gym maniac who worked out six days a week. He was proud of his physique and referred to his swollen biceps as 'shock' and 'awe'. He was tanned deepest walnut from weekends spent out on his boat, he wore his grey hair in a tight crew cut and it was rumoured he had once tossed a smart-mouth journalist through the window of his office for not turning in a story on time.

'I'm afraid I have bad news, Lee. Jessie Conway has turned us down again.'

'What do you mean she *turned* us down?'

'She's not ready to talk about what happened.'

'You mean she doesn't want to talk to you.'

'She doesn't want to talk to anyone.'

'Who reached her? Was it those fucking CNN sharks? Fox? Which of those lousy sons of–'

'No one has reached her. That's just it. She has refused to speak with anyone.'

'Whaddya mean, *refused?*'

'I don't know what else to tell you, Lee. I've requested an audience with her three times now. I even got Pastor Williams to try, but so far, nada, zip.'

'You *requested* an audience?' Popeye leaned his massive forearms on his desk. 'Is she the fucking Queen of England?'

'No, I mean I–'

'What the fuck is this, D? Amateur hour? Don't ask, don't *request*, go talk to her. Get me my story.'

'It's not that simple, Lee. I can't just barge in there and demand she start talking. It's impossible.'

'Don't give me any bull about impossible.' Popeye removed the cigar from his mouth and jabbed it in her direction. Bits of tobacco sprinkled across the blotter on his desk, leaving behind dirty yellow stains. 'Impossible is bullshit for people too stupid to build a bridge over possible. You go out there and you *make* it possible, that's what you do, make it possible, that's what you're paid for Darla, am I right?'

'Yes.'

'So stop fucking around. I want an interview I can put out tomorrow morning.'

Darla bristled. 'I have gotten plenty of interviews over the last few days and I think I can use them to piece together exactly what took place in the cafeteria. I have an exclusive with Cheryl Hogan, one of the girls Conway told to leave the cafeteria. She's a–'

'She's a kid, that's what she is, a scared kid. I know she has something to say, great, but we need to hear from the horse's mouth. So do me a favour, don't come back here without Jessie Conway's story. Jesus Christ, Darla, I have people calling me twenty-four-seven for quotes. Are you trying to make me look like a fucking joke?'

'Of course not.'

'Goddamned paper is being flooded with calls about that woman and we've got nothing. We've got to hook her before anyone else.'

'Yes sir.'

'What's the word on her injuries?'

'She was moved out of intensive care this morning. They've operated on her and removed the pellets from her skull. She is expected to make a full recovery.'

'When's she out?'

'I do not have that information.'

'Why the hell not?'

'The doctors don't know yet, Lee. How would I?'

'Don't get sassy with me Darla, you're the one with something to prove here. You broke this story, now you're letting this story break you. Fix the damn thing.' Lee moved the cigar from the left side of his mouth to the right without touching it. 'Get a goddamned camera into that room Darla, that woman *is* the news now.'

Darla kept her face neutral. 'I am aware of that.'

'People want to hear her perspective. They want to know her views. Goddammit, we need to talk to her before one of the others can secure a deal.' He stopped talking for a moment and looked stricken. 'Or worse, an exclusive.'

'She's not talking to *anyone.*'

'Yet,' Popeye said sourly. 'You wait until those big fish start flashing their chequebooks. Listen to me Darla, I know this game; any putz that doesn't know this game is worm shit. You want to be worm shit, Darla? You think your old man would let this golden opportunity turn into worm shit?'

'No, Lee.'

'Story's already cooling down, Darla. Next week some other doped-up popper-headed shit for brains with mommy issues will take out half a cheerleading squad for not blowing him and the press will move on. The window of opportunity,' Popeye held up his hand and brought his thumb and forefinger together slowly, 'is closing, Darla. Closing.'

Darla smiled stiffly. 'I'll get the story, Lee.'

'You do that, because if you don't you better start to get real acquainted with the local housewives round these parts, cause I'll have you covering bake sales and sob stories about goddamn missing poodles until one of us rots.'

Caleb rose at dawn and worked out for half an hour. He show-ered and then stood in the living room, eating a bowl of cereal, watching the news. Again, the Rockville shooting dominated the headlines. More photos of Jessie Conway appeared, including one of her on her wedding day. She was more than just pretty, Caleb thought. He didn't normally think much of redheads, but this one was pleasing on the eye. He listened to an eyewitness account of the struggle she had embarked upon to save 'her beloved pupils'. Caleb thought the story hyperbolic and overtly mawkish. He wondered why Jessie herself had not yet been interviewed.

He washed his bowl and dressed. As he left the apartment building, he stole a newspaper from the doormat of one his neighbours. Jessie Conway's face smiled at him from the front page.

He collected Maryanne's gold '01 Taurus from the garage and drove to his part-time job at the Happy Home Depot. Caleb worked in the stock room and on the floor. He liked the job: it was easy and informal, and he was allowed buy hardware at cost. He had fixed up much of the cabin using materials he had bought cheap or helped himself to over the months he had been there. It was a very satisfactory arrangement.

The morning went by quickly. Lunchtime found a number of the female workers discussing the shooting in the break room. Gloria, an obese loudmouth and the queen bee of the service tills, was holding court. Gloria always held court; she was the type of person who equated being loud with being interesting.

'Two've been released so far, but mark me y'all, there will be more to die.'

'How do you know, Gloria?' asked Mandy, Gloria's sidekick. Caleb despised her in equal measure. She was ugly and vapid and blew kisses at the kid who watered the plants in the gardening section. She thought she was being cute. She was too stupid to see she was a fool and the kid was embarrassed and made uncomfortable by her antics.

'I have a cousin married to a guy whose sister works at the hospital. Least another one for sure is going to go. He says only a machine is keeping that poor girl alive now.'

'It's so hard to believe these things keep happening. I mean what is *going on?*'

'Why, ain't it obvious?' Gloria lowered down her turkey, cheese and mayo sub. 'The evidence is right there for y'all to see. This society is what's wrong: it is sick at heart and getting sicker every day. I can't scarcely watch the television no more it is so filled with evil. It just about breaks my heart.'

A number of heads nodded in agreement.

'You know who is to blame – it's the government.' Gloria said in that imperious way she had of talking that made Caleb want to grab her throat and squeeze until he crushed her windpipe into dust.

'Why's that, Gloria?'

'Well think about it for a minute,' Gloria said, adding Sweet'n'Low to her coffee. 'This country is suffering from drought, a spiritual drought. *They* demand God is removed from our schools, so why should we be surprised when tragedies like this happen? They are forcing the Lord to turn away from His people.'

'That's right,' another woman said, tapping her hand to her chest three times in quick succession.

'How can we expect to be in *His* grace when we reject Him at every turn?'

Caleb filled a cup with black coffee. He turned and leaned against the counter, unsurprised to see a general bobbing of heads now. Oh that Gloria!

'When you reject Him you leave the door open for the other. Everyone knows that, but we have let our schools be overrun by the godless and *people*,' – she sneered – 'people with unhealthy *agendas*.'

'Did you see the teacher who stopped them, Gloria? She's only a slip of a thing.'

'I did and I tell you what, I believe the Lord was guiding that woman's hand.'

'I saw the video of her being led out from the school. Did you see her? My Lord, she had blood all over her.' Mandy shuddered violently, but Caleb guessed from the look in her eye her horror was just for effect. 'I think you're right Gloria, that woman had a guardian angel with her that day and that's for sure.'

'The Lord *will* watch over his flock.'

First a hero, now serving the community as a personal lackey from God, complete with guardian angel no less. Caleb stirred his coffee slowly and made a big production out of putting sugar in it, but as usual the women did not appear to take any notice of his presence. This amused him. These women with their talk of capricious personal gods, devils and spirits; yet here he was, the greatest devil any of them could imagine, flying easily under their radar.

It wasn't that they liked him: it was insultingly easy for a man of his talents to be accepted by any demographic readily. He understood people; he knew what made them tick. On his first day he had iden-tified and assessed the herd. He made it his business to be pleasant to every fat-assed cat lover in the place. Not overtly nice, nor obse-quious, but certainly pleasant. He was still male after all and did not want to give them ideas. But he remained *pleasant* enough so that they dropped their guard around him. They bought his story, swallowed his history. He was their quiet, helpful colleague. He was Arthur S. Weils: helpful, pleasant, safe. They thought him … toothless.

While the women talked, he sipped his coffee and fantasised about running Gloria through with his knife. It would be a gut wound, he decided, glancing at her vast stomach. It would be really something to see her try to push that mess back inside.

'Yo, I don't know about this,' Chippy said, from somewhere deep in the back of the cupboard.

'Shut up, for God's sake. Are you trying to get us caught?' Darla whispered fiercely. She opened the door a crack and peeked out into the corridor. A number of nurses and patients milled about, which was cool, but Doctor Saul Fraas, the snotty asshole treating Jessie Conway who had been so rude to Darla the night before was also floating about, which was not cool, not cool at all.

'Man, I don't like being in confined places. I got a phobia.'

'Will you *shut up?*'

'I'm gonna pass out or some shit, man; seriously, I have issues.'

Darla closed the door, reached into the dark, grabbed Chippy Gomez by his hair and viciously yanked him towards her.

'Issues? I paid $500 to get us onto this floor. If you don't shut up I am going to make you and your issues permanent residents here.'

'Okay, okay, *Dios.*'

Darla released him and returned to the door. The whole hospital was on some kind of media alert. Fortunately Darla had a friend who worked in the laundry department, and by friend she meant junkie stooge who always needed ready cash. Five hundred smackers and a promise never to disclose a confidence later, she and Chippy disentangled their legs and climbed from a laundry cart mere feet from Jessie Conway's room.

'Is that camera ready?'

'Yeah it's–'

It flashed, blinding Darla momentarily.

'Motherfu–'

'Yo, don't get mad. I'm sorry. I *told* you, I can't see shit in here.'

Darla gritted her teeth and waited for the rainbows in her eyes to fade. When she got this story, she decided, she would devote at least half an hour of every day to finding new and creative ways to make Chippy Gomez's life a living hell.

'Okay, here's the plan again. We walk in, I'll pull the curtains and you snap off a few rounds, then as soon as you have the pictures you walk, okay? Don't you wait around for some idiot to take that camera from you, got it? Photo and walk.'

''Kay.'

'Say it.'

'Photo and walk. I got it.'

'No waiting around.'

'I got it, I got it.'

'Doesn't matter who tries to stop you, you keep moving.'

'Yeah, yeah.'

Darla tried to relax her shoulders. She opened the door again and put her eye to the crack. Fraas was nowhere to be seen and – happily – neither was the big blonde nurse he had been talking with. It was now or never.

'Ready?'

Chippy belched in reply. Darla smelled onions and hot sauce. God, this had better be worth it.

'We're on.'

She opened the door and slipped out into the hallway as smoothly as possible. Both she and Chippy wore white coats to help them blend in with their surroundings. It wouldn't convince for long, but they didn't really need a lot if time.

'Shit,' Darla said, waving her hand behind her to catch Chippy's attention as the blonde nurse, the one that had been with Fraas when he had ejected her the day before, appeared at the end of the hall and began to walk towards them. Darla snatched up a clipboard as she passed a trolley and held it before her, flipping through the pages as though she had any idea what the words before her meant. She sneaked a look over her shoulder. Chippy was coming right behind her, trotting to heel her like some kind of ill-bred mutt.

'Stop making that face.'

'Huh?'

Darla slowed right down. Chippy collided with her.

'Sorry.'

'Idiot.'

They were almost at Jessie Conway's room. Darla dropped her head and pretended to study the chart in detail. Up ahead, an old man in pyjamas leading a drip on wheels stopped the blonde to speak with her.

'Move.' Darla grabbed Chippy by his lab coat; she hauled him with her through the door, closing it behind them.

The room was semi-private. Darla looked around. Four beds: two containing ancient, still-breathing corpses, and another with a sleeping woman who had a tube in her nose. Jessie Conway was by the window. She lay wan and small on the white sheets with her eyes closed. Her head was covered in bandages.

Darla crossed the floor quickly and drew the curtain around the bed. Chippy lifted his camera from beneath his coat and began to snap pictures from as many angles as the tiny space would allow. The commotion woke Jessie. As she opened her eyes, Darla elbowed Chippy behind her. Jessie squinted at the two people hovering over her.

'What's going on?'

'Hi, Jessie, how are you? You're looking fantastic. How are you feeling?'

'I'm okay … I'm sorry, who are you?'

Darla held up the chart she had been carrying. 'I've a few questions to run by you if that's okay.'

'I–'

'Surgery went well?'

Jessie lifted her hand to her head. 'Yes.'

'Doctor Fraas is very pleased. Did he give any indication when you might be released?'

'I don't know … maybe later this week. Look, I'm sorry I don't remember you. Either of you.'

'Memory's strange after a head injury.' Darla smiled reassuringly. 'What's the last memory you have before the shooting?'

'What?'

'It's a very simple exercise. What's the last thing you remember about the day of the shooting?'

Jessie's hands balled into fists on top of the sheets. 'I don't want to talk about this.'

'I understand, I do. But it's very important that you try.'

'The alarms…' Jessie's pupils dilated and her right hand began to tremble. 'I remember Adam falling.'

'Adam Edwards?'

'Yes, and his fingers … they were … he was trying to get up. I knew he was dying. I could see he was dying.'

Darla leaned in a little closer. 'He was shot right in front of you, yes? By Kyle Sanders?'

'Yes.'

'Do you remember if he said anything before he shot Edwards?'

'I don't know … maybe. There was another boy … the alarms were so loud. I remember I couldn't move.' Jessie closed her eyes and fell silent. Then she whispered, 'I heard laughing.'

'Laughing?'

'Kyle … he was laughing. Adam was dying and he was laughing.'

'Kyle Saunders was laughing.' Darla could barely contain her excitement. 'What can you tell me about him?'

When Jessie opened her eyes they were clouded with misery. 'I should have said her dress was pretty.'

'What's that?'

'I should have told her.'

'What about Hector Diaz? Did you remember him?'

'No … I …' tears spilled over and ran down her cheeks, 'I didn't know him.'

'Okay, can you run through the sequence for me? The alarms were ringing, Edwards was shot, and—'

'What the hell do you think you're doing?'

The blonde nurse dragged the curtains back with such ferocity two of the rungs pinged loose.

'Excuse me, lady,' Chippy said. He made his way to the door, not exactly running but moving fast. In the hallway he turned right and disappeared from view.

'Security!' The blonde hurried out into the hallway after him, bellowing. '*Call security!*'

Jessie wiped her tears with her hand and looked at Darla in confusion. 'I don't understand.'

'I'm sorry,' said Darla. Then she walked out of the room and turned left.

'I don't understand,' Jessie repeated, as the blonde nurse returned, her face like thunder.

Caleb sat on a stool, sipping a beer. Peripherally, he watched the raven-haired barmaid make small talk with a customer at the opposite end of the bar. She was leaning in towards the man as she spoke, flipping her hair and licking her lips; a leather-clad coquette with fake tits and a high-pitched fake laugh. She was working hard for her tips tonight, Caleb thought, watching the man's gaze travel down her cleavage and stay there.

The bar was a low-rent kind of dive; all scarred wood and split vinyl seats. It was loud too; the jukebox on the back wall was currently blaring 'The Ace of Spades' at a level so high the bass made Caleb's chest vibrate.

If the sound bothered the rest of the patrons, Caleb could not tell. The clientele was rough and ready; bikers mostly, with a few labourers and free loaders scattered though the mix to keep it interesting. Mostly, they were loud when sober; quick to snarl and square up to each other when drunk. They played pool and swilled beer from long-neck bottles; they chased shots, slamming the glasses down on hard surfaces, hooting with aggressive edges to their voices. Weed was freely smoked, other drugs taken too without fear of reprisal.

Women skirted the groups; brassy, tattooed females with painted lips and little clothing. They reminded Caleb of hyenas: cackling and shrieking, acting submissive when alone, brazen and confident when in numbers. Over the months, Caleb had gotten to know many of their faces and they his. At first he was a thing of curiosity; sometimes he endured the odd shoulder slam coming back from the john, the occasional insult tossed his way. But for the most part they ignored him, treating him as part of the furniture. To them he was just another dead-end loser drowning his sorrows in the bottle.

Tick tock, Caleb thought, rotating his arm a fraction to look at his watch.

At a quarter to nine the main door opened and a blonde came in carrying a motorcycle helmet in her left hand. She was tall and broad shouldered, with pale skin and kohl-rimmed eyes. Her name was Sonja. She was married to Bear, the leader of the Flaming Wheels motorcycle club and co-owner of the dump in which Caleb was now seated.

Sonja strode through the bar confidently. She returned hellos and performed elaborate handshakes before she swung under the service hatch. She spoke briefly with the raven-haired barmaid, releasing her for a break, which Caleb knew she would spend with one of the hyenas, hoovering up lines of coke off the dumpster out back. Caleb also knew that despite her flirtations and suggestive moves, the raven-haired barmaid had no interest in men, and lived to grind hips against the bull dyke in the red shirt playing pool in the corner.

'Hey Art, what's shakin' baby?' Sonja removed her leather jacket, rolled it and tucked it under the bar with her helmet. She wore a tank top tied at the waist, and her breasts were jacked halfway to her chin. A long leather necklace with a boar's tusk dangled outside her vest and a rose tattoo with the name Alex beneath it in gothic script covered her left bicep. Alex was her son's name. He had been killed in an automobile accident two years before, aged sixteen.

Caleb knew everything about Sonja: she had been pouring her grief over the Voice of Hope telephone lines for some time.

'Hello Sonja,' Caleb replied, tipping his bottle in salute.

'What's the haps?'

'Nothing really. You?'

'Same old, same old, my friend. Can I freshen that for you?'

Caleb nodded. Sonja opened a beer and set it before him. She smiled as she did, but it was a distracted effort. He knew she had other thoughts on her mind: chief among them, her husband's infidelity.

Bear had lately taken up with a busty, gum-popping tattoo artist named Suzi. He spent two afternoons a week holed up with her in a motel behind Safe-Cos. Caleb had been listening to Sonja raging about it over the help line for almost three weeks. Bear had promised he'd give Suzi up. Sonja had not bought a single thing he said.

Acting on a call from a disgruntled source, Sonja staked out the motel. She watched Bear and Suzi pull up and stayed still as her husband pawed Suzi's flat ugly ass like a rutting ape. She gave them enough time to get down and dirty in their room, crossed the car park and used Bear's own gun to blow the lock off the door before kicking it open.

The rest of the story was the stuff of legend. Sonja pistol-whipped the naked, screaming Suzi into the car park and shot Bear's beloved Harley full of holes. Everyone at the bar knew what had gone down. The patrons respected her decision, and those who didn't wisely kept their yaps shut.

Certainly Sonja had caught Caleb's attention.

He watched her pull a draught beer, her muscled arm smoothly drawing down the pump. It was hard to sit still when he felt like this; he wanted so badly to reach out and touch her.

The music stopped as the last song ended. The din and roar of voices did not lessen. Somewhere to Caleb's left, one of the hyenas shrieked a laugh with an undercurrent of anger. A glass was broken.

'Boys are rowdy tonight, huh?' Sonja said, catching his gaze upon her.

Caleb nodded. He was always careful not to speak too much around Sonja in case she recognised his voice. In a way, his silence seemed to appeal to the barwoman, and as he reached for his wallet to pay for his drink Sonja put her hand on his. Her skin was cool and dry.

'This one is on the house.'

Caleb looked into her brilliant blue eyes.

'I wouldn't hang about too late, Art; there's blood in the air, you dig?'

Caleb said, 'I dig.'

Sonja removed her hand. 'Hey, Bluey!' she yelled at a large man in a leather vest and biker boots. 'Play a fucking song man.'

'What you want, baby?'

'You want me to come hold your balls too? Pull your skirt down and pick one!'

The man grinned and walked to the jukebox amidst howls of laughter. Caleb drank the last of his beer, wiped his mouth and left as the opening bars of 'Highway to Hell' filled the air.

J essie stood before the mirror and stared at her reflection. It hardly seemed possible that ten days has passed since the shooting, but here she was, about to be released.

Why was she so terrified? What was scaring her so badly?

Fact: she was going home.

Fact: she should have been happy.

She pulled a smile but it was ghastly and only emphasised her hollow cheekbones.

Fact: she looked thin and washed out, a shadow of her former self.

She turned her head to the side and peeled back the gauze. She looked at the damage to her face. The surgeon said she had been lucky; a few inches to the right and she could have lost an eye, or worse. But to her it looked an ugly mess. The site was sore and swollen and the stitches were encrusted with dried blood.

Fact: she had been lucky.

Fact: she was alive. Alive when others were not; alive and relatively unharmed.

Fact: she was unravelling.

Jessie pressed the gauze back into place, furious with her self-pity. She dabbed at her eyes with her thumbs. When that didn't work she ran cold water onto her hands and splashed her face with it.

The sensation of the water hitting her skin shocked her and made her gasp. Instantly, she remembered the spray of blood, the stinging pain. She closed her eyes but the room spun and she struggled to remain upright. She could smell cordite.

She tried to fight it; a disconnected twist in her brain made her light-headed and nauseous. She gripped the basin with both hands to steady herself and tried to use the wall to slide her way back into the bedroom. She made it, and stood quaking, saturated in sweat. She gauged the distance between the wall and her bed. Ten feet, that's all it was, probably even less.

Fact: it might as well have been one hundred feet.

Her breath shortened. She thought she was going to vomit. She clung to the wall with her legs braced against the floor as though it was pitching like a ship in a storm. Move, she told herself, step out. But she could not. Jessie Conway slid to the floor in a sobbing mess, defeated by ten feet of tiled floor.

She was still there when Mike arrived.

'Hey, what happened?'

'I don't know,' Jessie shook her head. 'I felt faint. I couldn't walk.'

Mike got his hands under her arms and lifted her to her feet. Jessie swayed for a second, took a deep breath and straightened.

'Want me to get a nurse?'

'No, I'm okay. I need a moment.'

'I'll call a nurse.'

'No, Mike, I want to get out of here. Would you please pass me the scarf from the locker?'

Mike fetched the pale lemon chiffon and handed it to her. Jessie folded it into a triangle, wrapped it about her head and tied it at the nape of her neck.

'How do I look?'

'Like one of them old-school film actresses.'

'Oh sure.' She smiled at him, grateful for the lie.

'You ready to go? Do you need to see anyone or sign anything?'

'No, all taken care of.'

'Okay, I got to warn you though, there are reporters outside.'

'What? How did they know I was being discharged today?'

'Someone must have tipped them off.'

'Damn it,' Jessie sagged. 'Why does everything have to be public knowledge?'

Mike lifted her suitcase.

'Ready?'

'If I say no would it matter?'

He offered her his hand, and, after a moment, she took it.

As Mike had warned, a number of photographers were camped nearby and they swarmed the moment they caught a glimpse of her.

'Hey Jessie, Jessie, how you doing? Jessie, look this way. Jessie!'

'How are you feeling, Jessie?'

'Jessie, do you have any words? What have you to say to the families?'

'Are you going to return to work when Rockville reopens next semester?'

'Jessie! Jessie!'

Jessie shielded her eyes from the flashes with her arm. She heard Mike growl and swear at one man who tried to block them with his thigh.

'Just give us something.'

'How do you *feel* Jessie?'

'What do you think about gun control?'

'Did you know Kyle Saunders?'

'Jessie, Jessie, *Jessie.*'

Jessie felt panicked and hemmed in; she stumbled slightly, but Mike tightened his grip on her and kept them moving and finally they reached the truck. Mike helped her get inside, his lips drawn into a tight line. He climbed in and they drove away.

'Pack of wolves! I'm sorry about that.'

Jessie nodded and looked out the window, shaken by their actions.

'You okay?'

'What do they want? I have given a press statement. What more can they want?'

'Try not to let them get to you.'

'Is this what it's going to be like?'

'They'll get tired of it eventually.'

'Did you see that woman back there, Darla Levine? Does she really think I'm going to talk to her after what she did?'

Mike's grip tightened on the steering wheel. He was furious about what had happened in the hospital. Darla Levine had published photos of Jessie's injuries along with an op-ed piece created from innuendo and mindless gossip. She had then dressed the betrayal with a feel-good ending about hope and rebirth. An orderly had been suspended from the hospital, but what had hurt him most was that Pastor Williams had also appeared in the piece, pontificating and speculating, offering up his private thoughts for public consumption. Jessie had been beside herself; his mother upset and defensive. Mike had wanted to go down to the office of *The Gazette* and tear Darla Levine a new one. In the end, under his mother's advisement and as a result of her pleading, he lodged a formal complaint with the press office.

'Is it true?'

'Huh?' Mike glanced over.

'About the school, is it true they're holding a ceremony?'

'I believe so.'

'Life goes on, right?' Jessie could not keep the bitterness from her voice.

'Jess, there's only a few days left until summer break. They need this; they need some kind of closure.'

'I missed Alan's funeral.'

'I know it.' He drove on for a moment. 'You thought about what you want to do about that?'

'I am going to go and pay my respects to Irene and Francis.'

'Okay then.'

'Tracy is being buried tomorrow.'

'Okay.'

'I am going, Mike.'

'You sure?'

'Yes.'

'Nobody would think less of you if you didn't attend.'

'I would. I would think less of me.'

The following day Jessie and Mike drove to church. Waiting across the road from the main cemetery gates, a number of reporters and cameramen stood, smoking and snapping pictures of the crowd.

'They'd be here anyway,' Mike said as they parked as far from the prying eyes as possible. Jessie adjusted her sunglasses. The day was unbearably hot and she was upset and fretful.

Mike watched her carefully. 'You okay?'

'No. But I am going to pay my respects to my friend.' She got out and began to walk, keeping to the inside of the parked cars, her head bent low. But within seconds a cry went up and she was surrounded.

'How are you, Jessie?'

'Were you and Tracy Flowers close friends, Miss Conway?'

Cameras flashed inches from her face.

'My God, don't you people have any respect?' she said, furiously. She could see other mourners inside the grounds glance in her direction. 'This is a funeral.'

'Jessie–'

'Get away from me.'

She recognised a blonde inching her way to the front of the group.

'Jessie, how are you?' Darla Levine shoved a micro recorder in front of her face. Jessie tried to push past. Up ahead she saw her friend Lou-Ann Granger walking towards them and she heard Mike telling people to back off.

'Kyle Saunders' parents have spoken of their sorrow. Did they contact you when you were in hospital?'

Jessie glared at Darla. 'Why don't you head on back to the sewer you crawled from Miss Levine?'

Darla flushed as a number of reporters tittered and gawked at her. 'I'm sorry you feel this way, Miss Conway. I understand you must be going through a difficult time.'

'I am trying to say goodbye to my friend and colleague. Please, let me through.'

The press group broke enough for her to slip past and she practically fell into Lou-Ann's arms.

'You okay?'

'Those people are too much.'

'Calling them *people* is too much,' Lou-Ann said, linking her arm with Jessie's. 'Hi Mike.'

'Lou-Ann.'

They gave each other a kiss on the check. Lou-Ann leaned in to Jessie. 'Have you spoken to Irene Edwards?'

'I called her last night.'

'How is she?'

'She's pretty cut-up, but she's doing her best. She said she'd be here today.'

They passed though the gates and walked along the gravel path leading to the chapel. The gravesite was covered in green tarp, next to which was a fresh mound of soil covered in wreathes. A large number of people were in attendance. Jessie moved on jellied legs. She felt eyes on her at every step as she walked slowly towards Tracy's mother, Lorena.

'Lorena?'

'Hello Jessie.'

Lorena Flowers wore a long black tunic, with a veil drawn over her thick glossy hair. Her eyes were dry, but her voice was raw with grief.

'Oh Lorena.' Jessie began to cry. Immediately she felt ashamed. She had not wished to make a spectacle of herself.

Lorena hugged her, hard. 'I know, I know. My baby girl, I know.'

Jessie pulled herself together as best she could. After paying her respects to the rest of Tracy's family, she and Mike drifted to the rear of the crowd, where they found Irene Edwards standing with her son James by her side. Irene looked exhausted and her eyes were swollen from crying. She and Jessie embraced.

'I am so sorry for your loss. Both of you.' Jessie stepped back and laid her hand on James's arm. James was twenty-one, tall and softly spoken. A gifted musician, he was studying music at college in New York. Jessie thought he looked a lot like his father and she told him so.

Mike and Lou-Ann were offering their condolences when Pastor Williams rocked up, resplendent in a light summer suit, his hair suspiciously *freshly* golden. He greeted them and hugged Irene, holding her tight against his chest. When he turned to do the same to Jessie, she took a step back and pretended to watch the crowds. Without missing a beat, Pastor Williams grabbed Mike's hand and pumped it up and down.

'May God's grace keep you all this day. Irene, James, I want you to know my heart grieves with you. Alan was a fine man, an upright man. His loss is our loss and the Lord's great gain.'

'Thank you,' Irene said, her voice tight with pain. Jessie took her hand and squeezed it.

'So much grief,' Pastor Williams said. 'Jessie, how are you? It is good to see you up and about. So many people called the show offering prayers for you and your family, it was truly something to behold.'

With enormous effort of will, Jessie managed to force out a thank you. She was heartily glad when someone called the Pastor and she and Mike made good their escape.

Soon the funeral began. Pastor William spoke at great length about the mysteries of life and the suffering of man. He decried the loss of faith, of compassion, of youth and innocence. He pontificated on 'God's great plan' and spoke with a passion so fiery Jessie wondered if he thought himself on stage. In any event, Jessie paid scant attention to his sermon. She found no solace in his words, no comfort in his dramatic delivery. She thought of Hector Diaz, how he had smiled through his bloodstained teeth. She thought of the look of confusion and disbelief on Alan Edward's face as the first of the bullets struck him. She thought of his fingers scrabbling for purchase while the life leaked from his body. She thought of all these things and she wondered about 'God's great plan'. She wondered what His plan had been the day a red stain spread across a bright yellow sundress.

Caleb read the article on Jessie Conway twice and then a third time. It had been written in a style he associated with tabloids but was no less engaging for it. The woman intrigued him. She had single-handedly taken on not one but two shooters and won – unarmed. Such a thing was something so rare, something so Hollywood, he genuinely struggled to believe it. But no one had come forward to contradict the story and now here she was, head to toe in black, standing by the grave of one of the fallen; alive, red hair fiery in the sunlight. 'Hero,' Caleb said, tracing his finger over her image.

He folded the paper and leaned back in his chair, still thinking about her. His shift on the Voice of Hope help line was drawing to a dull close when he glanced out the window and spotted Pastor T. Creedy pulling his customised silver Mercedes into his parking space.

Caleb watched him walk up to the main doors, noting his wingtip cowboy boots, which probably cost more than the average monthly take-home pay. Creedy did not bother Caleb unduly; the man was a complete huckster, of that he was certain, but then in Caleb's opinion that might well be part of Creedy's job description.

'Blessings to you, Art,' Creedy called out when he entered the room, flashing the megawatt smile he normally reserved for the blue rinse brigade. He dropped a canvas sports bag on the floor by Caleb's chair.

'Pastor.'

'How are we this fine day?'

Creedy flashed him the smile again. Caleb waited, irritated. He knew there was something coming down the line.

'Phones busy?'

'Nope. Not a single call.'

'Well now, that in itself is a reason to be thankful.'

Creedy perched a butt cheek on the edge of the table. His pants stretched so tight Caleb could see the outline of his balls against the material, and it made him wonder why men like Creedy thought they were so enigmatic. Short of humping his leg, Caleb couldn't imagine the pastor pulling a more blatant, or more laughable, attempt at dominance.

'You're a compassionate fellow, Art. I can tell. I *know* people.'

Caleb waited.

'How would you feel about spreading The Truth to those less fortunate?'

'Say what now?'

'I could do with more men like you, Art; moral, upright, unafraid to be active in the community. I tell you, the world is a very dark and lonely place and when we step forward we are the bringers of the light.'

Caleb got the smile again.

'What we do here, Art; what we do is truly God's work. But I have been in reflection of late. Jesus did not wait for the people to come to him. He did not keep them at arm's length. No! Jesus *went* to the people. He was not afraid to get his hands dirty, he was not afraid to walk among the sick and the dying to show them the light of His love.'

'You want me to try healing sick people?'

'You are a hoot!' Creedy threw back his head and laughed and tapped the side of his nose. 'I have a friend who works over at the clinic on Druid's Hill. I was hoping you might be free to volunteer some of your services to help her out.'

'A clinic?'

'Yes. It would be one night a week, two at the very most.'

Caleb let his cogs whirl for a moment. He tried to figure out what Creedy's angle was in this, but came up blank.

'What about the phone lines?'

'Well, it's true that we offer solace and compassion to those who reach out to us. But to be really in His light, we need to be *visible* and *among* our people. Pass me that bag there, would ya.'

Caleb did as he was asked. Creedy unzipped the bag, rummaged inside and tossed Caleb a sealed plastic bag.

'Open it!'

Caleb opened it and withdrew a bright yellow t-shirt. Printed on the front was 'Let the Light of the Lord Guide You', on the back was 'Voice of Hope'. Caleb lowered the t-shirt and stared at Creedy.

'Aren't they something? It was Helen's idea for the colour. We need to let a little light shine in the darkness, that's what she said. Wonderful woman. So what d'ya say, Art?'

The following night, Caleb stood resplendent in bright canary yellow, staring into the ear of the director of the clinic as she fanned a set of photos with various names and aliases before him. Her name was Dorothy. She was a short dumpy woman in her fifties, with a smell as sour as her face.

'See now, you really need to learn these faces, Art.'

Caleb glanced over the photos. 'Who are they?'

'These are those that the Good Lord has sent to test us. Believe me.'

'Are they … clients?'

'They are when it suits them. Look, all you need remember is that whatever any of these people tell you, it's bound to be a lie. Do not, and I must stress this Art, do not lend any of these people money, no matter how plausible or heart-rending a story they lay on you. You hear?'

He kept his expression carefully neutral.

'I won't, Dorothy.'

'You'll be working with Steve tonight. He's an old hand and he'll show you the ropes. But I mean it, these people here,' she tapped the photos again, 'they see a fresh face and the first thing they do is hit you up for something.'

'Okay.'

She folded her arms across her ample chest. 'Okay, and another thing, there's a photographer coming here shortly with Creedy. He's going to take a few photos of you in that get-up, but once he's gone you can remove that shirt. You look like Big Bird.'

'Pastor Creedy's idea.'

'I'm sure it was,' she said, drawing her mouth into a thin line. 'But he's not the one wearing it and as far as I'm concerned it marks you out in a way you don't need to be marked.'

Caleb nodded in complete agreement.

'It's going to be a long night ahead. You ready for the madness?'

Caleb nodded again.

'I wish more people felt the same way you do, Art. The world would be a heck of a better place.' Dorothy retired to the back office, leaving instructions with Caleb to call her if he needed her.

At twenty to eleven, a blonde woman he recognised from the photos shoved the door from the street open and entered, half carrying a complaining struggling junkie with her.

'Uh-oh,' Steve, his co-worker, said. 'Here comes trouble. Think you can handle this one, Art?'

Caleb watched as the blonde deposited the junkie on a plastic chair and marched straight up to the counter. He remembered her name: Marcie Ingram.

'I can handle it.'

She leaned on the ledge in front of the glass partition that separated them.

'Hi.'

'Hello.'

'You're new.'

'Yes.'

'That's Amber,' she said, jerking her thumb over her shoulder towards the other woman. 'She's in a bad way. Had a helluva time getting her here, but y'all got to help her.'

Caleb gazed past her. The other woman was considerably older. It was pretty obvious to him that she *was* in a bad way, most likely on a hard comedown. She was worn and beat down, with ruined skin covered in sores. Her cheeks were sunken from where her teeth had most likely long fallen out of her head. She was scratching at her arms and when she looked their way her eyes rolled in different directions.

'What would you have me do with her?'

'I don't know. Can't you give her some money for some food or somethin'? You can see her, right? You can see how she is. She ain't eaten in days and her asshole boyfriend has kicked her out of her own damn house. She ain't got nowhere to go.'

'There's no point in me giving you money; she won't eat.'

''Scuse me?'

'She's not going to eat.'

'Says who?'

'I can see she's tweaking.'

Marcie eyes hardened but her voice softened. 'Okay beardy, how bout you give me some money and I'll get her a room 'til she's down.'

Caleb nodded over her shoulder.

'I think your meal ticket is about to split.'

Marcie snapped around. The other woman was up on her feet, weaving towards the door.

'Don't you move, Amber. I swear you I will plant you in the dirt if you try.'

Amber stopped and scratched at her arms miserably.

'Ah gotta get out ah here.'

'I *told* you to wait. Now sit your ass back down.'

Marcie turned back to her sales pitch.

'What's your name, honey?'

'Arthur.' Caleb looked at her a little closer. She was five eight, with naturally thick, dark blonde hair. Her skin was clear and she appeared to have all her own teeth. Underneath the wear and tear she could have been pretty. She certainly had the blueprint for it. Her edgy defiance interested him. She had spunk.

'Well now, see, I know you're a good person, Arthur. I can see that. I just need a little help. Look at her; she ain't slept in hardly three days. She *needs* to clean up tonight. If you could just lend me some money for a room I'd sit with her, help her out of this fix.'

Caleb began to speak but she cut him off.

'This is a Christian centre, ain't it?' she said slyly. 'Wouldn't it be *Christian* to help a body out?'

'I can't give you any money. If you want you can stay here for a while–'

'*Here?* For what? She ain't slept in three days, she ain't eaten. You sayin' you can't do nothin'?'

Caleb shrugged.

'Then what use are y'all? What the fuck you lookin' at, Steve?'

Steve glanced over. 'Nothing.'

'You been bad mouthin' me?'

'Marcie, I never–'

'Alls y'alls can go hump a pig.'

'Bring her to the cop shop,' Steve said. 'They'll likely give you room and board until she's back on land again. For free too.'

'Fuck you very much,' she replied. She turned on her heel, grabbed the wretched Amber by the arm and hauled her to her feet. Amber started to babble some nonsense but Caleb couldn't make it out. At the door, Marcie turned again.

'Some fucking use y'all are, this will be on you if shit goes wrong.'

He watched her clatter through the door and into the night, her strong pale legs spiriting them away to God alone knew what hellhole.

He spent the rest of the night thinking about her. She was Category A for sure. What fun he could have with her. When Steve took a toilet break, Caleb searched through the in-house files and found her name. It took him no time at all to learn what he needed to know about her. She was twenty-five and the mother of three kids, all of whom were being cared for by the state. She worked out of a motel beyond the river and would tell you up was down if she thought there was a buck to be made.

No one would miss her, he thought, and if they did, they would assume her big mouth had run against the wrong John one time too many.

Caleb put her file back and smiled. If anyone had witnessed this particular smile, they would not have enjoyed it at all.

Mike listened to Emma gabbing away on the office phone and wondered briefly who she was talking with. It was hard to tell with Emma – could be friend or foe, since she treated everyone with the same mild disdain. He knew he ought to speak to her about that, but Ace had not turned in that morning and Mike couldn't raise him. Energy wise, Mike figured he did not have the surplus needed for dispute. He'd already had one with Jessie and one was plenty.

He pushed open the office door and stood outside, watching the street. The day was already hot as hell and getting hotter by the minute. Heat rose and shimmered from the asphalt in the distance. Mike lit a cigarette and smoked for a while, thinking how hard it was to know what to do or what to say anymore.

Jessie had collapsed that morning. She had given neither sign nor indication that she was unwell; she had simply fallen down. By the time he had carried her to the sofa she had come round again, but was white as a sheet and clammy to the touch. Mike had wanted to bring her to the hospital, but she refused to go, telling him she was fine, that her blood sugar must have dropped.

Mike didn't buy it. Jessie was not herself. She jumped at shadows, cried in her sleep – if she slept at all. She hardly ate a thing and spent most meals picking at her food with disinterest before pushing it away.

It was the silence that bothered Mike the most. Since the funeral, he had watched her withdraw into herself. She hadn't attended the remembrance ceremony for fear of another melee of journalists. She was listless and deeply unhappy.

Mike felt as useless as tits on a bull. He spoke to Dr Fraas, who thought Jessie might benefit from talking to another doctor who specialised in trauma. But when Mike ran it past her, Jessie shot it down immediately, saying she did not need to speak to anyone. When Mike had pushed her with it she had grown furious and tearful, before retreating into silence. She was sinking and he had no idea how to save her.

Mike noticed Emma watching him and moved to the side of the door. Sometimes it felt like the whole town had him under the microscope, waiting for him to do something. But what? Everywhere he went people approached him and gripped his hand. They asked how he was holding up. They asked after Jessie and passed on their best wishes and their prayers. Between the curious, the well-wishers and the press, he was beginning to feel like a treed bear. Night and day: there seemed to be no respite, it left him on edge and prickly. He couldn't move on, not like this, not feeling that something terrible waited in the wings, a black presence preparing to make itself known.

He was sick and tired of watching the news channels; sick of repeated shots of the school. Sick of seeing Jessie's shocked and bloodied face appear on the screen. It felt like a violation of sorts.

Worse still was the lack of real closure. Kyle Saunders had left behind videos where he ranted and raved about perceived injustices and how it was payback for all the wrongs perpetrated against him. Mike had watched them all, hoping to gain some insight into what had happened, but to no avail. In reality, Kyle Saunders was a spoiled white kid from a middle-class background whose issues were of his own making. The tapes had been unoriginal, filled with boastful anger and dumb cunning.

Hector Diaz offered even less. The youngest son of Treo Diaz, the Saunders' gardener, he was a shy kid by all accounts – everyone said so – but in thrall to Kyle Saunders. He was a follower; a follower who had followed the wrong person to his death. A death by Jessie's hands.

Mike leaned one foot on the wall behind him. A blacked-out Escalade pulled partially across the main entrance to the scrap yard opposite the garage. A slender blonde woman he immediately recognised alighted from the passenger side and, after fixing her skirt, made her way across the road towards him. She smiled as she stepped onto his porch. Barracuda, Mike thought, a barracuda wearing frosted-pink lipstick.

'You got some nerve.' Mike pitched his cigarette out into the dirt and straightened up.

Darla Levine wore a tight black skirt, high heels with a red inner heel, and a pristine white wraparound shirt. Though the day was muggy, her makeup was flawless, and if the woman had sweat glands Mike couldn't tell.

'I left you a message yesterday.'

'I got it. The one at my house too.'

'Is there somewhere we can talk?'

'We got nothing to talk about.'

The smile never wavered, not even for a second. 'I am glad to hear Jessie is doing better.'

'I'll send your regards.'

'I sent flowers.'

'She got them.'

'I was rather hoping if she was feeling up to it she might like to give me a statement of–'

'She's not feeling up to anything at the moment except healing.'

Darla Levine nodded in a sympathetic manner. 'How about you, Mike – I can call you Mike? How are you holding up? It must be difficult for you at the moment.'

When Mike did not reply Darla did the smile again.

'You must be so proud of Jessie. She's an amazing woman, a real inspiration to the town.'

Mike shook his head and released a breath that was part exasperation and part disbelief. Darla Levine reminded him of a coonhound his father had once owned. Once it got the whiff of a scent wild horses couldn't drag it away. He wondered how long she would keep dogging them.

Across the street, Harry Carling, the owner of the scrap yard appeared. Mike watched as Harry approached the driver, a skinny-looking man with black hair and a thin beard grown only around the rim of his jaw. Mike knew Harry did not take kindly to non-paying folk parking on his property.

'You should probably move your vehicle.'

'It will be fine,' she said, without turning. 'Look Mike, I want you to know I understand the concerns you might have about talking to the press, I surely do. But Mike, people are interested in Jessie's side of the story. I was right there when this tragedy unfolded. I heard those children scream. I've read Sheriff Clay's report and I've read some of the files. What Jessie did was beyond heroic. I think people really want to know the woman *behind* this amazing act. They would like to hear her tell her story in her own words. And as a local I think I am in the unique position to get to the heart of this, to treat your wife's story with the sympathy and empathy it deserves.'

'Like the empathy you treated her with at the hospital?'

'I understand you're angry and I apologise. I promise we would only take a few moments of her time. Truthfully Mike, with the way the town is suffering, her courage is more than just inspirational. Really

Mike, if I can be honest here, the town needs to begin the process of healing. It needs to look to someone. Jessie could be an integral part of that process. Her story would go a long way towards giving people hope and closure.'

'Closure?' Mike snapped his eyes in her direction. 'What kind of closure do you think people are going to get? Don't you get it, Miss Levine? People are torn up. They're in shock, grieving. You can't paper over that with a fluff piece.'

'I can *assure* you I would not stand over a fluff piece.' Darla Levine's eyes narrowed. Mike saw he had needled her. 'I would treat Jessie's story with the weight it deserved.'

'The people that *count* already know Jessie and her story.'

'But the public–'

'I don't give a *damn* about the public, and tell the truth I don't think you do neither.'

In the background, the driver gesticulated at Harry, a universal sign, dismissive and crude.

'I understand Jessie's reluctance to talk. It might be hard to speak about what happened but I believe talking could be cathartic for your wife. I'm sure as a survivor Jessie is suffering from many mixed emotions. Fear, anger, guilt –'

'Guilt? Let me stop you right there, Miss Levine. You don't get to piss on my leg and tell me it's raining. I don't know what more might have happened that day. I sure as shit don't want to think about how bad it might have gotten neither. But whatever Jessie is feeling, you can be sure it's for the people who died, for those who are suffering *now*. You need to quit bothering my wife.'

'We are prepared to offer her a considerable sum for an exclusive interview, Mr Conway.' There was an air of desperation to Darla's voice, and yet still a trace of petulance.

'You people,' Mike shook his head. He tucked his cigarettes into the top pocket of his overalls and was about to go inside when across the street the driver got out of the Escalade and shoved Harry Carling in the chest hard enough to send the old boy sprawling. Mike was off the steps and across the road in a flash. He grabbed the driver by the shoulder with one hand, spun him on his heels, and decked him with the other. The driver went down, hard. Mike hurried to Harry, who was struggling to get his feet under him.

'He knocked me down, Mike. You see that?'

'I saw him all right.' Mike hauled him upright and brushed some of the dust from his pants.

'Damn, I lost my teeth.'

The teeth lay near the front tyre of the Escalade. Mike picked them up and handed them back to their owner. Harry spat on them, wiped them against the front of his overalls and popped them back into his mouth.

'He got the drop on me Mike, 'nother day I woulda had him.'

'Yeah, I've no doubt.'

'I'm so sorry about this,' Darla Levine came up behind them. She held out her hand to Harry. 'Please accept my apologies.'

Mike Conway looked past her to the driver who lay in a patch of weeds, holding his jaw. 'Your driver there might need some of that empathy and sympathy you're so keen to dish out.'

Darla flushed and dropped her hand.

'Come on, Mr Carling, let's go inside.'

Mike and Harry Carling went into the scrap yard together. Darla walked over to Chippy.

'You idiot,' Darla said. 'What the hell was that about?'

'He didn't hear what that old fuck called me.'

'*So what?* You need a fainting couch now because you hear a bad word? We've got half the big networks in the country circling Jessie Conway like sharks. Whatever chance we had is now gone! My fucking chance at an exclusive is gone!'

Chippy touched his face with his hand. 'I think he might have broken my jaw.'

'Pity it wasn't your neck!' Darla turned and stormed away.

It would be impossible to explain to another person, Caleb thought as he packed a few belongings into a holdall and locked the apartment door, the thrill hunting brought him. They would never understand what it was that drove him; that it wasn't the kill, or the butchery, or even the release he felt afterwards. How could he explain the anticipation or the tension that rushed through him? Who would understand the twisting unknown variables that sent the blood coursing through his veins? Perhaps another hunter, but he had been with other hunters before and felt no kindred spirit.

Caleb went downstairs and collected the gold Taurus from the underground car park. He drove out through the electronic gates and indicated left. He pulled in behind a dark sedan, slipped into the late evening traffic and drove at a law-abiding pace across town to Marcie Ingram's address.

While he drove, Caleb ran through the various scenarios that might shape his evening. He figured that a woman like Marcie would be unpredictable and possibly a little dangerous.

He liked that.

When he was a younger man he had hunted all over country, travelling to where the game drew him. He had always enjoyed solitude.

Being alone in the woods, with nothing to distract or bother him, set him free. He'd killed elk and goats in Montana, mulie buck and coyotes in Wyoming. He'd shot white tails, sika, partridge, wild turkeys, geese – hell, when short of decent targets he'd kill raccoons and stray dogs just for practice.

The first time he'd hunted another human, something in Caleb had shifted, some internal spring had been sprung. After that he shot animals only to keep the freezer full and over time his interest in this *other* sport consumed him completely.

Caleb liked to think of her, his first. Though five years had passed he could recall every detail.

Her name had been Angie. She had been hitchhiking illegally just outside Ashville when he stopped and offered her a ride. She told him she'd hitchhiked all over America, that she had been on her own since she was fifteen. She offered him some weed and laughed when he told her he had never done it. She was vibrant and flirty. She asked him was it cool to play the radio and then she sang along to every song at the top of her lungs.

He had not intended to kill her.

Not at first.

Ten miles before they reached Hickory, he'd pulled off the road, aiming to get to know her better, thinking he might try a kiss and if she refused he'd just dump her and leave her to walk to civilization. But something had triggered her alarms. Maybe she had been too street smart for him; maybe hiking carried its own rules. All Caleb knew was that when the truck slowed, she leaped out, hit the ground and took off running.

At first Caleb thought he ought to drive away. He told himself he hadn't actually done anything wrong. But then he panicked. She might recognise the truck and report him for kidnapping or attempted assault. Kidnapping was a hard cloud to shake. Caleb had already spent time inside for petty larceny and one case of ABH, and had nearly gone stark raving mad with the confinement. He vowed never, *ever* to let that happen to him again. He wasted almost five minutes in this state of panic until it occurred on him that he had other options.

Once the decision was made, Caleb's nerves settled rapidly. Streetwise or not, she was in his domain now. He grabbed his bow from behind his seat and set off after her, embarking on a path that would change the course of his life forever.

Caleb located Marcie as she grabbed a cab outside her home and trailed her northwest to a motel, Brookshire Boulevard on Interstate 85. She went inside and did not appear again until after midnight. Caleb waited, watching the car park. He noted the steady trickle of single male drivers who came and went with perfectly timed regularity.

Blatant.

Her shift over, Caleb trailed Marcie back across town. This time the cab dropped her outside a 7-Eleven half a block from her home. She went inside and bought a few things. When she came out, she put a cigarette in her mouth, lit it and started walking, blowing twin streams of smoke into the air from her nostrils.

Caleb put the car into drive and pulled onto the street. She quick-ened her pace as he drew alongside her, without making it obvious she had noticed him. Caleb let the window down. 'Marcie!'

She slowed, glanced at him using a side eye, and stopped.

'I know you,' she said bending to the window. 'What do you want?'

'To talk.'

She looked up the street, her hand resting on the door. Her finger-nails were coated in metallic green nail varnish, some of them chipped.

'I'm sorry about what happened with your friend. I felt bad.'

'Yeah?' Her head dropped into view again. 'How'd you know where I was at?'

'I asked around.'

'Asked who?'

'Someone at the clinic told me you lived near here.'

Marcie looked at him again, suspiciously. 'So you're feeling kind of ... sorry.'

'I could see your friend was hurting. It's just that Dorothy–'

'That big-mouth bitch.'

'–warned me about you; she said not to help.'

'She was sufferin' bad, man, real bad. Nearly flipped her switch.'

Caleb said nothing. He wasn't sure what there was to say to that. Marcie looked at him, licked her lips and took another drag from her cigarette. 'Sorry don't come cheap.'

'Can I buy you a drink?'

Marcie hesitated again, mulling him over. Caleb smiled at her goofily. After a moment, she pitched her cigarette away and opened the door. She slid into the front seat and turned to him.

'You got a place we can go?'

'I do,' Caleb said.

Darla Levine watched the news headlines slumped in her chair, her bare legs crossed at the ankle.

'Lee was right. The story is not even top quarter of the hour.'

Chippy shrugged. 'They ain't gonna wait forever, the dead are buried. What more do they got to say?'

'This story was my chance, you dumb shit. You think Rockville's going to throw up another like this again?'

'I hope not, man. I could live without that kind of thing.'

Darla rested her chin on her hand. 'There's got to be something I'm not seeing, some angle I can use to flame the embers a little longer. If I could put together some … something kind of special…'

Chippy yawned and rubbed his jaw. 'So what you wanna do?'

'I don't know yet. Find a new angle.'

'I'm gonna go get some coffee. You want?'

'Sure. Make sure it's decaf would you, I have a splitting headache.'

'What time we gotta go see that woman about the – what you call it – swige? The shit that's killin' her pond.'

'You had it right with shit.'

'What time?'

'What does it matter? Time we have at our disposal, don't we Chippy?'

Chippy looked confused, but he knew better than to push her, so he left her office. Darla remained in her chair, brooding, her fingers drumming on her desk.

Sewage … yep, just like her career.

Her thoughts inevitably returned to Jessie Conway. The teacher confused and confounded her. She'd learned from a number of sources that the bigger networks had offered Jessie a literal fortune for her story and that she had turned them down. Who did that? Who ran from fame and money like that? No one – at least no one she had ever met. Darla simply could not fathom the teacher's position. It didn't make any sense. None of it did. Darla did not believe in pure altruism and she sure as hell did not swallow the reluctant hero act. So why was Jessie Conway so reluctant to talk to the press? Why duck glory? It was almost as though she was ashamed to be a hero. But why? What was she afraid of?

Darla chewed the inside of her cheek. Then she grabbed her phone and dialled. Her call was answered on the second ring and an irritated voice said, 'Whut?'

'Hey Dallas. It's Darla, I need to speak to him.'

'He ain't here.'

'Where is he?'

'How should I know where he's at? I ain't his fucking keeper.'

'Okay.'

'You *do* see the gutless coward, you tell him to come collect his shit before I burn the lot of it out on the front yard.'

Darla disconnected and dialled a different number. If Billy and Dallas were on the outs it stood to reason he had gone back to his second wife, again.

A gruff forty-a-day voice answered after a number of rings. 'Yeah?'

'Sally, it's Darla. Billy around?'

'Hold on.'

She heard the phone being lowered and few moments later a voice said, 'Yo.'

'That is one complicated life you lead, Billy. How on Earth do you find the time?'

'Darla! How nice to hear from a little ray of sunshine on an otherwise shitty day. How you doing, doll?'

'Doing good, Big B. I've got a job for you if you're interested.'

'What kind of job?'

'Digging.'

'Usual fee?'

'Sure.'

'Then I'm interested. But I'm going to be tied up here for a couple of hours. Want to come by the office later?'

'Sure. I'll swing by say about six.'

'What's the gig?'

'I want you to chase up a woman for me.'

'She good-looking?'

'She's married.'

Billy laughed. 'Can't say that ever dissuaded me none. Swing by, we'll talk.'

'How is Jessie holding up?'

Mike accepted the coffee Fay offered him and carried it to the breakfast bar. Fay's kitchen was bright and sun filled. It smelled of cinnamon and apples from the pie she had baked earlier, and her ancient Labrador, Ollie, lay sleeping soundly in the doorway leading to the internal courtyard. It was a beautiful day. Everything was as it should have been. Yet nothing was.

'Well?'

Mike sipped his coffee, stalling for an answer. It was hot and burned his lip. He winced and put it down. 'To tell you the truth I don't know. I can't really say how she is.' He thought of Jessie as he had left her that morning, curled up with their dog Rudy on the end of the sofa in the living room. She had been sitting there, staring into space. The television had been on, but she was not watching, and when he spoke to her she had barely acknowledged him.

'Well,' Fay said, turning her cup. 'Tough times never last, tough people do.'

'Has that reporter been on again?'

'She called the other day, but not since then.'

'What did you tell her?'

'The same thing I told her the last time she called, I asked her to stop pestering my family. I complained to the paper too. For all the good I think that will do. I think Rosemary Keel from Keel Furnishings has some sway with their advertising department. I'm going to give her a call. They might sit up and take notice then.'

'I hope so. That Levine woman is like a dog with a bone.'

Fay wiped her immaculate counter tops with a clean cloth. 'Truthfully, Mike, I understand her interest.'

'Do you? Those people are vultures. Jessie gave her statement to the relevant authorities and she gave a press release – that ought to be the end of it.'

'Folk are hurting, Mike. They are trying to make sense of what happened. Like it or not, Jessie is a part of that.'

'Jessie can't fix them,' he said. 'She can't even fix herself.'

'You know I've been thinking about that.' Fay put down her cloth and looked squarely at him. 'Might be good to get her out of the house, bring her out of herself a little.'

'She doesn't want to *go* anywhere. I don't know what else to do about that. I don't … I can't *make* her go places.' Mike looked at the sleeping dog for a while. When he spoke again he sounded tired and defeated, even to his own ears. 'I don't want to keep pushing her either, Mom. She's real fragile right now.'

'I could ask Pastor Williams to speak with her?'

'I don't think that would be a good idea right now.'

'Oh she's not still mad about that little old talk he did, is she? My Lord, the man was *asked* his opinion. He had to say something.'

'She's not mad about that,' Mike lied, 'she's not up for visitors.'

Fay laid her hand on his and patted it. 'You look worn out. How have *you* been doing?'

'I'm doing fine.' It was a lie and they both knew it, but they were family and what passed between them did not always need to be spoken aloud.

'Tell you what,' Fay said, brightening, 'why don't we have a barbeque here on Saturday afternoon – nothing too formal, food and family.'

Mike hesitated. The way Jessie was, he figured a barbeque would not be high on the agenda. On the other hand, Fay was right, Jessie needed to start interacting with people again. 'I'll run it by her.' Mike finished his coffee and kissed his mother goodbye.

He drove into town to the hardware shop on Granard Street and parked out front. He bought a roll of chicken wire and some heavy-duty clips to mend a tear in the perimeter fence around the property. At the desk, he paid his money and politely answered enquires after Jessie's wellbeing from the well-meaning proprietor. He left the shop, loaded his purchases into the back of the truck, climbed into the cab and drove towards home.

Halfway to the house, he turned left instead of right and found himself heading out of town to where his brother lived, fifteen miles north of Rockville in a shabby trailer park near the county line. When he got there Ace's truck was nowhere to be seen and the trailer, dusty and sagging in the sunlight, was empty. Captain, Ace's dog, came out from under the trailer to the end of his chain and gave a few unenthusiastic barks to let Mike know he was aware of his presence. Captain hated to be left behind, and Ace rarely did so unless he had plans of various shades on the go.

Mike checked there was water in Captain's bowl and then sat on the wooden steps, rubbing the dog's head. He had no idea why he was there. It was not like Ace would offer him advice, even if he had any; that was not his brother's way. Hell, Ace could barely take care of himself. Or maybe Ace had the right idea. Maybe being unfettered and beholden to no one was how the game ought to be played.

Two little kids with dirty knees and deeply tanned faces pedalled past the trailer, making sure they got themselves a good look at the stranger in their midst. They rode to the end of street and back. The bigger of the two pulled up, popped his bike stand and dropped one foot to the ground.

'You looking for Ace, mister?'

'I was.'

'He ain't here.'

'I see that.'

'He went off this mornin'.'

'I see.'

'With his friend with the wonky eye.'

'Right.'

The boys glanced at each other. Clearly they expected this information to be enough to get Mike moving.

'Why're you waitin', mister?'

Mike shrugged. 'Seems the thing to do.'

'You say so.'

They pedalled away.

Mike listened to the breeze move through the branches of the trees behind Ace's trailer. He rubbed Captain's ears and noticed a fine dusting of grey on the hound's snout. He thought of how fleeting life could be. He thought of Alan Edwards and Tracy Flowers, people he had not known well, but liked and respected. Finally he thought of Jessie, of how her eyes drifted whenever he tried to talk to her, of how she flinched at sounds, of how she moved away from him if he touched her at night and cried silently when she thought he was asleep. He thought of all that she had lost – her friends, her dignity, her peace of mind – and he felt angered and guilty. He thought about the future, and for the first time in his life, Mike Conway could not see where it might lie. Everything had been blown apart the day two boys decided it might be something to show the world the power of their savagery. Now the wrongs they had felt rested on everyone, on the lives of the families trying to cope with the death of their loved ones, the survivors, the wounded. Everyone had lost something irretrievable.

Mike watched as a bank of clouds moved across the sun, briefly darkening the valley. He stood up and walked to the truck, and felt as he walked, his own heart fall into shadow.

Jessie stared at the television screen but neither saw nor heard what was playing. She was dazed from exhaustion and felt hollow and wrung out. The night before had been another in a growing line of sleepless hours. The air had been still, her bed was comfortable, but whenever she reached a point where she might fall asleep an image would rise from her memory and jolt her to wakefulness again. In the end, she had gotten up, preferring to wander the house than lie there listening to Mike breathing steadily and deeply beside her.

Hector Diaz. She did not know why his face haunted her dreams, but every night he was there, waiting for her. Every night she saw him raise his arm, watched him fall and saw the bright bubbles of blood and his stained teeth. Every night he smiled at her until the light went from his eyes and she sat up feeling hot tears on her face.

'Hey.'

Mike stood in the doorway of the living room in his boxer shorts, hair tousled, still puffy faced from sleep.

'Hey.'

'How long you been up?'

'A while?'

'You sleep at all?'

'A little.'

Mike crossed his arms and studied her. She knew he wasn't buying what she was selling.

'There's coffee made.'

'How's your head?'

'Oh,' she lifted her hand to her temple, 'better I think.'

Mike looked as though he might say something else, but he turned and headed for the kitchen.

Jessie attempted small talk until Mike was ready for work, but she was glad when he backed out of his space and drove up the lane out of view. She had something in mind and could not bear to have him scrutinise her. After he had gone, she took a shower, got dressed, climbed into her car and drove towards town. She knew where she was going, even if she had no idea what she would do once she got there.

Jessie turned into a small dusty street that backed on to the old railway lines. She counted houses, then pulled over and switched off the engine. Jessie looked at the house through her windscreen, drinking in the details. She had never been there in person, but had seen it many times on the television. It was a squat, flat-roofed building with a plastic corrugate porch. There was a racing bike double-chained to the railings that led to the front door. It was rusty and the saddle was torn so badly that much of the yellow foam stuffing was visible. The windows were closed tight, the curtains drawn. The woodwork was in need of fresh paint and the garden, little more than patchwork scrub, was littered with broken glass and dried dog faeces the colour of cedar ash.

Someone had spray-painted 'killer' across the front of the house. It had been whitewashed over, but the outline of the words remained visible.

Jessie sat immobile with her hands on the steering wheel. She looked across the street to the neighbouring houses, wondering who had targeted this one. Did they blame the family? Did they ask themselves how had they not known what moved amongst them?

What was she doing there?

She wished she had an answer, but she did not.

She got out and closed the car door. It sounded heavy in the still warm air: a solid clunk of metal on metal. Jessie walked up the garden, knocked on the door of the house and waited. Nobody answered. She stood listening for a moment and released the breath she hadn't realised she'd been holding. She turned to leave, but as she did, a curtain on the window nearest the door was pulled back and a woman looked out. She was heavy set, with long thick hair to one side in a plait. Jessie recognised her from the newspapers: Ana Diaz, Hector's mother.

Jessie nodded and the curtain dropped back into place. She waited. Nothing. She began to feel foolish, then flustered. This had been a mistake. She had taken a half turn from the door when it was yanked open and a rangy young man wearing a bandana stepped out onto the porch.

Jessie cleared her throat, startled. 'Hi, I'm—'

Without pausing to break stride, he raised his two hands and shoved Jessie in the chest, hard. Jessie fell off the porch and landed on her back in the scrub yard. Before she could catch her breath he jumped down the steps and began swinging his fists. Jessie threw her hands over her head to protect her face as blows rained down.

'Fuck you, bitch, you killed my brother.' He punctuated every word with another blow.

Jessie rolled onto her stomach and tried to crawl towards the street.

'Oh now you wanna go? You wanna go, bitch?

He grabbed her by the collar of her shirt and began to haul her across the dead grass towards the sidewalk. Jessie choked and gagged from the pressure on her neck. Buttons pinged as she scrambled to get her feet under her. She heard someone screaming.

'Javier!'

Her shirt ripped. Jessie pitched forward on to her knees, gasping and sucking air. She curled into a tight ball but he managed to deliver a vicious kick to her ribs. Jessie cried out in pain. She tried to cover her head and caught a glimpse of a young girl flying down the steps, with an older man on her heels. The older man threw his arms around the young man who had attacked her and the girl disentangled his hands from what was left of Jessie's shirt.

The older man was not large, but he was strong, and he hoisted her attacker into the air, away from Jessie towards the house. Jessie rolled onto her knees and managed to get to her feet. She staggered out to the car where she collapsed against the passenger side. She spat, wiped dirt from her mouth, and looked up. The older man was half pushing and half carrying the screaming Javier up the steps, where Hector's mother now stood motionless. They passed her by and she leaned and closed the door behind them. After a moment, she walked down the garden to the fence. The younger girl fell into step behind her.

People had come out of their homes. They stood on their porches, silent, watching. Jessie used the car to haul herself upright. She was badly shaken; she realised most of her upper body was exposed. She pulled the tatters of her shirt about her.

'I– I am…'

Jessie leaned against the side of her car, struggling to find words. She realised she had no idea how to begin, or how to articulate her thoughts. In the end, Ana Diaz spoke first.

'You are the woman who shot Hector.'

'Yes, I am.'

'What do you want?'

'I wanted … to see you, to tell you that I'm sorry about what happened.'

The woman's gaze did not waver, nor did her expression change in any way. She turned and began to walk towards the house.

'Please, you must believe me. I am so sorry,' Jessie cried. 'He gave me no choice.'

Ana Diaz stopped walking. She said something in Spanish to the younger girl, and then went inside.

The girl retrieved the collar of Jessie shirt and carried it to her.

'Thank you,' Jessie said.

The girl dropped the collar into her hand, leaned back, and without warning spat in Jessie's face.

Jessie wiped the spittle away with the collar. She pushed her hair back from her forehead and limped round to the other side of her car. She got in and tried to start it. It took her a number of attempts before she managed. At the end of the street she slowed for a stop sign and sat there, shaking. Another car drove up behind her and blasted her with his horn. Panicked, Jessie stalled the engine. He honked again. Then he pulled around her and drove away, leaving a blue plume of impatience in his wake.

18

Billy McCann's 'office' was a small rough-and-tumble bar on the outskirts of town called The Rookery. Darla pulled into the car park shortly after six. She made sure there was nothing of value visible in her car, locked the doors and set the alarm. She had learned this particular lesson the hard way from previous visits.

Billy McCann was of Protestant Scottish stock. He was notoriously hot tempered and a monumental drinker. He had been a good lawyer once, way back in the days before he decided he preferred the company of loose women and hooch. Not that Darla could really remember – he had been disbarred long before she left high school – but he and her father had been tight. So when Teddy Levine needed someone he could rely on to garner information on his third wife, the much hated Stacy, it was to Billy he turned. When Teddy died three years previously Darla had inherited Billy, along with the family home.

She found him now, seated with his back to the wall in his usual alcove inside the main door of the bar. As she approached he lifted his head and she was not entirely surprised to see that he had not one, but two black eyes.

'What happened to you?'

'Marital dispute.'

'Dallas did *that?*'

Billy grinned. 'Nah, I you know ain't gonna let no eighty-pound nut job get the drop on me. This here is a present from Ginny's new beau.'

Darla thought for a second and then started to laugh. 'Your first wife's new husband?'

'Yeah. Though how much longer they're gonna stay hitched I can't say.'

'*You didn't.*'

'Well, a man would be a fool to turn down what's freely offered.'

Darla shook her head as she sat down. How Billy McCann was like catnip to so many of the women of Rockville was something of a mystery to her. She looked him over: Billy was six four in his socks; he had pale freckly skin and sparse reddish hair, turning grey, she noticed. He was still big man, but what had once been rock hard muscle was now soft and running to fat, yet he never seemed to lack female company.

Billy drank a third of his beer in one mouthful and sighed with satisfaction.

'So, what's the job?'

'Jessie Conway.'

'That the school teacher?'

'Yes.'

'Well, what about her?'

'That's just it. I don't know what; I just know there's something not right about her.'

Billy rested his massive scarred hands on the table. 'Feelings are running high about that woman, Darla. If you're planning on bringing down the hatchet you want to make sure you have a clean swing at the neck.'

'I don't think that neck's as clean as people think.'

'What has you figured on that?'

'A hunch.'

'That it?'

'Yes.'

'You're getting more like your old man every time I see you.' Billy thought it over, then shrugged. 'Okay, I'll do some digging.'

Darla opened her bag and passed him a sheet of paper. Billy lifted the page and squinted at it through his swollen eyes.

'This it?'

'This is all anyone's been able to get so far.'

'Huh.'

'She's married to Mike Conway; he owns the auto repair shop over on Teal. She's only lived in Rockville eight years. I spoke to Alice Carmichael, the Principal at the school and she told me Jessie used to teach in Blowing Rock, which I have managed to get confirmed. Thing is, when I contacted them they said Jessie had been recommended to them from some employment agency over in Tennessee. That agency is now closed down and I haven't been able to find the last place she worked before that.'

'Did you ask her?'

'She won't talk to press. Hell, she hates the sight of me.'

'Maybe she was overseas or something.'

'I don't think so. And that's not all. Jessie Conway says her maiden name was Dalton and that her parents were killed in a car crash twelve years ago.'

'Sucks.'

'I spoke to an old colleague and asked him to do some checking. It's true that an Anthony and Rebecca Dalton were killed twelve years ago coming back from a friend's house and that they lived in Lake City, Tennessee. Only thing is, he could not find any mention of them having a daughter. Only a son.'

Billy looked a little more interested. 'You spoken to him?'

'No, there's no line on him either. But I made some discreet inquiries; Jessie Conway has never mentioned having a brother to anyone, as far as I know. Certainly no family appeared around the time of the shooting, save only her husband's family.'

'So what do you need from me?'

'The Conways have complained about me twice now and old Mrs Conway has the ear of a few businesses around town, businesses that are now threatening to pull their advertising revenue over a piece I ran,' Darla said, feeling heat rise to her face. 'Popeye won't give me any more rope and I can't be seen to be digging, but here's a hole in that woman's history. I want you to get me whatever I need to fill it in.'

Billy put down the page and thought about it. After a moment, he raised the fingers of his left hand and touched the swollen skin around his eyes. 'Can't hurt to take a break from Dodge for a while.'

19

Caleb dabbed iodine on his cuts, then carefully applied plasters to them, smiling as he did so. Even mortally wounded Marcie had fought him like a tiger, drawing blood and forcing him to finish the job far quicker than he would have liked. Afterwards he had been on a high for hours, recounting every moment, every furious gasp of her mangled body. She had invigorated him.

But now, back at the apartment, his high was fading fast and he was bored and restless. He hated the city: the cloying heat, the traffic, the noise, the sense of being walled in. His dreams, when he managed to get some sleep at all, were vivid and epic: he saw himself in the woods, carrying his bow, running strong and free.

And now, he discovered to his annoyance, a new problem had surfaced: his funds were running low. This would have to be rectified before he gave any more thoughts to hunting.

To do this he decided to concentrate on a twenty-two-year-old student named Barbara Cross. Barbara was a Category B, pure and simple; a moving target like Arthur S. Weils, just waiting to be picked off. She had called the Voice of Hope help line two months before, weeping over some boy and threatening suicide. Her threats had not rung true to Caleb, but it had been a dull night so he'd let her ramble on. She had called a number of times since then to complain about a myriad of things, usually drunk. During one call she claimed she had been date raped by a fellow student and that it had left her withdrawn and frightened. She claimed that was why she drank the way she did.

On her last call, she had told the profoundly bored Caleb that she had phoned her rapist and demanded an apology, but he had laughed at her accusations. She said she was lonely and depressed. She had terrible taste in men, she said. She wept as she explained why she believed them when they told her bad things about herself. She said she guessed she knew why a previous boyfriend had cheated on her with a close friend and dumped her so heartlessly. She told Caleb she felt utterly betrayed and close to some kind of breaking point. She threatened suicide again. This time, Caleb decided if she didn't kill herself he might take the matter into his own hands,

'You know, after the last time we talked I told my father about the rape. Do you know what he said to me when I told him?'

'No.'

'He said it was my own fault. He said if I hadn't wanted to have sexual relations I had no business inviting a man up to my bedroom. Can you *believe* that? My own father!'

'He said that?' Caleb stared at the ceiling, thinking her father was right.

'Dad's such an asshole. Just 'cause he's paying for college he thinks he owns me. I didn't even want to come here anyway, that was all his idea. I wanted to do an art degree in New York. I mean how could he say that?' she sobbed down the line. 'I'm his little girl, he's supposed to look out for me, he's supposed to believe me. I just ... I just want to *die*.'

Caleb let her cry, figuring – correctly – that she enjoyed the theatrics.

'What you're feeling sounds normal to me,' Caleb said, when she finally dribbled to a halt. 'I'd be angry if someone let me down like that.'

'I *know, right?*'

'That is a harsh view he's taken.'

'That's so true,' she wailed. 'It totally is.'

'This boyfriend–'

'Chris.'

'–sounds like a real piece of work, no wonder you're upset.'

'Right, right,' she said, her voice becoming steady again, her tears being replaced by indignation. 'Totally. I mean like, I *knew* he liked Silvia and shit, but she was my friend, right? Your boyfriend is supposed to *like* your friends, right?'

'He oughta respect your judgment, sure.'

'Right! Like her, great, but not *fuck* her behind my back!'

And off she went again, wailing.

Caleb watched a cockroach walk across the tiles towards his boot; he kicked at it, but at the last moment it changed direction and scuttled the other way. Even the cockroach, he thought, had more presence of mind than Barbara.

'Barbara?'

He waited for her tears to subside once more. They were always so pathetic when they cried, so utterly pathetic. For a brief moment he considered hanging up.

'Now you need to get yourself a pen and a piece of paper.'

'Oh, oh okay.'

'I want you to write out two notes. I want you to write one to your Daddy and one to this Chris fellow.'

'But, I don't know why–'

'Barbara, I'm *tryin'* to help you here.'

'Oh … okay.'

'This is what you do. Write two letters. You tell them how you feel Barbara. I mean really let 'em have it, both barrels. Can you do that, Barbara?'

'Yeah, okay. I can do that.'

'Everything you told me, Barbara, you put it down.'

'Okay … um, do I send them?'

'No, you write the letters and then you seal them in two envelopes.'

'Oh, okay.'

'Put their names on the front of each and leave those envelopes somewhere you can see them, like a side table or–'

'I can put them on the mantle. I have a fireplace here.'

Caleb made a note of that. Fireplace. Most likely she was in a house and not an apartment. He had already gleaned from their conversations that she lived directly across the road from Latta Park, and that the drycleaners her boyfriend worked in was on E. Worthington Avenue. It would not take much more information to pinpoint her exact location.

By the time Caleb got off the phone with her twenty minutes later, he knew the street she lived on and the car she drove. It was that easy.

Darla Levine slid into one of the red vinyl booths at Ray's Diner and ordered a black coffee. When the waitress brought it, she added three sugars and stirred it lethargically. She watched the ebb and flow of customers, her thoughts dark, but her humour darker still. Popeye was making her life a goddamned misery. She had spent the entire morning at a cat sanctuary forty miles east of Rockville, interviewing some old hippy and her creepy husband about their various rescued fur balls. Her best pumps reeked of cat piss.

She watched the door of the café. Her big chance had come and gone. Over. It was hard enough to get a hot story in a town like Rockville, but one that stretched across the country in such a profound way was a once in a lifetime opportunity. Everything now hinged on Billy, and that was surely a most depressing thought.

She drank her coffee and waited. Shortly after twelve, the door opened and Billy McCann entered, looking every inch the sleazy genius she knew him to be. He wore gold-rimmed aviator sunglasses, crumpled cargo shorts to his knees, what might have once been white towelling socks, and moccasins; he topped this egregious combination with a loud, canary yellow dress shirt. He carried a small brown leather satchel under his arm. Without invitation, he plopped into the booth opposite her and grabbed a serviette to mop the sweat from his face. Various curious heads glanced his way.

'Shit, hotter than Haiti out there.'

'You've been to Haiti?'

'Fuck no, why the hell would anyone want to go there?'

He removed his sunglasses and laid them on the table. His eyes looked a little less swollen, although they were still pretty bruised.

'Hey Darlin', can I get a cup of coffee here?' he called to the waitress, who was serving people at a different table. She glanced at him in irritation. 'Be right with you, sir.'

'None of that fancy foamy crap; I want a regular cup of regular Joe.' He turned his attention to Darla. 'Who pissed in your cornflakes?'

'Excuse me?'

'The face, what's eating you?'

'Work-related anxiety. What have you got?'

He lifted the satchel onto the table and undid the buckles. He removed a slim manila folder and slid it across the surface to her. She reached for it, but he pressed down on it with his thumb.

'This one is going to cost a little extra.'

'We already agreed a price.'

'That was before. None of this information was cheap to come by and you know I don't like to be out of pocket.'

'How much out?'

'You want receipts now, kid? Maybe a neat little ledger of all my expenses?'

Darla's eyes drifted down to his hand. 'How much?'

'Another three.'

'Are you kidding me?

'Hell no, I never joke about money.'

'This is my dime, Barry. Popeye didn't authorise this.'

'Come on Darla, you know me how long?'

'Long enough.'

'Exactly. So what makes you think I'd wanna stiff you? That's not business. Trust me, this is good stuff, but it cost me, so now it's costing you. You wanted a story; well believe me, you've got one.'

Darla leaned back in her seat and studied him carefully. Despite their long relationship, Billy McCann was a devious shit whose first and only loyalty was to Billy McCann. Still, what he said made a kind of sense. Even if it hadn't, there was no point arguing. The truth was she needed a toad like McCann and he needed a regular pay cheque like her. While she mistrusted him on a personal level, she respected his abilities. He was like a ginger aardvark; he could dig through any layer of dirt to uncover any hidden gem. The truth was he couldn't have cared less what she did or did not think. He was honest that way, she supposed.

'I'll have it for you by the end of the day.'

'Drop it to the office?'

'Sure.'

She tugged at the folder; eventually he released it and sat back. 'Hey honey,' he called the waitress, 'better give me that coffee to go.'

While he collected his coffee, Darla opened the file. She read down the first page, flipped it over and read some of the way down the second. She jerked her head up. Billy was standing by the counter, watching her.

'Are you shitting me?'

'I told you it was good stuff.'

Darla grinned. 'Good? This is *dynamite*.'

'Well then, go blow a story out of the water and quit looking like a wet weekend.' He tipped an imaginary hat to her, collected his coffee and left.

Darla continued to read, devouring the details of Jessie Conway's history, all the while thinking about how much she was going to enjoy the look on Popeye's face when she showed her hand this time.

Chippy could not remember a time he had seen Darla Levine smile quite as much as she was smiling right at that moment. It made him nervous.

'Didn't I tell you there was something suspicious about her? Didn't I say her aversion to the press was odd? Nobody turns down that kind of press. *No one* is that humble. No one.'

'I thought Popeye say he want us out of her business.'

'That, Chippy, was *before*; before we had this!'

'I dunno man, he seem pretty mad to me.'

'Are you kidding me?'

Chippy held up his hands. 'I'm just saying.'

'Well don't say. I don't want to hear it.' Darla grabbed her purse from the top drawer of her desk. 'Go get your camera. We need to hit the road.'

'I haven't even ate yet.'

'Jesus, didn't you hear a work I said? How can you think about food at a time like this?'

''Cause I'm hungry.'

'We'll get food on the road. *Come on*, we're burning daylight.'

Darla and Chippy left the office and hurried downstairs to the Escalade.

'Should we tell him where we're going?' Chippy asked, pausing by the driver's door.

'No.'

'Aw, man. I'm s'posed to take pictures of the shopping centre for J.J.'

'Get in, will you. I'll handle J.J.'

'He's gonna be mad.'

'*Get in.*'

By the time they had reached Lake City, Tennessee, the sun was low in the sky and Chippy, who still hadn't eaten, was sullen and anxious. His phone had rung countless times until Darla had grabbed it, switched it off and tossed it over her shoulder onto the back seat. They turned off Route 75 and cruised through a well-appointed suburb while Darla checked the GPS for confirmation.

'Next one over, according to this piece of garbage.'

'Left or right?'

'Left.'

They pulled onto a wide, tree-lined street. The homes here were large, but not ostentatious. A number of them were in darkness and shuttered up tight.

'Quiet,' Chippy said.

Darla glanced at her notes. 'Number 148, there! Pull over.'

They parked outside a large clapboard house set back from the sidewalk by a square of lawn surrounded by neatly maintained bushes. Lights glowed from deep within the house and a Toyota sat parked in the driveway behind a yellow Volkswagen Beetle.

'Wait here,' Darla said.

'Yes sir,' Chippy said, as his stomach rumbled in complaint.

Darla climbed out, checked her hair in the wing mirror and approached the house. She rang the doorbell and heard a dog barking somewhere out back in response. After a minute, a tubby teenager wearing shorts and a tank top opened the door and peered out.

'Yeah?'

'Good evening,' Darla said, smiling. 'My name is Darla Levine and I'm a reporter with *The Rockville Gazette*. I'm investigating a person who may have lived at this address at some point. I wonder are either of your parents home?'

The girl looked past her to the street. 'Is this, like, a joke? Did Mark put you up to this? 'Cause if he did you can tell him it's not freaking funny.'

Darla kept her smile in place as she removed a card from her purse and passed it over. The girl read it, popped a gum bubble and said, 'huh'. She turned her head and bellowed, '*Dad!*'

Within seconds a large man with hair to his shoulders, wearing jeans and a baggy white shirt, appeared at the door. He did a double take when he saw Darla and she knew immediately he would give her any information she required. It turned out all she needed to know was the name of the old lady who lived down the street.

'Really, Mr Blench, I sure do so appreciate you talking the time from your busy evening to make introductions,' Darla said, laying it on thick as she hurried down the street to the house. 'But it is really not necessary to accompany me.'

'Oh it's no trouble, Miss Levine. Call me Kevin.'

Even by streetlight Darla could tell he was blushing. 'Are you sure Miss Millar will remember the Daltons?'

'Oh sure, Miss Millar's near eighty now, but she's still as sharp as a tack.'

They stopped outside a house at the end of the road. It was smaller than the others and in need of some repair. Together, Darla and Kevin climbed the creaking wooden steps to the porch. Mr Blench rapped on the door, hard.

'She's a little hard of hearing,' he said, by way of explanation to a question Darla had not asked. They waited. Crickets chirped. Darla tried to ignore the smell of rising damp, or Kevin Blench, whichever it was.

'Must be exciting being a reporter.'

'Mm.'

'I imagine you get to interview all sorts of famous people.'

'I sure do.'

'Who's the most famous person you ever interviewed.'

'George Clooney,' Darla lied.

'The actor?'

No, the builder, Darla thought, wondering why it was that the gods seem to conspire against her at every turn. She reached out and knocked the door again, harder than Kevin had.

'State your business,' an aged voice said. 'I have a loaded gun and I am not afraid to use it.'

'Miss Millar, it's Kevin. From 148?'

'I know which house you live in, Kevin. I am old, not dumb.'

Kevin glanced at Darla and flushed. 'Ma'am, I've got someone here who would like to have a word with you if you had the time.'

Darla heard a number of bolts slide back. Then a very small old lady carrying a very large old gun looked out.

'Well, what do you know,' she said, looking Darla up and down. 'You finally took my advice, Kevin. You bought yourself one of them mail-order brides.'

Yep, Darla thought in a surly fashion, at every turn.

Caleb parked the Taurus a little way down the street from Barbara Cross's home and waited patiently until dusk set in. If he guessed her habits correctly, he figured he would not have long to wait. Sure enough, shortly before ten, Barbara Cross left her townhouse, dolled up to the nines, and began to walk east.

Caleb got out of the car, crossed the street and trailed her two blocks to a small, funky-looking bar. He waited for a few minutes then entered after her. He eased his way past a number of people and found a seat at the bar. It was crowded; the patrons were young and hip, mostly students from the local college.

Caleb ordered a beer and watched Barbara do the rounds, flitting from one group of people to another, steadily drinking as she did so. She was animated, laughing loudly and gesticulating, but Caleb could sense her desperation from across the room. She was downing vodka – straight with a twist of lime. She was drinking a lot of it.

The fifth time she came to the bar to order a drink, he made his move.

'Excuse me, ma'am.'

She glanced at him, sized him up and disregarded him in seconds.

'Yeah?'

'Can you give me the time?'

'Sure, it's …' she squinted at her watch, 'just gone eleven.'

'Oh, okay, thanks anyway,' Caleb sighed and shook his head. 'I should have known this would happen.'

She leaned her arms on the bar and looked at him quizzically.

'I've been stood up.' He gave a small shrug of his shoulders. 'It happens.'

'That is does.'

'Guess some people think it okay to treat folk like dirt.'

That was all it took to get her to sit by him and start talking. Of course, it helped that he had known what buttons to push. But even without the firsthand knowledge, Barbara Cross was ridiculously easy to manipulate. By the time she had put away another four vodkas she was as pliable as wet clay.

The next part was trickier. Caleb needed to leave the bar alone in case anyone asked questions later on. He waited until she went to the toilet, then gathered up his things and signalled to the barman.

'For my bill,' Caleb said, tossing some notes on the counter.

'What about your date?'

'Not my scene, man.'

The barman shrugged. Caleb stood up and left quickly. He waited in the doorway of a shop front. As he had anticipated, she left the bar soon after him, weaving down the street heading in the direction of her house. He caught up to her one block over.

'Hey, wait up!'

She turned towards the shout and he could see from the mascara tracks on her face she had been crying.

'What's wrong?'

'I thought you were different. Guess…' she hiccupped into the back of her hand, '…guess I was wrong.'

'I'm real sorry I had to leave that way. But when I went to order more drinks I saw I'd left my wallet in the car and had to go get it.

When I got back the barman said you'd paid your tab and hightailed it. Why didn't you wait?' He raised his hand and tucked a loose strand of hair behind her ear. 'I thought we were having a good time.'

Barbara frowned and squinted up at him. 'You told him you'd be back?'

'Yes ma'am.'

'He didn't say that. He said you'd split.'

'If I'd split I wouldn't have had to run all this way to catch you up.'

'Oh.' She looked confused. 'You're not lying, are you?'

'I don't lie.'

She smiled a little uncertainly. 'Do you want to have that drink? My place is real close by.'

'I'd like that.'

'Come on.'

She linked his arm and Caleb wondered idly what is was about Category B people like Barbara and Art. Why was their value on life so low that they were eager to relinquish it freely? He thought of them, and the many like them, drifting through life with a big bullseye painted on their back. If they were lucky, the predator was not looking as they drifted by. If not ... well, if not there were people like him.

'You have to come, they're expecting you.' Mike stood in the door of the bathroom wearing nothing but a towel wrapped around his waist. His body looked lean and brown; his hair lay wet and flat against his head.

Jessie put the book she had been pretending to read down beside her on the bed. Their dog, Rudy was asleep at her feet, his chin resting on her ankles.

'You go. You'll have just as good a time without me.'

'Mom is doing this *for* you.'

'I didn't ask her to do anything for me.'

'Jess.'

'I don't want to go. I don't feel up to it.'

'Up to what?' Mike said, his voice rising slightly. 'You don't have to do nothing except sit there and–'

'Mike–'

'–eat some food, drink a beer or two and relax.'

'I'm perfectly relaxed right here.' Jessie picked up her book again but now her hands were trembling.

'You know what, Jessie. This is not how it's going to be!'

Rudy opened his eyes and whined softly at the raised voices. Jessie lowered her book and stared at Mike in surprise.

'*Excuse* me?'

'You think I don't see what you're doing? You're holed up in this house avoiding people. You've been doing it for weeks. But I've had enough; this is not how it is going to be. I won't let you do this to yourself.'

'I don't see–'

'We don't have to stay there long. We can–'

'I don't fucking want to go, Mike. Okay?'

Mike looked surprised: Jessie almost never swore.

'It'll look funny if you don't show, set them tongues wagging for sure.'

'I don't give a damn about their *tongues* neither.'

'Yeah, well I do, and I don't want to be stuck fending off questions for the evening.'

'Oh, so it's all about you then?'

Mike took two steps into the room. 'It's about *us*. It's about us doing something together. Doing something normal for a change.'

'What are you talking about? Normal? *Normal?* Are you kidding me?'

'I'm not kidding about anything. I know you're going through something rough, Jessie. Believe me, I get it. But let me tell you something, *you're not the only one.*' Mike looked away for a moment. 'We've got to try get a handle on what happened. How are we supposed to get through this if you won't talk to me? If you won't talk to someone?'

'I did talk to Dr Fraas.'

'Once! Once! After that you refused to go back to him.'

'He can't help me.'

'You didn't give him a chance. You think you're dealing, Jessie, but you're not. You don't sleep, you hardly eat, and you're popping pills like there's no tomorrow. I can hear you crying at night. You won't talk to me, you … Look, I'm not asking you to do anything out of the ordinary here, except come with me tonight and eat some food.'

Though she tried to stop them, tears began to spill from Jessie's eyes. Mike looked at her, anguished. 'Please, Jessie.'

'All right.'

'Well all right.' Mike tried his hand at a smile, but it didn't quite work. 'You should wear that green dress of yours, that looks nice.'

Jessie wiped her tears and rubbed the top of Rudy's head. 'Since when have you ever taken notice of my wardrobe?'

'I've got eyes, don't I?'

'I guess you do.'

While Mike shaved, Jessie pulled out the dress and held it against her body. She looked at her reflection in the mirrored door of the wardrobe, trailing a critical eye over what she saw. She looked sickly and wan. Her cheekbones were more prominent than ever, and while that might look fantastic on some Hollywood starlet, it did not please her in the slightest.

She took a quick shower while Mike fed Rudy and left some food out in a bowl for the cats at the back of the house. By the time he had done that and locked up, she was dressed and ready to go.

'See,' Mike snaked an arm over her shoulder and kissed her on the forehead before releasing her, 'green suits you.'

'Thank you.' Jessie checked her reflection in the hall mirror and dabbed some lip gloss on her lips.

You're dolling yourself up while your friends lie rotting in the earth, while parents are crying over their injured babies, while children are learning how to be people again.

She shivered. What she was doing seemed ridiculous and offensive.

'You can't be cold?' Mike said.

'A little,' she said, 'I think I'll take a shawl.'

'I'll go start the engine up.' Mike kissed her lightly on her forehead again. 'I'm glad you decided to come.'

'Me too.'

Jessie walked to the bathroom and closed the door. She barely made it to the toilet before she vomited. She retched until her stomach was empty. When she was sure nothing else could possibly come up, she washed her face and hands, reapplied her lip gloss and went to join her husband.

Fay lived on the opposite side of the Rockville to them; the 'gentrified' side, as it was laughingly known amongst those that could not afford to live there. Mike's father, George, had built the house some time in the early '70s, following a memory of an elaborate house he once stayed at in Europe. Unfortunately, George hadn't been much of an architect and as a result, the single-storey house was an odd expanse of strangely shaped rooms built in an almost hexagonal shape around a central courtyard.

The house was gaily lit up when they arrived. Mike drove up the long fenced drive and parked to the rear of the property.

'I see Waldo is here.' Mike nodded to an out-of-state Lexus. Waldo was Walter Hynes, Karen's – Mike's sister's – boyfriend.

'Don't call him that. He hates being called Waldo.'

'I don't think much of that fellow.'

'You mean he's not local.'

'That's got nothing to do with it.'

'You know I'm not local either,' she reminded him.

'That's different.'

'How?'

Mike shrugged. 'It just is.'

They got out of the truck. As they climbed the steps to the patio, Fay flung open the doors. 'There you are! I was starting to think you weren't coming.'

'Hey, Mom, good to see you.'

'Come in, come in. Oh for heaven's sake, Mike, I'm glad you're here, could you please go help your brother get that grill going some time this evening. I do not know what is wrong with it.'

'I'm sure Ace has it under control.'

'Mike,' Fay said, tilting her head.

'I'll go take a look.' Mike stepped past his mother and into the main house. Fay gave Jessie an expansive hug.

'I'm *so* glad you're here. The girls are inside. My, isn't green just darling on you. Come on through, I sure hope you're hungry.'

Jessie allowed herself to be shepherded through the house. She spotted Walter by the fireplace in the living room, standing stiff and formal with a bottle of beer in his hand. He tipped the bottle to Jessie and she raised a hand in return. Jeb Orville, husband to Penny, Mike's other sister, was sprawled on Fay's white sofa, pink-faced from sun, wearing a cream polo shirt and cargo pants. Jeb's father Vernon Orville was one of the richest men in Rockville, owing to the timber trade. Jeb worked in the business as little as possible while drawing down a considerable salary. He was not a person Jessie had a lot of time for.

Jessie offered to help Fay in the kitchen but was refused, so she made small talk with Penny and Karen. After a while, she excused herself and drifted outside to where Fay had set up a long table under a green awning in the courtyard. Mike and Ace stood over the now lit barbeque. Ace turned drumsticks over the coals, a cigarette dangling from his lips, a beer in his other hand. He was deeply tanned and wearing clean jeans and a clean shirt. Jessie drew alongside them. Ace had a zoned-out look that Jessie guessed was from a certain level of self-medication. Well, if that's what it took to get through these family reunions, who was she to judge?

'Hey, Ace.'

He turned to her and smiled shyly. 'How you doin', Jess?'

'Fine, thank you. You?'

'I have been a whole lot worse.' His eyes drifted down to her empty hands. 'Mike, your wife could probably do with a drink.'

'Jess?'

'I'd love a glass of white wine.'

Mike went inside to fetch her drink while Jessie took a seat at the table, enjoying the warm air and the rich scent of the honeysuckle growing all around the courtyard walls. Ace cooked the rest of the chicken, and then placed several potatoes wrapped in foil over the coals. He hummed under his breath while he worked. The ash on his cigarettes grew perilously long between tips. Neither of them spoke, but the silence between them was natural and comfortable. Jessie always felt at ease around Ace and he around her. She knew he had his demons and thought they were none of her concern. She had long before decided it was not her place to judge people for how they lived their lives. Ace was his own man. That didn't suit *some* folk in the Conway clan, but *that* wasn't her concern either.

The evening drew on and for the most part it was perfect: nothing but easy company and light conversation. For the first time in a long time some of the tension ebbed from Jessie's body. That was until Jeb, brimming with scotch and entitlement, felt the need to pontificate on the subject of violence. Penny attempted to draw him away from the topic, but Jeb, standing under the awning gnawing sticky chicken wings, talked over his wife.

'See, kids these days, they get too much handed to 'em,' he said, sucking dark brown sauce from his thumb. 'That's why they go nuts.'

'For God's sake, Jeb,' Penny said, with a mortified glance in Jessie's direction. 'Nobody needs to hear this.'

'That's the other problem,' Jeb wiped his mouth with the back of his hand. 'We pretend like this shit don't happen. Well it's happening. Kids got no sense of … ethics. Why would they? Everything comes too easy to them.'

Mike took a sip of his beer. 'Unlike, say, how you struggled to find employment?'

It went quiet for long moment. Inside, Jessie heard Fay clattering around with the dessert plates.

'My daddy built that mill from the ground up,' Jeb said petulantly. 'I know I was raised well; that's not the point I was making.'

Ace lit a cigarette and folded his arms across this chest, his expression neutral. 'What was your point?'

'Ace–'Penny hissed.

'My point is we're breeding a generation of fags and layabouts. Like them kids that shot up the school. Kids like them Columbine freaks in the trench coats and all the weird music and stuff. Back in my day, if you saw a kid wearing make-up you saw someone touched in the head. Now we're all supposed to act like we don't see 'em and pretend we're okay with stuff we used to be proud to stand against.'

'Jeb, honey, could you see if there's some more coleslaw in the fridge?' Karen said.

'There's some right there,' Jeb pointed to a tub by a stack of stripped ribs. 'Now I know these days folk like to say it's all, what ya call it … social conditioning or some shit – excuse me – some bull crap like that, but it is no such thing. We didn't have no shootings in our days, did we Walter?'

'I'm sure people got shot plenty in our day.' Walter opened a bottle of beer and threw Karen a look. Karen shrugged, helpless.

'Yeah I know, but not like now. We didn't have kids going in and shooting up a place or bombing the heck out of schools. We didn't have that sort of–'

'Jeb, I'm not sure we need to talk about this right now,' Penny said.

Fay returned carrying ice cream. 'I hope everyone kept room for some dessert?'

'Well see that right there is part of it,' Jeb said, ignoring his mother-in-law. 'If we don't talk about these things … if we don't face up to the peril this generation is suffering from, and I mean peril, a peril of the soul … see if we don't face up to these things … they get swept under the carpet.'

Fay frowned and glanced at her daughters, then to Jessie, who had grown still and pale. 'Give it a rest, Jeb, would you?' Mike said.

'Now hold on here, that's what happens. We duck and dive and bob and weave, but we know what's out there and we need to face these fears, we need to face them head on, we need–'

'I faced it head on,' Jessie said.

Jeb looked at her as if seeing her for the first time.

'I faced it head on, Jeb, and you know what I learned from it?'

Jeb stared at her.

'Absolutely nothing, that's what I learned. Nothing.'

Jessie stood and pushed her chair back from the table. Her face was alabaster pale, her eyes glittery and overbright. 'Good night, Fay, it's been a lovely evening and thank you for having me.'

'Jessie, please don't go.'

Jessie grabbed her shawl and walked through the house. She walked straight out the door without stopping.

Mike joined her after a few minutes, his face flushed with temper. He climbed into the cab and slammed the door. 'There's no cure for stupid, Jessie. You know Jeb, a few drinks down him and that man is stupid to the core.'

'Can we go home?'

Mike drove them home. When they pulled into the yard, Rudy got to his feet and stood in the headlights yipping a delighted greeting.

'You okay?' Mike asked.

Jessie stared out the windscreen at her home, at her dog standing in the beams of light. She realised then what it was that had been bothering her. She had spoken in anger, but, she realised with a shock, it had been the truth. Everything she had said back at Fay's was true.

Everything she had once believed had been swept away on a wave of screams and blood and pain. No insight to the universe had been revealed to her; she had learned nothing. She *knew* nothing. She felt nothing. She might as well be dead inside. She might as well have died in a hail of bullets on the cafeteria floor.

Maybe that was the truth of it. Maybe there was nothing to be learned.

Absolutely nothing.

'Jessie?'

'I can't do this any more.'

'Do what?'

'Any of it.'

Mike took her hand in his. 'Don't talk like that.'

She pulled her hand away. 'I'm sorry.'

'He didn't mean it. Damn fool talks too much.'

They sat for a while, saying nothing. Rudy plonked his rump down in the dust, bored from waiting.

24

Darla Levine was hot, tired and sticky. Worse than that, she felt perilously dull-witted from the enforced company of Chippy, who, when he wasn't yapping at her, insisted on playing a Los Tigres del Norte CD, singing along at the top of his lungs for most of the trip.

'How much longer?'

'Should be right up ahead,' Chippy said, peering through the dusty windscreen.

'You've been saying that for ages.'

They had been on the road since early that morning and were now deep in the highlands of Tennessee. Darla was sick to the back teeth of looking at trees.

'*Mira!* There!'

Before them the road snaked around to the right and set back off it about one hundred feet was 'Misty's', a diner and rest stop for weary travellers. Chippy pulled across the highway and drove into the compact dirt lot.

'Park behind the trucks.'

'Why?'

'I don't want him to know I have a photographer with me.'

''Kay.'

He parked near a row of dusty trees. 'Man, I'm starving. You think they do tamales?'

'Stay here, I won't be long.'

'Why you say I gotta stay all the time like a dog or some shit? I ain't no dog.'

'I need you to walk by the windows and make an identification. When he comes out I need you to take his picture. Don't let him see you.'

'But you said this was an assignment.'

'I said you're to take his picture. That's all.'

Chippy looked fleetingly puzzled, then his features crumpled. 'Aw, Popeye don't know about this one?'

'Make sure you get a good clear shot of him.'

'Aw, shit.'

Darla gathered up her things, climbed out and moved towards the diner through rigs parked three deep.

It was a ramshackle affair. The original building was prefabricated, with a single-slope roof and two window walls overlooking the fore-court. Clearly, over time there had been a number of additions added to the main structure; more than Darla guessed were legal. She figured that out this way building inspectors had to be as rare as liberals.

Darla pushed the door open and stepped into a long room with double booths running the length of one wall, a bar at the other, and free-standing tables on the floor in the middle. The place was busy, wall to wall with road travellers, truckers, sales folk, small families with tired-looking faces and bored children picking at chips.

Darla scanned the place and spotted her target within seconds. Though she had never met Clint Robinson in person, she recognised him from the photos Billy had managed to acquire. He was seated in the second to last booth near the toilets. Darla made her way towards him, aware that many sets of eyes were following. At the booth she stopped walking and said, 'Mr Robinson?'

Clint Robinson looked up from his food. She put him around his late forties, but he might have been older. He was thin, with washed-out blue eyes, a week's growth on his face and a busted nose. There was grease on his chin and oil on his shirt. He looked like a man who had been shit on by life so often he had learned to like the smell.

'You Darly?' His voice was high and nasal.

'Darla. Yes, we spoke on the phone.'

He let his eyes roam over her body, from her head to her toes, slowly, disrespectfully taking his time. 'You sure do fit your clothes.'

'May I sit down?'

'Still a free country, ain't it?'

She slid into the booth opposite him and opened her bag. She took out a notebook and a digital recorder, which she placed on the table between them.

'You want some food? This place does a mean steak.'

'I'll have a coffee.'

He signalled to the waitress. She brought a cup over and laid it before Darla without exchanging a word. Darla wondered how in the hell she had understood exactly what the hand gesture had meant. The waitress poured the coffee and left. Darla looked at her cup. The coffee was the colour of tar. She added milk and sugar and looked at it again. Now it was like lighter tar.

'Mind if I eat? I got to get back out on the road.'

'Please, carry on.'

Robinson picked up his burger and took a huge bite. He chewed it for a while, looking at her across the top of it. Darla waited. She had met men like Clint before. He didn't intimidate her in the slightest.

When he was finished his food, he wiped his mouth, belched loudly and slid his coffee cup closer to his side of the table.

'You got the money?'

'I brought it.'

'Well let's see it.'

Darla took an envelope from her bag. She opened it and let him see the wad of cash inside – one thousand dollars to be exact. Robinson's eyes widened.

'I guess I shoulda asked for more.'

'We agreed a price,' Darla said, beginning to put the envelope back in her bag. 'If you don't want to talk I am sure I can find someone else interested in–'

'Aw now, hold your horses. I never said I weren't interested. So whaddya want to know?'

Darla pressed the 'on' button on her recorder.

'Like I told you on the phone, I want to know everything you can tell me about Jessie Conway.'

'Conway,' he sniffed out a laugh. 'When I knowed her she was Vedder, Jessica Vedder. Before she was Robinson, that is. Not that she kept *that* name long.'

'You've known Jessie how long?'

'Long enough.' He sipped his coffee. 'Since she was in school. I shoulda known it was her when I saw them news pictures. She's changed her hair. She used to wear it blonde.'

'You said she was married to your brother, Doug was it?'

'Yeah,' his expression darkened. 'You met her, right? Bet she still looks like butter wouldn't melt in her mouth. But that devious bitch killed my brother; shot him same as she shot them kids in that school. There ain't nothin' soft about that woman. You best believe it.'

'How long were she and Doug married?'

'Three years, thereabouts.'

'When did she and your brother marry?'

'Straight out of school, round, oh, late '89. They were sweethearts, even though she made out she was better than him. Doug was sweet on that girl from the moment he met her. Back then Jessica Vedder didn't have a pot to piss in. Doug wanted to provide for that woman, start a family of his own.'

'So what happened next?'

'Next? Nothing, they rented a place over in Rutherford. Doug had a job at the mill there and she worked a job at the market. Didn't get to see much of 'em, but they seemed happy enough.'

'Something must have happened between them.'

'I told you, she had notions.'

'Notions?'

'Said wanted to go to college.'

'Hardly a notion.'

His eyes narrowed to slits. 'Maybe not to you, but who'd y'think was gonna pay for all that? Her daddy hadn't two cents to rub together. He weren't gonna pay for it. He didn't pay nuthin' for them kids.'

'Kids?'

'Her and her dumb brother.'

'I didn't realise Jessie had a brother. Is he still around?'

'Dunno, ain't seen him in years. Used to work down the valley with a road crew, could be scattered to the winds by now.'

'What about her folks?'

'Gone.'

'Left the area?'

'Naw, dead.'

'They're dead?'

'Yep, fire took 'em out.'

'What year was this?'

'Oh, '92 I'd say. Not long after Jessica and Doug split.'

'That's awful.'

'Yeah, they reckon the old man had rigged up some kind of generator but it blew. Burned hot too, don't think there was enough of them to fill a matchbox when it was finished.' He was watching Darla carefully as he spoke. She wondered if he was trying to shock her with his description. He had a mean streak, Darla could see that. She wondered if it ran in the family.

'So her parents were poor and she was married, broke, but ambitious.'

'My brother worked hard for that woman, but like I say, she had notions. I told him, that woman ain't for you, but he wouldn't listen. He wouldn't listen. Now Doug is dead and buried and she's supposed to be like some kinda fuckin' hero. She ain't no hero, what she is is one devious bitch.'

'She's a hero to a lot of people.'

'My ass. You got witnesses to back up her version of events? 'Cause that woman likes to say things, she likes to paint a picture that makes her look like a peach, but Jessica Vedder, I can tell you right now, she ain't no peach. That woman could fool a snake.'

'Is that what happened with your brother? She fooled him?'

Robinson looked at his plate, his brow furrowed deeply. 'Everyone knew he was stupid over that woman, couldn't nobody tell him nothing about her. Then she took up with this other bozo, but she wasn't finished playing Doug. I knew it and everyone else knew it. Everyone except Doug.'

Darla flipped through her notes. 'Not long after they separated, Jessie filed a police report saying your brother was stalking her.'

Clint raised his head, his expression one of derision. 'Stalking my ass. Shit, they lived in the same town. Stands to reason they'd run into each other.'

'You don't think she was afraid of him?'

'I tell you what I do know. I *know* she killed him. I *know* she shot him dead like a rabid dog. Point-blank range. I *know* Doug never stood a chance.'

Darla leaned forward. 'I read the police report, Mr Robinson. On the night your brother died his blood alcohol was .28. I also read the hospital records on Jessie. She was battered black and blue and had cuts and lacerations to her scalp and hands.'

'Yeah, they had … disagreements. Look, she knew what buttons to push with Doug and she pushed 'em. I know folk say a man ought to keep his hands to himself, but she was like a flint. And let me explain something to you, Darly, maybe damp down that judgement I see in your eyes. You can talk all you want about fightin' and whatnot, but only one of them is in the ground.'

Darla looked down at her notes. 'I'm sorry, Mr Robinson, I didn't mean to be rude.'

'I ain't saying my brother was some kind of saint, but neither was she. She's cold, that woman, cold as stone.' Clint Robinson sat back in his seat and shook his head a little. 'People can say all they want, but if I ever cross her again I'm gonna make real sure to keep *my* back to the wall.'

Caleb's sleep was fitful and filled with dreams. He woke early the next morning and worked out but could not shake the feeling of claustrophobia and unease. This was unusual after a successful mission and it troubled him.

He drank a cup of coffee and drove the Taurus across town to the apartment of one Frank Fulchano, or 'Frankie the Fence' as he was also – and perhaps better – known. Frank was a small, twisted little bird, with skin the colour of molasses. He was a forty-eight-year-old street hustler with foul teeth and a fouler disposition. He lived in a small walk-up in Tuckaseegee. Caleb had met him months before at Sonja's bar.

Caleb had been to the apartment only once but found it easily. He parked one street over, eyeballed a group of youths watching him from some nearby steps and walked back to the flat. He climbed the metal stairs to the third level, carrying a black gym bag over his shoulder.

Frank lived in the last apartment at the end of a graffiti-soiled walkway. Caleb passed apartments, noting that all the windows had bars over them. The air was filled with music and the smell of fried food. Caleb rapped on Frank's door and took a hasty step back as an explosion of barking came from within. Something big and solid struck the door.

A few moments later the door opened on the chain and a Hispanic woman of indeterminate age wearing just a t-shirt and panties looked him up a down. A massive dog with cropped ears rammed most of its head through the gap and barked throatily.

'What you want?'

'Frank's expecting me.'

'He didn't say nothing about expecting no one.'

'I got business with him.' Caleb opened the bag and partially withdrew Barbara Cross's laptop.

'Wait here.' She closed the door.

Caleb waited, feeling the back of his shirt grow clammy and stick to his skin. He was thirsty and the heat and dust disturbed him. He thought of the cabin, of the cool creek filled with sweet cold water and he licked his lips.

Minutes ticked by. Caleb eased his weight from one foot to the other. His mind wandered a little. He had a shift later that morning in the Home Depot. Maybe he'd try to pick up some more sheet metal afterwards, assuming the floor manager was nowhere around. That Polish prick had it in for him, although Caleb, who usually did his best to avoid hassle, did not know why.

The woman returned to the door with the dog. She stuck her hand out. 'Give me the bag.'

'No.'

'*No?* What you mean, no?'

'I mean no.'

'What you got?'

'Various things.'

She narrowed her eyes. 'Like what?'

'Electronics, jewellery, a jacket.'

'He don't do clothes.'

Caleb shrugged. 'You keep it then.'

She looked at him and closed the door. Caleb heard the chain rattle and then she opened the door just enough for him to slide past. She held the dog by its chain. It stood on its hind legs and tried to sniff him. Caleb doubted she'd be able to hold it if it meant business.

'He down the hall, last room.'

Caleb walked past two open doors. The first one led to a kitchen and in it sat another woman, younger than the one who had let him in, a daughter maybe, pudgy, wearing denim shorts and flip-flops. The second room was empty, but fresh cigarette smoke drifted on the beams of sunlight and there was a trace of a man's cologne.

Frankie was in the last room as she had said. It was a small office of sorts. Two of the walls were covered from floor to ceiling with crowded shelves. There was a sofa propped up against the third and the fourth held a widescreen television that looked very new and very out of place. Frankie sat on the couch. He wore a white vest and jeans; on his head was a straw cowboy hat with a bandana tied around the rim. His bare feet were propped up on a coffee table littered with cables and assorted electrical equipment. He smoked something from a plastic bottle. The air was thick with the cloying stink of it.

'I told you 'bout comin' here, man.' He inhaled deeply, held it and released, tilting his head all the way back, exposing his throat. Caleb shrugged one shoulder.

'I have something.'

'Shit, we coulda done business at the bar.'

'I don't want to do business there.'

'What the fuck … this ain't about what you wanna do, chico.'

Frankie put the bottle down and grinned at Caleb.

'You're still sweet on Sonja, heh?'

Caleb narrowed his eyes. 'What?'

'I see you watching her, man. I know you interested in some cream. Don't let Bear know you sweet on his bird. Man liable to clip them wings.'

Caleb saw a shadow move in the hall outside. Frankie's pupils were black and massive. He was sweating up a storm and his jaw muscles twitched rapidly. Something was not right.

'So what you got?'

Caleb opened the bag and emptied the contents onto the coffee table.

Frankie glanced at what he laid out, waved a hand. 'I give you two for the lot.'

'Two hundred?' Caleb frowned. He had done business with Frankie before. He didn't like the filthy dick but he had never been slighted like this. He picked up the fine gold watch he had removed from Barbara's wrist. 'This is a Cartier. These go for real money.'

'Then take it to a *real* fucking shop.'

Caleb noticed Frankie's eyes dart to the door behind him and back again. Caleb always, even as a child, had an innate sense of danger, and he felt it now. Yes, the look could mean nothing, or it could mean plenty. Pretending to gather his goods, Caleb reached down into this boot and withdrew his grandfather's knife. He snapped to the right and turned as a thin wiry man with bad skin lowered a gun to where his head had been seconds before.

Caleb swung the knife in a backwards arc and drove it straight into the man's left eye. He twisted his wrist, feeling the blade crunch around in the socket. The man dropped the gun and began screaming, as blood and fluid splashed across Caleb's skin. Caleb bent, grabbed the gun and shot the man in the side of the head.

Frankie tried to scramble to his feet but he was out of shape and wasted. Caleb shot him twice, knocking him backwards onto the sofa. He swiped his stolen goods into the bag, yanked his knife from the dead man and stepped into the hall.

The woman came into the hall from the kitchen, blocking his path of escape. She stared at him, released the dog and it charged without hesitation. Caleb shot it mid-stride, the woman during the next, blowing half her face off in the process. He looked through the rooms for the girl and found an open window in a bedroom. She was gone.

'Shit.'

He used the bottom of his t-shirt to open the door handle and hurried along the walkway, leaving the apartment door open, the smell of cordite in his nostrils.

D arla paced the corridor for a while, but finally she returned to her office and remained there, trying to force her left leg into submission as it jiggled up and down with nervous anticipation.

It was early in the morning and the station was almost empty. Darla had been there since five thirty and had managed to bribe Kath Hilson, the features editor, out of bed to read over her piece before it landed on Popeye's lap. Now it was a waiting game. Darla hated waiting. Shortly after eight, the door to her office opened and Kath's tousled head appeared.

'Well?' Darla stretched.

'You checked out all the sources?'

'Yep.'

'Verified all the accounts? Including the police and hospital reports?'

'All that could be, yeah. Any that I couldn't I left out.'

Kath pushed her glasses up onto her head and leaned on the door, her expression one of mild disapproval. She was a stern-faced woman in her forties, but fair and well liked in the office by everyone.

'What's the matter? Why the face? You don't think it's good?'

'It's red hot, but are you sure the angle is one you want to run with, Darla?'

'What do you mean?'

'This piece,' Kath jerked her head towards Darla's computer. 'Are you prepared for the shit storm this is going to cause when it gets published? *If* it gets published.'

'Why wouldn't it be published?'

'There are a lot of people in this town who think Jessie Conway walks on water.'

'I know that,' Darla said, nodding. 'So what? She lied about who she is. She shot and killed her husband. She hid her identity. You don't think that's relevant to what happened here in Rockville?'

'I don't see how.'

'*Really?*'

'You know my nephew goes to that school.'

'So?'

'If it wasn't for Jessie Conway he might very well dead now.'

'Speculation. You don't know that.'

'What has that poor woman ever done to you?'

'Nothing,' Darla threw her hands up in exasperation, 'this is a genuine public interest story.'

'This looks like a hatchet job, Darla.'

'There's nothing personal in this. I'm reporting the facts and that *is* my job.'

'On your head be it, girl,' Kath said and closed the door.

After another quick rewrite, Darla emailed the entire file to Popeye and went to the cafeteria for coffee. Her stomach felt upset and she was more than a little aggrieved by what Kath had told her. Yeah, fine, it was no secret that she was ambitious and that Jessie Conway and her family had been of interest to her, but to accuse her of *personalising* a story was way out of line.

Darla carried the coffee to the bathroom. She washed her hands and dabbed the back of her neck with cooling water before she reapplied her lipstick. When she retuned to her office she was a little surprised to find Popeye sitting in her chair.

'Morning, Lee.'

'Come in.'

She did not remind him that he was, in fact, in her office; something in his expression made any word that crossed her mind evaporate. She closed the door, and, being left with no option, took the chair normally reserved for Chippy.

'Something the matter, Lee?'

Popeye eyed her from across the desk. 'I don't know, is there?'

Darla spread her hands. 'I don't think so.'

'I've got a few reservations.'

'About what?'

'This story.'

'Oh no,' Darla shot out of her chair, 'this story is rock solid. I've confirmed every assertion made with different sources. I've got the legal documents to back up everything I've written. I've–'

'I know all that. '

'Then what?'

'It's … there's a lot of emotion tied into this situation, with the Conway woman.'

'Oh really?' Darla put both hands on the desk and leaned across it. '*You* were the one who told me that emotion had nothing to do with the news.'

'She's a local hero.'

'She's also a liar. I checked with Carmichael, the Principal; she had no idea about Jessie's past.'

'So she omitted a few details. That doesn't change the fact that the people of this town regard her as a goddamn hero.'

'That's because they don't know her! She could be a complete sociopath.'

'Shit, don't say that.'

'You know how she was able to do what she did? Because killing comes easy to her.'

Popeye sighed. 'Even going by what you found, it's not killing that comes easy is it?

'No?'

'No, defending herself is what she's good at.'

'To-*may*-to, to-*mah*-to'

'I'm serious, Darla. You open this can you need to be prepared for the worms that come out.'

'I'm ready, Lee. I'm prepared to stand by what I say; my cards are on the table. You don't run this story, then, by God, I'm going to take it elsewhere.'

Popeye linked his stubby fingers together. He puffed air from his cheeks.

'Are you prepared to stand by me and my story?'

Finally he looked her square in the eye. 'Run it.'

J essie lay in the shuttered bedroom, watching the shadows cross the
ceiling. Despite the multitude of tablets she had taken, sleep eluded
her. Her thoughts were jumbled, confused. She could not escape
them, even with narcotics. Shortly before dawn she gave up trying.
She rose quietly, dressed into shorts and a t-shirt and left the house,
pausing only to collect a sleepy but excited Rudy.

She walked up the drive and stepped onto the road. The air was heavy
and warm, but tolerable. She walked a mile until she reached a trailhead
and slipped into the woods, feeling strangely calm and removed from
her surroundings. Jessie began to run; slowly at first, and then gathering
pace as her muscles remembered their previous role in life.

Twenty-five minutes later she crested the ridge behind her house
with her heart yammering in her ears. There were a number of routes
to take, but she had deliberately chosen the most difficult and least
used. She was not sure why she was hitting the trail so hard, but she
wanted nothing more than to run. She wanted to run away from her
quiet house, to leave behind the husband with the watchful, doleful
eyes. She wanted to run away from calls and visitors, from enquiries
and questions. She wanted to run from her own mind, from her own
thoughts, from her guilt and her despair.

'Come on, Rudy.'

She attacked the next rise with gusto. The terrain was steep and thick with scrub bushes and shoulder-height ferns; the earth underfoot compacted hard from the summer heat. She pitched forward and used her weight to stabilise her ascent. Her muscles ached and the sweat ran freely now. She felt light-headed and breathless, but still she ran.

She would keep running.

She would not stop.

If she could run she could leave it behind. She needed only to figure out where her foot went next, which section of slope would hold her weight, which root could she grasp. This was easy. This was primal.

Jessie glanced up. The crest of the rise was within reach, two hundred yards above her. The path grew steeper, now the clay began to crumble underfoot. Rudy fell behind. She dug her feet in and swung her elbows. *Keep going. Please don't stop.*

She slipped, grabbed some crab grass and pulled. The sweat ran down her back, into the waistband of her pants. Her lungs screamed for air. Her muscles sang in protest. She was slowing, exhausted. She dug deep; her feet scrabbled as loose pebbles rolled away down the bank to the trees below. There was less to grab here, she was out in no man's land, between the last few scrubby yards and the thickly covered ledge. The soil here was no longer red, it was paler, sun bleached. Dust. Earth. Dead.

She threw everything she had into the last few feet, up one long agonising stride at a time, another, then another, and then, finally, with a partial scream, she made it to the ridge, where she collapsed onto the parched grass, her chest heaving.

Jessie rolled onto her back and watched a cloud move lazily across the washed-out blue of the morning sky. It never stops, she thought. If I live, if I die, the clouds still go by, the sun still rises. Life will go on with or without me. It was a revelation of sorts; one she tested again.

I am not special.

I am not unique.

I am here.

After a few minutes, she sat up, wiped the dust from her t-shirt and looked down the valley. Dawn had fully broken now and although there remained some pockets of darkness in distant corners, the sun's rays stretched across the valley floor. She searched but could not locate her house. For some reason this pleased her.

Rudy thundered up the rise behind her, his tongue lolling out of the corner of his mouth. She watched the old dog scramble his way to her, thinking that there was a time he would have been under her feet the whole way. When had he gotten so old? He reached her, puffing and blowing like crazy, and threw himself down at her feet. Jessie let him rest. She sat with her hand on his ruff, watching the valley, thinking about time. For the first time in weeks she felt something within her lift.

She felt present. Not worrying about the future, not burning from the past. She was here, on a ledge over looking the valley with her dog. The sun was overhead and she was here, alive. Present. No Earth moved; no crack of celestial thunder passed overhead. There was nothing to mark the occasion, but in that moment Jessie Conway suddenly felt that maybe, just maybe, she might make it out the other side after all.

Mike was helping Ace dismantle the interior of an original Mini Cooper when Emma appeared at the passenger door and cleared her throat. 'Hey, Mike. Listen, I got a call from my mom a short while back.'

'What is it?' Mike asked.

She stuck her thumb in her mouth and chewed on the nail. She looked nervous and uncomfortable.

'Spit it out, Emma, I don't have all day.'

'She said there was a, um, thing … in the paper. She said it was about your wife. So I went out and got one.'

Mike climbed out of the Mini and towered over her. Ace put down his screwdriver and watched them silently.

'And? What about her?'

'Um … I … it was about Jessie. How she, um … has been married before and stuff.'

'What in the blue blazes are you going on about?'

Emma's cheeks flushed pink under the weight of Mike's gaze. Her other hand whipped around from behind her back. 'Well don't get mad at me, I thought you should know is all. Here.' She rammed a copy of *The Rockville Gazette* into his hands and started back towards the office.

Mike stared at the front page. The headline read, 'Tragic History of Hero'. Under it was the photo of Jessie in the hospital bed but beside that was another, larger, photo of a youthful looking Jessie with blonde hair, smiling goofily into the camera. She was holding hands with another man. The man was young too; he had a bad haircut and hard eyes.

'What's going on?' Ace asked.

Mike ignored him. He opened the newspaper and began to read. At each line he heard the sound in his ears deepen; felt a rising sensation from his guts. 'Son of a bitch.' He walked into the office, with Ace following hot on his heels. Emma was in the street outside, smoking and pacing in a circle. She was on her cell phone and looked rattled. The phone in the office began to ring. Warily, Mike picked it up as Ace stepped outside to join Emma. 'Mike Conway.'

'Mike.'

He closed his eyes. 'Hey, Mom.'

'Have you seen the paper?'

'Just now.'

'That journalist, that Levine woman, she's run some story on Jessie. I have it here in front of me. She says Jessie killed her first husband.'

Mike glanced out to the yard where Emma was talking with Ace, her arms gesticulating wildly as she spoke. Ace had a cigarette in his mouth but had not lit it. Mike could tell from how he stood his brother was not taking any pleasure in what he was hearing.

'Mike?'

'Yeah?'

'She says that Jessie has been married before, that she shot her first husband dead. I don't understand. Did you know anything about any of this? Is it true?'

'I have to go, Mom.'

'Mike?'

'I'm gonna have to call you back.' He hung up and called his house. Nobody answered. He hung up again and was about to call Jessie's cell when the phone rang under his hand. He hesitated briefly, and then picked up.

'Mike, it's Penny. Mom called.'

'Jesus.'

'Is this true?'

'I don't know.'

'*You don't know?*'

'That's what I said.'

'How the hell can you not know something like that? Are you really telling me Jessie never told you she was married before? *Really?*'

'It never came up.'

'Are you kidding me with this shit? *It never came up?*'

'Are you deaf, Penny?'

'Are you stupid, Mike? Everyone's talking about this. Mom's in hysterics.'

'I've got to go.'

'Don't you dare hang up on me, Mike Conway. This is serious. We need to get the family together and talk this over. We need–'

Mike slammed the receiver down. He ripped the phone from the desk and flung it through the window. Ace looked at the shattered glass and at the phone lying in the street. He said nothing, but picked it up and carried it back inside. Emma stayed outside. She looked terrified.

'Go on home,' Ace said, jerking his head towards the street. 'I'll take care of shit here.'

'Thanks,' Mike said, trying to breathe, feeling as though someone had just kicked him square in the guts.

Caleb ditched the gun in a stinking dumpster in Hidden Valley and returned to the other side of town as fast as the law allowed. As he drove, he noticed that he had blood spattered all over his clothes and he swore. If he got stopped now he'd have questions to answer.

He managed to get home without meeting anyone. Once inside, he paced the apartment, trying to think. He was furious at Frankie and worse, furious at himself. Frankie had been nothing but a piece of shit but the cops would be all over the killings. People had seen him park the car; the girl had seen him come in. The cops would canvass people who knew Frankie, which meant they would be at the bar in no time. It would not take long for them to put two and two together and come looking for him.

They would speak to Sonja. They would offer her a description. She was not a stupid woman; she was Category A to the core. She would know exactly to whom they were referring. She would be shocked: kind, shy Art? Then she would wonder, then she would think about her security.

Caleb had monumentally fucked up his entire game plan. He had lost a Category A over a goddamn maggot like Frankie. He kicked a chair over and punched a hole in the plaster. *This* was what happened when a person relaxed. He had grown sloppy, too comfortable in his new skin, and *this* was the result. He reeled and caught a glimpse of his reflection in the hall mirror. He stared at himself, imagining his features morph and slide. It was time to ditch Arthur S. Weils. It was time to ditch Charlotte.

He went to the bedroom and sat on the end of the bed, which he had made perfectly that morning. Thoughts swirled about his brain: Sonja, the cabin. He considered just snatching her, but it was impossible, not even he could risk that. To be captured now would be the death of him. It was no good. Sonja would not be his.

He closed his eyes and forced himself to think. He would need to leave Charlotte. He would head to the cabin to regroup and reorganise. He would need to replace Sonja.

Caleb tilted his head. Replace her with another.

Who?

The redhead.

With each slow inhale and exhale he thought of Jessie Conway. She was Category A, he was sure of it. He needed that; he needed affirmation now more than ever. Why not her?

Another problem presented itself. He needed money. Without Frankie he was stuck with Barbara's useless crap. He looked at the calendar on the wall. It was two days from payday, but he needed that money.

He looked at his watch. His shift at the Depot had already started by twenty-five minutes. If he wanted to collect he would need a story to roll out on the sad sack of shit owner. He thought for a moment, drumming his fingers on his chest. What could he use to open his boss's wallet? Something sentimental would do it.

Caleb packed as much as he could as fast as he could. He carried everything to the car downstairs and loaded it, then used a screwdriver to exchange the number plates with a rust-coloured Honda Civic belonging to another resident before returning to the apartment.

There was, he realised standing in the living room, the issue of finger-prints. He definitely did not have the time to clean the whole place down.

He went to the kitchen and rummaged through the drawers until he found a box of matches. He set fire to the chintz curtain in the bedroom, then returned to the living room, where he pulled some of the stuffing from the sofa and lit it. He watched as first it smouldered, then bust into a strangely coloured flame – blue first, then brilliant orange. By the time he closed the apartment door for the final time the apartment was a furnace.

Caleb drove to Home Depot and parked in the customer car park instead of the staff one. He walked through the shop floor, ignor-ing the curious looks from the rest of the staff. He went upstairs and knocked on the door of the manager's office.

Stuart Gilmore had a light system bolted onto the doorjamb, like the kind you'd see at a bank with a holding porch. If the light was red you could not enter, if it was green you could. The fact that the panels to either side of Stuart's door were bubble glass, allowing the waiting party to see Stuart twiddling his thumbs, did nothing to dissuade him from using the stupid system.

Caleb rapped on the door and waited for the green light. While he waited, he ran through his story once more in his head. He did not like Stuart Gilmore. He reminded Caleb of a landlocked walrus. He was large and obscenely fleshy and he always seemed to be sweating, no matter the weather. It sure wasn't from the amount of manual work his did about the place. It took a lot of effort to be as lazy as Stuart Gilmore.

The light flashed green. Caleb arranged his facial features and opened the door.

'Hey there, Art.' Stuart leaned back in his custom-made leather recliner and folded his hands across his prodigious stomach. The heat in the office was stifling and the floor fan by Stuart's chair did nothing but move the warm air around. 'I thought you might not be joining us today.'

'Sorry, Stuart, I've had a bit of a crisis.' Caleb smiled and waited to see his boss's reaction to it. It was a well-practised, friendly smile, not too wide, not too many teeth. But sometimes men reacted differently to it than women. He had once been asked what the fuck he was smiling at by a man who had taken offence to his toothy grin. Caleb had replied, 'not a whole lot', before leaving the man holding his guts in place behind a parked station wagon.

Stuart smiled back and looked at him inquisitively. 'So what can I do you for?'

'I'm sorry to have to lay one on you Stuart, but I'm handing in my notice, and I'll need my pay.'

Stuart's face fell. He sat forward in his chair. 'That's a … well that's a hell of a request, Art, all things considered. I thought you liked it here.'

'I do, I surely do.'

'What's going on?'

'It's my mother. She fell the night before last and broke her hip. She's okay insofar as I can gather, but she's pretty shaken up. I need to go make sure she's being looked after right.'

'Oh jeez, I'm real sorry to hear that, Art. What age is she?'

'She's seventy.'

'Awful, that's just awful. Gosh their bones are so brittle at that age.'

'I know it's short notice and I hate to put you on the spot like this Stu, but I'm really in a bind.'

'I know, Art, I understand. You may not know this, but my own mother,' and here Stuart's voice quavered with emotion, 'Lord bless her, she lives with me fulltime so I know how it is. Believe me when I say that.'

'Oh, I had no idea,' Caleb lied. He had known about Stuart's mother; that was why he had chosen the mother line in the first place.

Stuart sniffed and snuffled. 'Oh yes, it's hard when they get older, yes it really is.'

'So you see the position I'm in.'

'Sure, you'll need to square your hours with Tom and I'll sort out your cheque. Boy it's just awful when they get older, I know. Which hospital is she at?'

'She's not in hospital.'

'She's not in hospital?' Stuart frowned. 'Oh, I thought–'

'She couldn't afford to stay there.'

'They didn't *keep* her? With a broken hip?'

'Insurance won't cover her for much more than a trip to the emergency room.'

'Blood-sucking leeches, I'll bet not.'

Caleb endured a long-winded diatribe on the evils of insurance companies before he was able to remove himself from the office. He went downstairs to the main floor to seek out the manager, Tomas Vorkenski. He found Tomas standing near the entrance of the loading dock with a clipboard in hand, talking to one of the forklift drivers. Caleb stood to one side and waited for him to acknowledge his presence. He waited a full two minutes before Tomas made eye contact, though he knew the foreman knew he was there.

'What?'

Caleb did not use any form of smile with Tomas. Tomas was a humourless second-generation Pole and had made it clear from the first day that he did not like Caleb, and no amount of smiling was going to change his mind on the matter. For his part, Caleb was cautious around Tomas. The man was no fool and Caleb had more than once wondered if Tomas sensed some of Caleb's more twisted thoughts. Sometimes Caleb thought he might have to do something about Tomas. Sometimes he thought he would enjoy that a lot.

'What?' Tomas repeated, his pale eyes boring a hole through Caleb.

'I'm taking off. I need my hour sheet.'

'You're taking off?'

'Yeah, I quit.'

'That so? I'll do one up for you; you can have it end of day.'

'I need it now. I spoke to Stuart, he's expecting it.'

'You talked to Stuart without talking to me first?'

Caleb did not reply. It was a redundant question and not worthy of a response. He looked steadily at Tomas, playing eye chicken as he often did. He knew the foreman would try to jam him up if he could find a good enough reason to do so.

Tomas looked away first. 'Fine, I'll drop it in to him. Nice knowing you.'

'I don't think so.'

'Feeling's mutual.'

Last-word merchant, Caleb thought as he walked back across to the main building. He glanced at his watch. It was almost noon. Soon as he had the cheque he could get out of there. Now that his plan was in motion he felt re-energised, filled with secrecy and excitement.

He walked directly to Tomas's office and paused at the door. He glanced around. When he was certain no one had noticed him, he stepped inside and shut the door behind him. He unzipped his pants, pulled out his penis and urinated in the corner of the room. The carpet was dark blue and showed no discernable colour change, but it would sure stink like hell by the end of the day.

When he was finished he zipped up, left the office and went to the staff room to do a number on a turkey sandwich belonging to a woman named Gloria.

Mike slammed the truck into a sliding stop outside his house and ran up the steps, ignoring a startled Rudy who had been asleep in a patch of sunlight on the porch. Jessie was at the counter in the kitchen making a sandwich. Her hair lay wet on her shoulder, her face lightly flushed. Her greeting died on her lips when she saw Mike's expression. He strode towards her and slammed the newspaper down on the counter. 'Read it.'

Jessie looked down. Mike watched her eyes skim over the front page, feeling the skin on the back of his neck prickle as she read downwards. He wanted so badly for her to react angrily, to dismiss the story as nonsense. He wanted her to take his hand and shake her head and put him out of his misery with a word.

She raised her head. Mike saw her eyes go wide with fear and shame and felt the bottom slide out of his world. 'Is this true?'

She said nothing.

'*Is it true?*'

'Mike, listen to me…' she reached for him, but he reeled away with an agonised howl.

'Oh my God. Oh my God. I can't believe this. Everything, everything we have together, everything we have is based on a fucking lie.'

'Mike, please, let me explain–'

Mike spun round and grabbed her by both arms. 'Explain? Eight years, Jessie. You had eight years to explain. *Eight years!*'

'*Stop it!*' She yanked herself free and took a step backwards. 'You're scaring me.'

Mike pointed a trembling hand at the paper. 'Why didn't you tell me about him?'

'I ... I couldn't.'

'What do you mean, couldn't? What the fuck does that mean, Jessie?'

She flinched. His voice was venomous, something she had never heard from him before. 'Well, when was I supposed to broach it? The first time we spoke? What about on our first date or the first time we slept together? What was I was supposed to say, "Gee, Mike, I like you a lot. By the way, I shot and killed my first husband, could you pass the salt?"'

'That's your answer? The timing was off?'

She lowered her head and stood silent for a moment. When she spoke again her voice was flat. 'Do you know what it's like to live in dread? Do you know what it's like to dread the sound of a vehicle approaching your home? Do you know what it's like to dread a certain look or a certain tone of voice? To spend your life terrified of making a mistake or saying the wrong thing at the wrong time? Do you have any idea what it's like to dread like that?'

Mike shook his head.

'Well I do. I wouldn't wish that on my very worst enemy.'

'You were afraid of him? Is that what you're telling me?'

'Yes.'

'You're not stupid, Jessie. You must have known what he was like before you hitched your wagon to his.'

'I was barely eighteen when I married him, Mike. I was only a kid. I didn't know what the hell I was doing, only that I wanted to get the hell out of my parents' home.'

'So what happened?'

'I don't know what happened.'

Mike pulled a face.

'I mean it. Somewhere along the line he changed. Or maybe he didn't. Maybe he was always the way he was and I was too dumb to see it until it was too late.'

'What way was he?'

'Mean.' Tears began to spill down her face. 'Mean and dirty to the core. I never met a man so mean in my whole life and I hope to never meet one again.'

'How long were you with him?'

'Three years.'

Mike pinched the bridge of his nose with his fingers. 'Ah shit, Jessie, what do you take me for? If he's as bad as you make out why didn't you leave him sooner?'

'I did, at least I tried. Thing is, no matter what he'd show up at my work or bug my friends. It was a small town, Mike, hard to avoid an ex-husband, especially one hell bent on running into you. He'd plead with me to come back, tell me he'd change. That he was sorry. I fell for that line a number of times before I realised that's all it was, a line.'

She reached her out to touch him. Mike pushed her hand away, though it almost killed him to do so. 'Please, Mike. I wish I could explain to you how … powerless I was back then, how vulnerable. He would not take no for an answer, he would not leave me alone. He had only one intention and that was to make me suffer for leaving him.'

'So you went back to him?'

'I did, and for a week or two it was okay. And then it wasn't.'

'Just like that?'

'Just like that.' Jessie took a shaky breath and wiped at her tears with her hands. 'I don't really remember what he was angry about, or what I said, but he … well, this time he really did a number on me.

That's when I realised that I would die if I spent another day with him. I waited until the next morning when he had gone to work, I packed whatever I could carry and I walked to a friend's house. I never went back.'

'And then?'

'She patched me up and she talked me into filing a police report. Took photos of my injuries to keep on record. After that I filed for divorce.'

'How'd he react to that?'

'He kept a low profile for a while. I waitressed during the day and started a night school course,' she shrugged, 'I thought I could go forward with my life. Stupid.'

Mike said nothing, but Jessie felt his gaze on her face.

'One night I pulled into the yard at my friend's house and he came at me, out of the shadows. He was drunk, belligerent, called me all sorts of names. He started to hit me, tried to knock me down, but I made it up the steps and inside the house. I was screaming at him, screaming for help, but Maxine wasn't home and I...' She blinked, her eyes unfocused, lost to her memories, 'I tried to wedge the door closed but he kicked it almost clean off the hinges. I remember thinking it was hanging funny. I fell, got to my feet and bolted for Maxine's room. I knew she kept a gun in the dresser by the bed. I just wanted to scare him with it, but he laughed at me.'

'So you shot him.'

'He kept coming. I had no choice.'

'You say that a lot.' As soon as he had uttered the words he was sorry, but it was too late. Jessie turned her head, bewildered, then slowly the meaning of what he had said hit home. Her features crumpled; eyes were bruised with hurt.

'You don't get to throw that at me.'

'I'm sorry,' Mike said, feeling like a heel, but angry too.

'You think that of me? Is that it?'

'No I don't.'

'My God, Mike, you think I wanted to kill my husband?'

'I don't know, did you?'

She took a step away from him, crying now. 'You can go to straight to hell Mike Conway, if that's what you think of me.'

'Tell you the truth, Jessie, I don't know what to think of you. I feel like I hardly know you.'

'You ought know me, Mike.'

'Yeah, I ought to but I don't.'

'You want me to beat myself up for you? Tell you how much it kills me to see you hurting? You think I wanted you to find out like this?'

'No, I don't.'

'I never asked for *any* of this. None of it, but I won't stand here and let you cast that kind of aspersion on me, and goddamn you for even thinking it.' She walked out of the room and moments later Mike heard the door of the bedroom slam shut.

Caleb cashed his final cheque from the Home Depot, burned Arthur S. Weils' licence and began using the licence of one George Graham, a rare identity he kept for emergencies. The real George had been a dumbass Category Z labourer Caleb had spotted hitchhiking after his truck broke down six miles outside of Atlanta, and whose body Caleb had left lying in fetid lowland swamp later that same day.

Caleb drove along the interstate, keeping the needle under the speed limit. He was in better humour now that he was on the road and had almost talked himself into believing that ditching Charlotte had been predestined.

He drove for a number of hours, planning his next course of action. Other than staying below the police radar, he was under no particular pressure, and now that he had some money he was in no real rush. He thought briefly about Sonja and wondered if the cops had spoken to her already. Would her white skin prickle to think she had stood so close to death so often? Certainly she would not forget him, not now. He would be a part of her thoughts forever.

That cheered him a little.

Close to 2p.m. he pulled off the highway at the service exit and parked the Taurus outside a diner. He went in and ordered a plate of grits, gravy, biscuits and some black coffee. He was waiting for his food when he saw Jessie Conway's face appear on the television behind the counter.

'Can you turn that up a bit?'

The waiter did as he asked.

Caleb listened to the breathless news reporter as she broke the news of Jessie's past, of her dead first husband, of her action again in Rockville High. There was an undercurrent to the story, a salacious edge that had not been there before. Caleb found himself enthralled. This confirmed it; she was without any doubt a *bone fide* Category A. By the time he'd finished his food, Frankie and Sonja and Charlotte were completely consigned to the past, and Caleb cared nothing for the past. The past was nothing, a dream; it could not be touched or altered. It was, in his view, worthless.

He hit the road, changing route twice more. By the time he reached the outskirts of Rockville it was after six in the evening. Caleb drove through neat suburbs, with their mid-sized homes and well-watered lawns, moving slowly into narrower streets where the homes needed the odd paint job and some of the cars sat low on patches of scrubby grass. No children played outdoors that he could see. On this scorching day the town seemed empty and tired.

He got out at the Dawn's Light Motel and stretched his legs. The motel was a two-storey affair with a wraparound balcony on the second floor and wooden stairs dead centre leading from the car park. Positioned directly in front of the main office, the stairs allowed the proprietor full view of who came and who went. This did not unduly bother Caleb. He was not planning to spend much time there other than to sleep.

He parked the Taurus next to a wilting scrub rose, entered the office and removed his sunglasses. A chubby young man wearing a pale pink t-shirt and a string of coloured beads tight around his neck glanced over the cover of *People* magazine at him.

'Hi, can I help you?"

'I need a room.'

The man put the magazine down and stood up. He had a fake diamond earring the size of a nickel in his left ear. 'Do you have a reservation?'

'No.'

'Single or a double?'

'Whichever.'

'Can I have your name and some identification?'

Caleb supplied the necessary, and while his invoice was being readied he read the notice board behind the clerk's back.

'Will that be cash or credit card?'

'Cash.'

'Would you like a room to the front or the back?'

'Front.'

'Any preference for a floor?'

'Ground.'

'Chatty one, aren't you?'

Caleb looked at him until the younger man flushed.

'Okay. How long do you want the room?

'Today through 'til Sunday.'

'You leaving Sunday?'

Caleb leaned on the counter with his elbow. 'If not I'll let you know.'

The clerk removed a cardkey from under the counter and slotted it into a cardboard envelope.

'Room will need to be vacated by 12 noon. There's a space for your car outside the room.'

Caleb took the key.

'Will you be needing anything else?'

'There a library in town?'

'Oh sure, it's over on Wellton Street. Imagine it's closed now but–'

'How much for the maps?'

The man snatched a map from a metal holder with a theatrical flourish. 'These? Six dollars.'

Caleb dug some change from his pocket and dropped it on the counter.

'You don't really need a map, you know?' said the man, 'I can tell you anything you need to know about Rockville.' He smiled and blinked a number of times. Caleb stared at him blankly before he took the map and shoved it into his back pocket.

'If you need anything all just call down, my name is Ritchie. I'll be here *all* night.'

Caleb nodded, tired of the interaction.

The room was situated second last from the end of the building nearest the street. Caleb moved his car down and parked in the allotted spot. He let himself into the room and locked the door behind him. It was small and the furnishings were a little dated but it was clean. There was a double bed and a bathroom to the rear. He set his bag on the bed and closed the curtains. He checked to see if there was a window in the bathroom. There was, big enough for him to fit through should he need to.

He drank some water from the tap and went back to the bed. He put his keys and the map on the dresser, lay on the bed and slipped his hands under his head. He listened to the cars pass by on the street outside, and heard doors opening and closing in the building. After a while, he slept.

When he woke it was getting dark. Caleb switched on the bedside lamp and rubbed his hand over his face. He opened the map, studied it, and after a while folded it and put it in his travel bag. He shoved the bag under the bed and left the room, carefully locking the door behind him. A black cat sat on the bonnet of his car. It flattened as he approached, pinning its ears close to his head.

'Move,' Caleb said. The animal did so immediately, racing off into the bushes. Cats are smart, Caleb thought as he got into his car and drove away into the night.

Rockville was not a large town, and it did not take Caleb long to scout it from end to end. He located the library first, then the school, which he recognised from the television. From there he tracked his way back to the town centre, thinking of Jessie Conway, getting a feel for her and the places she had to be familiar with.

When he was sure he had his bearings, Caleb's thoughts turned to food. He pulled into the parking lot of a place called Ray's Diner. It was only one block from the school and he figured Jessie had probably eaten there from time to time. He parked the Taurus in the farthest spot from the CCTV camera, went in and sat at the counter. He ordered a taco and a bowl of home cut fries. When the food came, he was surprised to find it was good and he understood why the place was filling up.

He watched the comings and goings without appearing to take much notice of either. There seemed to him a strange prevailing mood in the air. A lot of people appeared to be drinking heavily and the conversations, from the snippets he could hear, seemed forced and shrill. To the rear of the main floor was a set of booths, four on each side of the lane to the bathrooms. The booths were occupied by two groups of loud and vocally aggressive teenagers. He watched them for a while, amused at their posturing, but curious as to why their high jinks went on without comment, especially when one group started firing fries across the aisle at another.

He ordered another light beer and waited for the woman who had been watching him to make her move. She had been side-eyeballing him since he had sat down and in that time had consumed four glasses of cheap bourbon to his two beers.

She made her move when she came up to the bar to order her fifth glass. She casually bumped against him as she was going past.

'Oh sorry, sugar.'

'That's okay.'

'I would hope so.'

He smiled at her and smoothed his beard with his left hand. He watched her eyes scan for a wedding ring.

'Waiting on someone?'

'Nope, all alone.'

'Well now that ain't right.'

'I just ordered a drink.' He glanced at the barman. 'Can I get you one?'

'Well sure.'

'What are you having?'

'I'll take a Maker's Mark.'

He signalled to the barman and ordered the drink. The barman fetched the bottle down and smirked at the woman as he poured. 'You are getting *expensive* tastes, Louisa.' She shot him a dirty look.

'You don't worry about my *taste*, Ray, worry about your business.'

Caleb pretended to watch the teenagers as the barman poured, saying nothing. He had met men like Ray before, they noticed things: accents, faces. They struck up conversations easily and probed with abandon. He did not wish to speak with Ray.

When Ray eventually moved away, Caleb raised his bottle to Louisa, who had settled on the stool beside him. 'Cheers to you.'

'And to you, Honey.'

They clinked. She drained half the glass in one mouthful and set it on the bar.

'I don't recognise you. You're not from around here, are you?'

'What makes you say that?'

'I'd remember a handsome face like yours.'

He smiled, and tried to look bashful. It was not the best look in his repertoire and he seldom used it, but he doubted that she'd notice how out of practice he was. 'No, I'm passing through. My mother lives over yonder in Bridgewater. I'm on my way to see her.'

'Oh yeah? Bridgewater. Used to know a guy from there.' She touched her glass absentmindedly and licked her lips. 'Your people are from there?'

'Born and raised.'

'What's their name? Maybe I know 'em.'

'Vaughn.'

'Can't place them. But it's good that you keep in touch with your family. Lot of folk forget where they came from. You can believe that.'

Ray drifted back down the bar, looking up along the glass shelves towards the bottles as though he'd never seen them before. His curiosity was transparent, even to Louisa, who huffed and rolled her eyes.

Caleb waited until Ray returned to the other end of the bar. 'I haven't been back much, but my mother, she hasn't been too well lately.'

'I am sorry to hear it.'

'There are worse things in the world, right? Mom's a good age.'

Louisa was looking at her glass again. He knew she was probably wondering when it would seem appropriate to drink from it again.

'I mean look what happened here.'

She glanced at him.

'I guess folk are still pretty torn up about what happened up at the school.'

He sipped his beer, pretending not to notice her eyes on his face, trying to read him. She might be a drunk, but she was no fool.

'Bridgewater, huh? Did you go to Trenton High or St Columbus?'

He snorted. 'TH of course. My family couldn't afford to send no child to Columbus. Come to think of it, I don't know many folk that could.'

Right answer. She picked up her glass and took a delicate sip.

'You want a fresh drink?'

She looked surprised. 'Well sure.'

'Maker's Mark again okay?'

'It surely is.' She leaned in closer to him.

'I know it sounds kind of stupid, but with everything that's going on in the world, a man would be a fool to miss the opportunity to have a drink with an attractive woman.' He wondered if that was too much, but she didn't seem to notice how corny it sounded. He watched her signal to Ray, who came down the bar in a flash.

By the time he left Ray's Diner two hours later, Caleb had a phone number he didn't want and a headache from the five bottles of light beer he had consumed. His wallet was a good deal lighter from the seven bourbons he had paid for. But that was okay too. He had learned plenty of what he needed to know and there were always ways for a man like him to pick up some more money.

33

Mike fought for the oblivion of sleep but could not catch a wink that night. It didn't help that Jessie had refused his offer to talk and was asleep in the spare room. He hated the feel of the empty space beside him.

He tried to get a handle on what was eating him the most. He played Jessie's story over and over again, deciphering what she had told him, trying to make it more palatable. He believed her, or at least he thought he did. But even as he thought that, another niggling voice asked whether he could be totally sure when she had so expertly lied to him for so many years. He twisted and turned on his sheets, his hair and skin damp with troubled sweat. Finally he kicked the sheets to the floor in temper.

He and Jessie had met in the springtime. She had pulled into the garage with black smoke billowing from under her old Capri. When she got out she looked so forlornly at the car he could not help but smile.

'Help you, Miss?'

'Lord I really hope so. It gave a loud clunk a few streets over, next thing I know there's smoke everywhere.'

'Looks to me like your transmission.'

'Looks to me like the kiss of death. There's only dirt and prayer holding this piece of junk together.' She smiled at him, exposing even white teeth and dimples in both cheeks. Mike knew instantly that this was one woman he would like to get to know a little bit better.

Not that she had made that easy on him. She had been reticent in all her dealings with him and everyone else, deflecting attempts at conversation or enquires into her personal life with practised ease. But that was okay. Mike wasn't one to pry much one way or another.

She had been in Rockville for less than a month and had secured a job with Rockville High when Mike asked her on a date.

He had planned it right. He knew she liked strawberry milkshakes and often went to Ray's Diner for one after work. Mike had made it his business to run into her one afternoon and they had struck up conversation. She told Mike she was renting a room from old Melvin Cedar. Mike nodded, but he already knew. Melvin was an old friend of Mike's father and it was Melvin who told Mike that his latest tenant liked old movies and dogs.

Mike mentioned to Jessie that he was planning on catching a screening of *High Society*, part of the classic film collection Rockville cinema liked to show on Saturday afternoons. He asked if she might like to accompany him. To his delight, Jessie said yes.

That Saturday they watched Grace Kelly choose between John Lund and Bing Crosby; the following weekend, they watched *Roman Holiday*. Over time, Jessie and Mike found themselves relaxing into a gentle friendship that eased again into romance a few weeks later. But despite their blossoming love, Jessie had always kept a little piece of herself to herself.

Mike hoisted himself up and lay against the headboard. He felt the memories were making a mockery of him somehow. How dumb was he that he hadn't known she had been carrying something so huge for so long? He banged his head back against the board. That was quite the question.

If he was honest, he had known something. There was no point denying that now. Within his wife there had always been an unknowable story. She had bad dreams from time to time. Sometimes she was twitchy. She could be withdrawn or quick to anger, though she was always sorry shortly after.

She had told him her parents had died in an accident, but had refused to be drawn more on them or any remaining siblings. She was sparing with her history, glossing over her emotions in a way that he now could see was protective. She did not look for sympathy and neither did she wish to dwell on the past. Jessie was, he thought, an enigma, but one that he found himself drawn to in the most basic way possible. He loved her; it was as great and as simple as that.

His family had been delighted for him. His mother had, one night after too much peach schnapps, confided that she had – almost – given up on him ever settling down. His sisters liked Jessie too, although they had been initially a little put out at her unwillingness to shop or get her hair done as often as they liked. But Jessie was kind and thoughtful around them and over the years they had grown to love her as one of their own.

And then there was Ace. Ace had never been one to play his cards away from his chest. Mike had not sought approval for his choices nor asked his opinion on Jessie. It was not how it was done, and he would not expect much more than an offended grunt should he ask such a question. But Ace and Jessie had always been at ease in each other's company, and spoke easily. Jessie had fought Ace's corner on more than on occasion, defending him against Fay's undisguised disappointment. When Ace had gone back to jail on his last bust, Jessie had refused to hear a bad word against him, only to remark that 'it sure was hard to fly straight through an ill will'.

Maybe that was how it ought to be, he thought, feeling a flash of anger surge through him. Families stood shoulder to shoulder when things got tough, didn't they? What gave a jumped-up nobody like Darla Levine the damn right to judge Jessie on her past? The past was the past, wasn't it? It was not like any of it could be changed. What gave her the right to meddle in their lives the way she had? What was her agenda?

Long before dawn, Mike rose. He dressed and jumped into his truck and drove towards town, his jaws clenched tight, his knuckles white on the wheel. He parked illegally in a loading dock outside the office of *The Gazette* and took the steps three at a time. He hurtled through the revolving doors into the reception. A young man sat behind the reception desk. He was in his early twenties, rail thin and wore an earring and a headset. He glanced up at Mike's arrival and frowned.

'Sir, can I help you?

'I'm looking for Darla Levine.'

The young man looked in an exaggerated manner at a large ornate clock hanging on the wall behind him. 'Miss Levine has not arrived yet.'

'When does she get here?'

'Sir?'

'Are you deaf? I asked what time does she come in.'

'Sir, if you could tell me what this regards I'm sure I can assist you.'

Mike snatched his cap off and bunched it in his hands to keep from exploding. 'I don't need your *assistance*. I want to speak to that god-damned woman. Now call her up, you tell her Mike Conway is right here waiting on her. You tell her that.'

The younger man looked alarmed. 'Sir, I assure you I can give Miss Levine any message you wish to leave, but I can't call her a–'

Mike reached across the desk and grabbed the younger man by the ear that held the earring. He twisted it, bringing him up out of his chair onto his tippy toes. 'I didn't ask for your assurances. I asked you to call that woman.'

'Please, sir,' the younger man said, his face contorted with pain. 'Don't hurt me. I just work here.'

Mike released him and took a step backward. He put his hand out and the receptionist flinched. Mick felt sick to his stomach with shame for his actions. 'I'm sorry. I'm real sorry about that. I wanted to tell that woman to leave my wife be, you tell her to leave us alone. Okay?'

The receptionist nodded furiously.

'Okay then.' Mike put his cap on his head, turned, and walked out the door. Outside, the driver of a larger truck was parked behind Mike's with the window rolled down.

'That your vehicle, bud?'

'Yeah.'

'Can't park it there, fella, yer blocking the entrance. Didn't you see the signs?'

Mike waved his hand, climbed in and started the engine. No, he thought as he pulled away, he hadn't seen the signs; he hadn't seen them at all.

34

Mike Conway was not the only man up and about early.

Armed with Louisa's information, Caleb Switch left the motel and followed a road eight miles outside of the town. He turned left by the old converted sawmill onto a smaller secondary road. The mill, he noticed, had been remodelled into some kind of fancy bijou hotel. He knew without ever setting foot inside the door that it would be full of quirky memorabilia and 'authentic' tat. Rubes loved that kind of crap and paid top dollar for it. Caleb had never understood why folk got such a kick out of pretending to be hicks.

He drove along a narrower road for a spell, moving deeper and deeper into the countryside. The distance between properties began to grow longer, a quarter of a mile at first, then scarcely any homes for long stretches. He passed through a set of crossroads, and half a mile later he slowed and parked up opposite a bright yellow mailbox with the name Conway printed on it in neat black lettering.

Caleb rolled the window down and switched off the engine. He sat for a moment, savouring the scents, the sharpening light. He smelled conifers and deer. He imagined the woods around here were full of them.

After a few minutes he climbed out and crossed the road. There was enough light to make out the wrought-iron gate fastened across the top of a rutted lane. The lane sloped down and turned sharply a few yards further in. He walked along the side of the road. He had not gone more than a couple of feet when, through a gap in the trees, he saw the house in a clearing below. He lifted his binoculars and glassed it. It was a single-storey wood and stone house with a wraparound porch. There was an older model Volvo parked by a set of stone steps leading to the porch.

He remained standing, ears cocked for approaching vehicles. His patience was rewarded when a light came on inside the house. Someone opened the door and stepped out into the porch. Caleb's breath caught in his throat as he recognised Jessie Conway. She had a portable telephone pressed against her ear. She was barefoot and wore only a vest and underwear.

A dog appeared by her side and ambled out into the yard for a sniff about. It was large and black. Caleb squinted but it was hard to tell from there what it was, maybe a Labrador of some kind. Its movements were stiff so he guessed it was probably old. Even so, it was a problem, although not one he was unduly concerned about. After pacing the porch for a few minutes, Jessie called the dog and went back inside.

Caleb cocked his head, feeling that strange flutter he always got in the pit of his stomach when he made first contact with his prey. He glanced at his watch, returned to his car, pulled a u-turn and drove back into town, taking careful note of how much traffic he met and the distance and time it took to reach the highway.

Back in town, he made his way to a small diner far away from Ray's and ordered grits and hash browns and coffee. He ate a hearty meal, paid and set off to track down Mike Conway's garage. He would be surprised if the Volvo belonged to anyone other than Jessie.

At the garage, the double gates were locked and the shutters were down on the prefabricated building attached to the yard. Wherever the husband was, it wasn't work. Caleb was disappointed; he would have liked to see Mike Conway in the flesh. After all, he had seen him so many times on television he almost felt he knew him.

He sat for a while thinking about the dog and what he was going to do about it. Shortly after seven, an old man pulled in ahead of him in an ancient pick-up truck that was more rust than paint. He got out slowly and gave Caleb the stink-eye.

Caleb decided it was time to get gone. He waited for the local library to open and asked if they had a section containing local news, history and local records.

'Well sure,' the librarian said, looking over his glasses at the young bearded man before him, 'we keep records, but what kind of records might you be looking for?'

Caleb shifted his weight from one foot to the other. 'My Daddy's name was Vaughn, he's from Bridgewater, but his people – I believe – was from around these parts. I was hoping if I go back some I might find trace of 'em.'

'Vaughn?'

'Yes sir.'

'Don't believe I know any Vaughns, but you're welcome to take a look, son. Would you be needing to see the obituaries?'

'Yes sir, if that was possible.'

'You're in luck, son. We used to have those stored on index cards, but moved them all to microfilm two years back – easier to find names that way.'

Caleb smiled; if it was a poor one the librarian did not seem to notice. 'Appreciate that, sir.'

'Come on down the back. I'll show you how to operate the reel.'

Caleb followed him to the rear of the library and into a small room occupied by a desk and a projector. The librarian, whose name he learned was Elliot Pearson, set up the screen and the film and left him to it.

Caleb began to search through the deaths of Rockville, looking specifically for suicides. It took him the best part of two hours before he recognised a pattern. He investigated further and found it arose again, and then again. As with all small towns, suicide was addressed in terse figures of speech. People didn't kill themselves, they were 'found dead with no foul play suspected'. He read on, noting a particular place cropped up again and again.

When he was finished he returned to the librarian and said thanks.

'You find what you need, son?'

'I did surely,' Caleb said. He tipped his forehead with his right index figure and left.

He drove back to the motel and opened the map of the town. He located the area mentioned in the archives and decided to take a drive out there later in the day. He refolded the map, took a shower and lay on the bed. He drifted off to sleep listening to the crickets sing from the branches of the olive tree in the parking lot and dreamed of Jessie Conway running through the trees, her red hair streaming behind her.

He woke up a few hours later, refreshed and ready to begin work on the next step of his plan. All thoughts of his mess up in Charlotte were banished. He had a new mission now.

It felt like being reborn.

When Jessie got up she noticed that their bedroom door stood open and their bed was haphazardly made. She glanced out the window to where Mike had parked the truck the night before and suffered a little pang at the empty space.

Her eyes felt gritty and a dull-pressured ache was building behind them that seemed fitting for the occasion. She wondered how she was going to get through the day, how she was going to face everyone who knew her. She wanted to do nothing more except go back to bed and pull a sheet up over her head and wait it out until her life drew to a close.

She greeted Rudy in the kitchen, scratched him behind his ears and poured herself a cup of coffee. What was coming down the tracks next, she wondered, taking a seat in the breakfast nook. Where did she go from here? Bitterness was not her natural state, but right at that moment it was very hard not to feel bitter about the hand she was being dealt. All she had ever wanted was to live a peaceful life, one free from violence and judgement. Was it so ludicrous to want to get up in the morning and be happy? Was it so wacky to desire to be left alone in peace and quiet?

She sipped her coffee and stared unseeingly into space. She figured by now everyone in Rockville would have read that piece of tabloid garbage. There would be ladies hunched over coffees pontificating and gossiping about her, calling each other on red-hot lines. There would be a question mark over her head where before there had been none. It was the nature of a small town; it was the nature of people.

The argument with Mike had scared and upset her. What he had said to her was bordering on the unforgivable. But then what did she expect after the bombshell that had been dropped on his lap? The question was what happened now? Could they get past this? Would he even want to try?

She rested her chin on her hand, thinking. Old memories rose up from the deepest parts of her. Doug Robinson: she could barely bring herself to think his name let alone say it. She had told Mike he had been a mistake but he had been much more than that. There were hardly words to describe him, though demon might be closest.

From the outset, he had telegraphed exactly the sort of man he was, but she had been too young and inexperienced to see it. His jealousy she had thought mildly flattering, his need to know her business at all times, romantic. By the time she'd understood how messed up their relationship was it was too late to escape. Knowing her feelings for him had changed, Doug had tried to break her, of that she was certain. But she had not broken.

So how was it that even from beyond the grave he had managed to insert himself into her life again? Everything she had built was in jeopardy: her work, her reputation, but mostly her marriage.

Maybe she should have told Mike from the beginning, but hindsight was a wonderful thing. It was not easy to talk about the past. Nor had she wanted to see in his eyes anything like she had seen last night; the doubt, the disbelief, the fear. She had not wanted him to think any less of her, to hold her in the same contempt in which she held herself.

Jessie finished her coffee. She rinsed her cup, took a shower and brushed her teeth. She dressed in pale linen pants and a cream vest with white daisies on it. She was eating a slice of wholemeal toast in the kitchen when the doorbell rang.

She watched Rudy hurry down the hall to sniff the door, and saw his nubby tail wiggle with delight. Jessie put down her toast and smoothed her hair. She walked down the hall and unlocked the front door. Let her give it her best shot, she thought, she won't break me, I won't let her talk down to me neither. What is done was done before I ever knew her. I owe nobody an apology for *my* past.

'Hello, Fay.'

Fay wore navy blue pants, violet sandals and a cream lace blouse. Her hair was immaculate as always, but her eyes were puffy and her face was drawn with fatigue.

'Come on in,' Jessie gripped the door, taking a firm stance, her shoulders back and her spine ramrod straight.

'No thank you, I won't be stopping.'

They faced each other. Jessie's stare broke first. She lowered her head, waiting for the hammer blow.

'My son loves you very much.'

'I know that. I love him too.'

'Do you?'

'Of course I do. How can you ask me that?'

'How can I not? Love is not about lies,' Fay's voice cracked on the last word. 'Love does not keep secrets. Love does not break vows.'

'I broke no vows.'

'You vowed to *honour* him, didn't you? Does making a fool of him honour him?'

'Please Fay, I know you're angry with me, but I … I can't, there's nothing I can do or say that can change the past.'

'This is not about the past. This is about now, about yesterday, about last week. This is about Christmas and birthdays and coffees. We – all of us – welcomed you into our family … and this … this is how you repay us? You had so many opportunities to be straight with me, with Mike, with all of us, and you lied. You deceived us.'

Jessie wanted the ground to open up and swallow her whole. Her earlier resolve faltered and gave. Tears spilled down her face. 'I'm sorry.'

'You are certainly not the only one.' Fay turned to leave.

'Fay–'

Fay did not stop. She hurried down the steps, got into her car and drove off without another glance at Jessie. Jessie watched the car disappear up the drive and closed the door. Rudy looked up at her, his tongue hanging to the side, his nub still. Jessie slid down on the floor beside him, buried her arms in his fur and wept.

36

Not long after Fay had gone, Jessie plugged the phone back in and called the garage. Emma was weird with her when she answered, but she had expected that. When Mike came on the line she could tell he was not happy to hear from her. She had expected that also, but it still hurt.

'What?'

'If you're busy say so and I'll let you be.'

She heard Mike exhale, and when he next spoke his voice had softened some.

'How're you doing?'

'Fay was here.'

'At the house?'

'Yes.'

'What did she say?'

'She's angry with me. She's angry that I did not confide in her. Or you. She wanted me to know that. She said I have dishonoured you.'

'She ought not to have done that.'

'She's hurt,' Jessie leaned against the wall. 'She has every right to be angry. I don't hold it against her.'

'That's not the point.'

'You were gone early today.'

'I stopped by *The Gazette* looking for that woman.'

Jessie moved to the kitchen and stood by the back door looking out across the yard. High above the tree line, ominous dark clouds were forming over the hills.

'Why did you do that?'

'I wanted to talk to her. I want her to know the damage she was causing.'

'She won't care; she doesn't care about anything other than herself.'

'She wasn't there in any case.'

'Probably for the best.'

They lapsed into silence.

'Well I ought to go. I have a stack of jobs here that need doing.'

'What time will you be home?'

Mike paused, then said, 'I don't know.'

'You don't know?'

'I don't know, Jess. I might head over to Ray's with Ace and have a beer after work.'

Jessie felt tears prickle her eyes. The hurt and anger in his voice was hard to listen to and it cut her deeply to think that she was the cause. 'We need to talk, Mike.'

'I know that,' he replied, 'but truthfully I don't feel up for much talking right now.'

'Is this it, Mike?' Her voice trembled; she could not stop it from doing so. 'Is this how it's going to be?'

'What do you want from me, Jessie?'

She felt a sob slip from her lips and despised herself for it. 'Will you give me a call if you're going to be late back?'

'If you want.'

'I'm so sorry about all of this.'

'I know you are.'

'If I could change it I would.'

'I know that too.'

'Mike–'

'I need to go, Jess.'

He hung up. Jessie pressed 'end' and laid the phone on the draining board. She cried, feeling lonelier that she had ever felt before in her life.

Thunder rumbled in the distance and Rudy, who been lying asleep on the rug in the hallway, came to her, pressed his nose against her thigh and whined. Jessie wiped the tears from her face. 'It's okay, Rudy. It's only noise, right?' Rudy whined and scratched at her leg with his front paw. 'Easy, Rudy, take it easy old man.' Another rumble. The light under the grill flickered.

She figured she should check that the generator in the cellar was working. It was not uncommon for electrical storms to occur at this time of year, neither was it uncommon for them to blow the power. She opened the door to the basement and hit the lights. The bulb buzzed twice, flickered and popped.

'Great.' Jessie flipped the switch twice more for no good reason.

Rudy growled.

'It's a light bulb, Rudy, no biggie.' Jessie went to the kitchen to fetch a spare bulb from under the sink. The thunder rumbled again, a little closer this time. 'I think we might be in for a humdinger of a storm, Rudy.' The dog glanced at her and his nubby tail twitched. 'Are you really that scared? Oh come on now you big softy, it's only noise. Noise can't hurt you.' She changed the bulb, checked the generator for fuel and returned upstairs.

Rudy had moved to the living room. He stood at the picture window, looking out into the bushes. His hackles were raised and he alternated between a growl and a whine. Jessie watched him for a moment. Rudy was a rescue dog and had been fully grown when she and Mike had taken him in five years before. No one knew how he had been reared or even how old he was exactly, but he had always been anxious during storms. Still, she could not remember him acting this oddly before.

'Rudy. Come here, Rudy.'

He ignored her and gave two sharp barks. Jessie walked over to him and rubbed the soft patches of hair behind his ears. Rudy whined again and turned back to the window.

'You want to go out? Is that it? Okay buddy, but don't come crying to me when it starts to bucket down out there.' She let Rudy out and watched him bound away towards the trees to the right of the property. The clouds were so low now the air itself felt energised and static. Jessie shivered despite the heat and returned to the kitchen.

Caleb smiled as thunder rumbled overhead. He liked thunder; he always had, even as a kid. This was a good sign.

He opened the gate at the top of Conway's driveway, climbed back into the Taurus and drove on to the sheltered hiding spot he had earlier sourced. He parked the car and hiked through the woods to a narrow ridge. He carried with him his bow, arrows and a small bag slung over his left shoulder. He crested the ridge and removed his binoculars from the bag he carried. From where he now stood he could see directly into the Conway's front yard. He glassed the house, hoping to catch a glimpse of Jessie.

Thunder rumbled in the distance. It was hot and clammy and the air crackled with electricity. Caleb spotted the dog standing in the large picture window to the side of the main door. It looked anxious and it paced and circled a few times. Jessie Conway appeared by its side and laid her hand on its head.

Caleb watched her through his binoculars. What he saw pleased him. She looked lovely, more so than she had on television. She was finer boned, paler, her neck was long and graceful. Caleb swallowed, thinking what he would like to do with that neck.

Dark clouds tumbled in over the hills. Caleb ran over his plan again. Earlier that day he had hiked a different hill and found the area mentioned in various newspaper stories of Rockville's suicides. It had been difficult to find, hard to reach and was unlikely to be known by anyone other than locals. In other words, it was perfect. But that was only one tiny part of his plan; the rest depended on many factors, getting rid of the dog being the main one.

Another roll of thunder sounded, closer this time. Caleb waited. He was rewarded when Jessie opened the door and let the animal out. Caleb bent down and from his bag he took a short silver whistle on a length of fine chain. He placed it between his lips and blew three long notes. He glassed the yard again. Sure enough, the animal was standing stock-still, its ears alert and searching for the source of the sound that no human could detect.

Caleb blew again, three notes. The dog began to run and then disappeared from view amongst the trees. Caleb continued to blow at regular intervals, sure the dog would find him; sure that he would soon move on to the next stage.

And what a stage that would be, he thought as the first drops of rain began to fall, and from the trees below he heard an excited bark.

J essie opened the freezer, removed the sausage meat from its wrapping and popped it into the microwave to defrost. Maybe Mike would be late, maybe not, but either way she was going to make him the dish he loved. She felt it was the very least she could do. No, it was *all* she could do.

She switched the radio on to a music station to distract herself while she worked. She browned the sausage to seal in the flavour and placed it to one side. She began slicing vegetables, and sautéing onions and mushrooms. She added a chopped red pepper to the onions and stirred them in gently.

Try as she might, she couldn't put Fay from her mind. Her relationship with her mother-in-law had always been civil, if a little forced, but she knew Fay to be a good woman with a kind heart and it grieved her to have caused her pain and upset.

The phone rang on the draining board, scaring her half to death. She was annoyed that she had forgotten to unplug it again. She checked caller ID and breathed a sigh of pent-up anxiety as she recognised Lou-Ann's number.

'Hi.'

'Hi you,' Lou-Ann's voice was soft and so full of kindness Jessie felt tears again.

'Oh Lou-Ann, everything is falling apart.'

'It's all right, sugar. It's all right, come on now, talk to me.'

Everything poured out: the fight with Mike, Fay, her fears, all her grief over the past; the words tumbled from her mouth so fast she could hardly hold them. Lou-Ann listened in silence until Jessie was finished, then comforted her and offered solidarity.

'To hell with 'em!' Lou-Ann said. 'You think you're the only one in Rockville with a closet full of skeletons? Hell, can't you hear the valley rattling? There's not a one of them can be holier than thou and that's a fact.'

'Mike could be,' Jessie sniffed, drying her tears on a sheet of kitchen towel.

'Mike is a stand-up man Jessie, and there's no denying that. He won't turn his back on you.'

'You didn't see how he looked at me last night.' Jessie began crying afresh. 'I don't know what to do, Lou.'

'Hold your head up, that's what you do, and let anyone who doesn't like that go whistle.'

'It's not that easy.'

'Nothing worth doing ever is.'

They spoke for a while longer, until Lou-Ann remembered she had to pick up the kids.

'Want me to stop by later?'

'No, no thank you,' Jessie said. 'I appreciate the offer; I appreciate everything you've said.'

'Think nothing of it. Jessie,' Lou-Ann's voice became serious. 'I know you're hurting; I know you're hurting really bad right now, but let me tell you something my Mom used to say whenever things got tough. She'd say, "This too shall pass." I promise you, Jessie, this too shall pass.'

After they said their goodbyes, Jessie returned to the counter and finished making the stew. As she added the stock, drops of rain began to fall – a light spray at first, but within seconds it became a downpour. There was another loud rumble of thunder, closer this time. The lights in the house flickered and the hair on Jessie's arms rose.

Jessie turned down the heat under her food and went to the front door. She stepped out onto the porch and was surprised that Rudy was not already at the door, demanding to be let in.

'Rudy!' She turned her head to her left. 'Rudy! Come on, Rudy, let's go.' She waited, but Rudy did not come. She went back inside and stood in the hall for a moment, deciding what to do next. She grabbed her keys and a raincoat from the closet and went outside.

'Rudy!'

She walked towards the trees and whistled. Still there was no sign. She wondered where he had gotten to and hoped he was all right. He had once chased a rabbit off the property and had been missing for a day, but that had been many years previously, and not while there was a storm in the air.

Jessie returned to the house and tried to occupy herself, but when another hour passed and there was still no sign of the dog, she locked up and went in search of him. She searched all around the grounds and sheds, calling all the while. The rain was heavy now, driving hard against her face and hands.

'Rudy!'

Flickers of fear began to form into more solid shapes.

'Rudy!'

She made her way up the drive and noticed with dismay the gate standing wide open. She ran up onto the road and looked this way and that. Which way? She turned right and made her way along the ditch, calling every few yards, pausing to see if she could hear anything. She was half a mile from the gate when a gold car came down the road towards her and passed her slowly. Jessie had gone on a few paces when she heard the car stop and a door open. The engine was still running.

'Ma'am?'

Jessie turned around and wiped the rain from her eyes. A tall bearded man stood with one foot out of the driver's door.

'Ma'am?' he called. 'Are you looking for a dog? Black? Short tail?'

'Yes!' Jessie yelled, feeling an almost overwhelming relief surge through her body. 'Have you seen him?'

He looked down for a moment and Jessie felt her relief die.

'What is it?'

'Ma'am, I'm real sorry. He's laying up a ways yonder, looks to me like he was hit by a car.'

'Oh no.' Jessie stood rooted to the spot, feeling the rain run down her face onto her collarbone. She tried to find something to say, but all she could muster was a weak, 'Oh no, no.'

'Look, get in,' the man said. 'I'll run you up to him.'

Jessie walked towards him in a daze of misery. She was almost at the trunk when she thought she heard it pop and the bearded driver came toward her. Jessie stopped inches from the trunk and blinked.

'You know what, I think I'll go get my own car. Whereabouts did you–'

And then the world went black.

'Mike?'

'What?'

Ace wiped his hands clean on a rag and pushed the brim of his cap up a little higher on his head. 'I asked if you want to take a spin out to The Shack when we're finished up here.'

Mike sat back on his hunkers. 'Neville's place? Shit, is that dump still standing?'

'It's standing.'

Mike considered the offer. Though he had told Jessie he was probably going to head to Ray's for a drink, the longer the afternoon had stretched on the more he realised he did not in fact *want* to go to Ray's Diner. It was Friday, payday for most of Rockville. Ray's would likely be busy and Mike could not face the questions in the eyes of so many people he had known most of his life. He could not face their curiosity – or worse, their pity.

'Well?'

'Sure. Why not?'

'All right then.' Ace looked up at the sky as raindrops, big and heavy, began to fall onto the yard.

Mike attached the last wheel. Ace helped him pull a sheet of tarpaulin over the Mini and waited as Mike parked his truck out the front of the building and locked it. Together they drove out of town, turned east and began driving high into the hills behind Rockville. As they drove, Ace smoked and played some old-time music that reminded Mike of when they were kids.

'What is this music? It sounds familiar.'

'It oughta,' Ace said, blowing jets of smoke through his nostrils. 'It's Doc and Chickie Williams. Pop used to listen to 'em when he was working on the house. Don't you remember?'

'I remember now.'

'You used dance around the house to "Polka Dots and Polka Dreams".'

'Dance?'

'Sure, Pop would laugh and say, "Look at that one go!"'

Mick glanced at him sceptically. 'I don't remember no dancing.'

'Well you did, and it made Pop happy that you liked his music. He said you reminded him of a time when he was a kid himself.'

Mike laid his head back against his seat. The music relaxed and comforted him and he listened to the songs and thought of his father while Ace kept his eyes on the road, concentrating as the rain hammered against the windscreen. Visibility was reduced to a few scant feet before the headlights.

They reached The Shack shortly before seven. The varied beer signs were jazzily lit against the darkening air. Already there were a number of trucks and chopped-down motorcycles in the dirt parking lot outside.

'Busy,' Mike said.

'Friday,' Ace said, by way of an explanation.

They got out and ran through the rain into the building. Inside, the bar was crowded with pockets of drinkers; some dry, some steaming gently.

'Well hey there, Ace. Good to see you again.' Coraline Neville, short, round and cute as a button sashayed past carrying a tray loaded with whisky shots to a table of marauders seated in the corner. Ace nodded to her, but remained silent.

'Let's sit at the counter,' Ace said.

'Since you're so familiar. Lead the way.'

Ace scowled. Mike detected a trace of colour bloom on his neckline and hid a grin behind a cough. He understood now why they had travelled so far for a drink. He was strangely gratified that Ace had managed to blend his own desires with his brother's current needs.

They perched for a number of hours on a pair of stools, shooting the breeze with Coraline and then later with her father, Red Neville. Red was a cantankerous old coot long blown in from Nova Scotia. He was a born storyteller and liked nothing more than to regale anyone who might listen with wild tales of his days as a merchant seaman, before he got landlocked into what he affectionately called, 'this God forsaken shithole'. Red talked his talk and Coraline rolled her eyes and tenderly reminded him of whichever piece of the story he was forgetting. It was an entertaining double act, and after a while some of the tension eased from Mike's shoulders.

During a quiet spell, when Red was changing a barrel and Coraline was off collecting glasses, Mike leaned towards his brother. 'You like her, huh?'

Ace tossed a shot of Beam back and jammed a cigarette into his mouth. 'She's all right.'

'Why don't you ask her out?'

Ace shrugged.

'It's obvious you like her and she likes you.'

'Quit digging through sand, Mike. I ain't your project.'

Mike downed his own Beam and decided to keep his thoughts on romance to himself.

The storm had blown over by the time they left the bar and night had long fallen. Mike looked to the sky. Above him, millions of stars twinkled against the inky backdrop and the air smelled of pine and earth. He was drunk as a skunk. Ace lit a cigarette and opened the driver's door. Mike slipped and slopped gingerly over the muddy ground and came to a halt, resting both hands on the trailer. 'I appreciate this. I do, Ace, I want you to know that.'

'I know it.'

'It's all … a fucking mess, y'know?'

'This shit will pass over, Mike. You think it won't 'cause you're caught up in it, but it will. Next week, week after, something else will come along to entertain the masses.'

'And Jessie? What about her?'

'That'll die down too.'

'You think so?'

'If you let it.'

'She lied to me.'

'I'm thinking she must have had her reasons.'

'That's it?'

'What else is there?' Ace got in the truck and closed the door. After a moment Mike did the same. He was asleep before the truck made it to the first bend on the road. Next thing he knew Ace was shaking him by the shoulder.

'Home.'

He sat up blearily and fumbled for the door handle, but before he had it open he heard Ace say, 'There's no one here I reckon.'

Mike looked. The house was in complete darkness and Jessie's car was not where it should have been. 'Where is she?'

'Maybe she went out.'

Mike checked his watch. It was almost midnight. He sighed. 'Yeah, could be.'

'You okay?'

Mike patted Ace on the forearm.

'I'm good.'

He opened the door and slid out onto the ground.

'Shit.'

He used the runner on the truck to haul himself upright and slammed the door.

It seemed to take a while to locate his keys, and longer still to get them into the lock on the front door. He waved to Ace, stumbled to his bedroom and lay down on the bed to wait for the room to stop spinning. He'd lie there for a minute or two, then get up and wait for his wife to return home.

He was asleep in seconds.

40

Mike opened his eyes and lay perfectly still. He wondered for a moment what the licence plate of the truck that hit him might be and what critter had died in his mouth during the night.

He scratched his chest and smacked his dry lips together. The light filtering through his windows hinted at early dawn. He turned his head and saw that he was alone. He eased himself upright, went to the bathroom and gulped water straight from the tap. When he had enough, he rinsed his face and leaned shakily on the sink, breathing slowly until his stomach stopped rolling.

He couldn't remember the last time he had felt this bad. He closed his eyes and tried to remember going to bed. Despite his best efforts he could not quite nail the memory down, and was not sure if he had spoken to Jessie or not.

Feeling sick and vaguely uneasy, he made his way to the kitchen and stood in the doorway, squinting at the brightness. It took him a few beats to process the information.

Rudy was nowhere to be seen.

Maybe Jessie had let him sleep in with her last night; she did that sometimes when she was upset. He wondered how pissed she was that he had not come home after work. Maybe he should have called. He noticed the saucepan on the cooker and opened it. The smell of Italian sausage hit his stomach hard. He slammed the lid back in place with a groan.

He brewed some coffee, poured a cup and carried it outside to the back porch. The sky was brightening over the hills; oblong clouds tinged with red and purple drifted lazily by. It was warm and the air still held the faint trace of rain. He sat on the top step, sipped his coffee and watched the light grow stronger. One of the feral cats, a calico he knew Jessie favoured, crept from under the woodpile. She moved closer to him and swished her tail.

Despite his hangover, Mike realised he felt a little better about things than he had the day before. Maybe Ace was right. Maybe this shit *would* pass if he let it. He drank his coffee, eased himself to his feet and went inside. He poured another cup for himself and one for Jessie and walked down the corridor to the spare room.

She was not there and the bed was neatly made. Mike frowned and walked to the front of the house and looked out. Jessie's car was not where she usually parked it, and he remembered then that her car had not been there the night before. She had to be pretty mad to stay out all night.

Mike took a shower. Shortly before seven he phoned Ace. It was a while before his brother answered, and when he did his voice was thick with sleep.

'What?'

'Hey, can you swing by and pick me up on the way in?'

'Huh?'

'Jessie didn't come home last night. I need a ride.'

He heard Ace light a cigarette, inhale and exhale before he answered. 'Okay?'

'Probably she's at Lou-Ann's. I should have called her I guess.'

Ace offered no comment on this, so Mike hung up and chewed on his lip for a little while. He considered calling Lou-Ann but decided against it. It was too early in the morning to be broadcasting his business about town.

He made a slice of toast and forced it down, along with a glass of water. While he ate he stared at Rudy's empty bed. That troubled him some. Whatever about Jessie taking off like that, why had she taken the dog? But then he figured the way things were going, unlikely and likely were kit and kin. By the time Ace arrived he was less worried and more down in the dumps about the situation than anything else. He was certainly not in any humour for small talk. Fortunately, neither was his brother. Ace drove towards town, humming tunelessly under his breath.

'Do me a favour, swing past the Granger house.'

'Now?'

'Just do it, Ace.'

They turned off the main road and passed meadows and barns and numerous smallholdings. Vic Granger was a hog man, and ran a successful organic pork farm with help from his aged father, Vic Senior. Lou-Ann ran the Rockville Readers' Circle and together the pair were probably the closest thing to friends Jessie Conway had.

Ace pulled up by the main gate to the Granger property. The house was a two-storey clapboard farmhouse, with neat railings and flowerbeds out front and industrial sheds to the rear.

'I don't see her car.'

Ace shrugged. 'Could be she parked out back.'

'Could be.'

'Want me to drive in?'

'Nah, let's get to work. If she's there she's there, no point stirring up gossip.'

When Jessie came round she had no idea where she was or what had happened. Her head ached so badly she felt sick. It took her a few moments to work out two things. One, she was in the trunk of a car. Two, there was tape across her mouth and she couldn't breathe.

Immediately, she panicked. She thrashed and flailed from side to side, tensing her body against the binds that held her. She tried to use her tongue to push the tape but it was pressed so tight against her skin she could barely part her teeth.

Adrenaline flooded her muscles. She strained her neck and managed to lift her head upwards towards a tiny crack of light. There, she was able to detect a tiny ribbon of diesel-tinged air. She tried to roll one shoulder under her body to get closer to the air source. It wasn't much but it was enough to step back from the ledge of full-blown panic. Her nostrils flared as she sucked it deep into her lungs.

What was happening?

She remembered the storm. Rudy … he hadn't come when she called so she had gone out onto the road to see if he had left the property in pursuit of something. She had been worried something had happened to him.

A car had come out of the rain, a gold-coloured sedan of some kind. She remembered a man with a beard asking if she was looking for a dog. She had run across the road towards him. Idiot. She clenched her teeth.

Now here she was, in the dark; hot, terrified, trapped, trying to suck air into her lungs through her nostrils, one of which was semi-blocked. If the other one closed she…

She rolled onto her back and arched her neck as much as possible to keep her airways open. She found it impossible to remain on her back with her hands bound behind her. Her left arm went completely numb. She had cramp in both her calf muscles.

Fear would not help her; that much she knew. She forced her breathing to slow further. Fear was the enemy. *Breathe. Breathe.* Jessie concentrated on easing the cramp. She flexed and released her muscles, flex and relax, flex and relax. Slowly she began to regain some measure of control.

Think.

Where was she?

She was in the trunk of a car, a moving car.

How long had she been unconscious?

No idea.

Did she know the bearded man?

No.

Why had he taken her?

No idea.

What did he want with her?

She felt the flutter of panic again and clenched her aching hands into fists. Wrong question.

What did he want with her?

I do not know.

Why on earth had she kept walking towards him?

She closed her eyes.

The car in which she was travelling slowed and she heard the indicator come on. She felt it turn, heard a truck horn, then the car accelerated again.

Where was he taking her?

No idea.

Why had he taken her?

I don't know.

Mike would come home. He would notice she was gone. He would surely be sick with worry. Would he realise what had happened? She moaned, remembering how things had been left between them. What if that was the last time she ever saw him? When she allowed herself to picture Mike's face her panic increased and tears began to spill from her eyes. She snuffled and choked on them, realising too late they could be her undoing.

Jessie slammed her head against the floor of the trunk and jarred herself hard enough to see stars. It hurt, but had the desired effect. Do not cry, she ordered herself; goddammit if you cry you *will* suffocate.

The car bounced over a pothole. Her shoulders burned from constriction.

Forget the pain. *Think.*

She was alive. He obviously wanted her alive.

Why?

I do not know why. I am afraid.

She gritted her teeth. *Fear will not help you.*

What did he want with her?

Whatever it is, it cannot be good.

Was he going to kill her?

Jessie clenched and unclenched her muscles, grappling with her mind. She fought until she managed to push that question back.

Time passed. She felt the car slow and turn again; no indicator was used this time. Why was that? She heard gravel, then none. Were they climbing? It felt like it.

Time passed. The pain in her shoulder was travelling in waves. She imagined it red hot, like lava. The pins and needles in her fingers were excruciating.

She wiggled onto her side again. The pain did not lessen.

Focus.

She tried to draw her legs up closer to her body.

Breathe.

Do not think about Mike. Do not think of the pain. Focus on something else.

Breathe.

Concentrate.

Think.

Does the car seem to be travelling slower now than before?

Yes.

The surface … it's different. Doesn't it feel bumpy, a little rougher than before?

Yes.

Good, okay–

What does he want with me?

Stop that.

She squeezed her eyes shut.

The car seemed to be slowing. It rumbled over what sounded like planks of wood – a bridge, Jessie guessed. They picked up speed for a while, then slowed and took another turn. Now it felt like rugged terrain. She heard the engine growl in complaint and estimated they were travelling at no more than ten miles an hour. After a while, the car stopped and Jessie heard the handbrake being lifted.

Fear will not help you, she told herself. But when the engine was shut off she trembled all the same.

Mike arrived back at the house a little after six. He was surprised, then annoyed, to see Jessie's car was still not there. He parked and climbed out, observing that Rudy had not come to greet the truck as he did most evenings. His anger was fleeting: Mike was too tired and weary to sustain it.

He stepped up onto the porch and let himself in. He walked through the house to the rear. The saucepan with the Italian sausage remained on the cooker; the coffee pot from the morning was where he had left it. One of the feral cats sat on the windowsill, looking into the kitchen. It jumped down when he approached the back door and slunk across the yard to the woodpile.

Puzzled, Mike walked back through the house and checked the other rooms, but everything was as it had been that morning. There was no note, and when he checked the answering machine it was full: none of the messages were from Jessie. He called her cell phone and heard it buzz from its place on the charger in the living room.

Mike's hand hovered over the phone. Jessie had to be really pissed to stay away like this. Why had she taken Rudy? Was that some kind of sign? Was she telling him she was gone for good? He ought to call Lou-Ann; she would surely know something.

He decided to take a shower, figuring – hoping really – that by the time he'd washed up Jessie might walk through the door.

He showered and changed into sweats. He glanced at the clock in the kitchen. It was nearly eight. He made a sandwich and sat around. At nine o'clock he was worried enough to begin making calls.

He called Lou-Ann first.

'Lou-Ann, it's Mike.'

'Hello, Mike.'

He noted her formality and tried not to let it get to him.

'Hey, Lou-Ann, I know it's late and all but I really need to speak to Jessie.'

'Jessie? Jessie's not here.'

'She didn't stay over last night?'

'No, I haven't seen her. I phoned the house a bunch of times today, but she never answered, so I figured she was not in the mood for people.'

Mike felt a flicker of unease. 'When did you hear from her last?'

'We spoke early yesterday.'

'How'd she sound to you?'

'How do you think she sounded? Cut up. What is it Mike? What's going on?'

In the background, Mike heard Lou-Ann's children hollering and messing about.

'It's probably nothing. It's ... well, she's not here and I don't think she's been here since yesterday, so I was wondering if maybe she mentioned stopping by.'

'She didn't, but if I hear from her will I get her to call you?'

'Sure, she's probably blowing off steam somewhere.'

'Where?'

'I don't know, exactly. Maybe she's gone to a hotel or something.'

'Well, okay.' Lou-Ann did not sound convinced. 'I'd appreciate a call if you speak with her; let me know she's okay.'

'I can do that.'

Lou-Ann lowered her voice. 'Goddamn it Mike, I am so mad at you right now.'

'Excuse me?'

'No disrespect, Mike, but with everything that woman has been through, I don't blame her needing some time alone. I mean how much more is she supposed to take?'

Mike had no answer to that question so he said his goodbyes and hung up. He phoned a few other people Jessie was friendly with but no one had spoken to her or seen her. Finally he called his mother. When she answered she sounded half in the bag, which was unusual to say the least.

'Did you see Jessie at any stage today?'

'No, I did not. I tried to call her but she wouldn't answer.' Mike heard ice clink against glass, then his sister Karen in the background, asking who Fay was talking with.

'Karen's there?'

'Yes, she is.'

'Makings of a fine coven.'

'Don't you dare, Mike, don't you dare speak to me in that fashion.'

Mike glanced out the back window. The sun was behind the hills now, the sky the colour of a fresh bruise. Shortly, the valley would descend into complete darkness.

'Ask Karen has she seen her.'

'She hasn't, Mike. I'd know if she had. What is it, what's going on?'

'I got home from work and Jessie wasn't here.'

'I'm sure she's … maybe she's at Lou-Ann Granger's place.'

'I already called her. She hasn't seen or spoken to her since yesterday. Rudy's gone too.'

'Well there you go then.' Fay let out a small sigh.

'I don't think she was here last night either.'

'Your sister wants a word.'

'No.'

'Hold on, I'll put her on to you.'

Mike hung up. He took Jessie's cell phone and his own and left the house. He checked the barns and surrounding sheds, keeping a tight lid on any emotions that tried to rise. The cats shadowed him as he walked. They were clearly hungry. He tried to sell himself the story that she was visiting with friends. She had been angry and upset – stood to reason she might want some time alone – but to leave and not write a note or take her phone with her? That didn't sit right with him. If she was mad with him that was okay, he decided. She could be mad at him, she could be mad as hell. He only wanted to hear her voice.

Where would she have gone?

He walked back down to the house, stood on the porch and looked out into the gathering darkness. He had no clue what to do or where to start looking.

She seemed so down, so very depressed.

Shut up.

This is out of character.

I said shut the hell up.

But still the voice persisted.

She's been depressed since the school, you can't say you haven't noticed. Now with all this dirt from her past being flung in her face … Lou-Ann was right; how much more was she expected to take?

He balled his hands into fists. Inside the house the phone began to ring. He hurried into the house and snatched it up.

'Jessie?'

'Hey Mike, it's Karen.'

Mike glanced at the clock on the wall.

'Is everything all right? What's going on?'

'I don't know,' he said, 'I've got a bad feeling.'

'Oh Mike, I'm sure she's out somewhere, driving around. Mom said the dog was gone too.'

'Yeah.'

'Well there you go. She's probably staying with a friend until she can get her thoughts straight or something.'

'Maybe so.'

'Mom told me she had words with her.'

'She did.'

'Well, she's not the sort of woman who keeps things bottled up. She's sorry that it came to that.'

'I know she is.'

'I tried phoning Jessie yesterday and she didn't answer or anything, but I figured she didn't want to talk about … well what Darla Levine was talking about. Not that I have any real thoughts on the subject, although I do feel Jessie could have spoken to us about it. I mean we *are* family.'

'Karen, I need to get off the line in case she's trying to get through.'

'Okay, call me when you hear something.'

'Will do.'

Mike hung up and stood listening to the stillness of his home. Despite his best efforts, he felt a sensation rise within him and thought of how ironic it was that he recognised it so easily.

Dread, he was feeling dread.

Caleb climbed out of the car and stretched. His lower back was stiff and his legs ached. It had been a long drive from Rockville, but now that he was at the cabin he could unwind and shake off some of the fatigue.

He checked the perimeter of the cabin to be sure it remained undisturbed. Satisfied no one had been snooping around, he unlocked the front door and stepped inside the main room. He lit two kerosene lamps, deposited his bag in the metal trunk and returned to the car, carrying one of the lamps loosely in his hand.

He unlocked the truck, unsurprised to find her staring up at him. He lifted the lamp and ran it over her. She shrank from the light and made a whimpering sound behind the tape.

They all did that.

He grabbed her and hauled her out. He cut the plastic cables that bound her feet and shoved her in the direction he wanted her to go. She stumbled in the dark, but remained upright.

'Walk,' he said.

She walked.

He directed her towards a barn to the rear of the cabin. As he unlocked the doors she made more muffled sounds from behind the gag. He ignored this, disinterested in what she was trying to say. He had a fair idea what it was. He was pretty sure he had heard it all before. He pushed her inside and shut the door behind them.

'Stand still.'

She complied immediately. He hooked the lamp onto a beam and lifted a trap door set into the floor a few feet inside the barn. When she saw what he was doing she backed away, keening in her throat with fear.

'Get in there.'

She shook her head and folded in on herself. He advanced on her and grabbed her arm. She threw herself to the ground with surprising force. When Caleb reached to grab her again she drew her feet up to her chest and kicked out at him. Unfortunately for her, the range was too short to cause any real damage and he knocked her legs out of the way with a snort of amusement. He grabbed her by the legs, flipped her over onto her stomach and dragged her across the floor by her ankles. He paused at the trap door and flung her down the steps.

Caleb took the lamp from the hook and followed her down below. She was groaning, confused. He unlocked the door she had collided with and dragged her by the back of her shirt into a small room no bigger than a prison cell.

He attached the lamp to another hook set into the wall. Jessie sat up a little and looked around her. There was a fold-down bed against one wall and a metal toilet and hand basin like the kind you'd find on a train by the other. The floor was compacted dirt, and that was all that was in there.

He caught Jessie around her waist and lifted her onto the bed. He took a knife from a sheath wrapped to his ankle and sliced through the binds on her hands. He flipped her over and ripped the tape from her mouth so fast tiny pricks of blood appeared on her upper lip where her skin had come away with the tape.

'Please don't hurt me.'

'Shut up.'

'Please, what do you–'

He slapped her across the face hard, snapping her head to one side.

'I said it once already.'

She was silent. Caleb grabbed the lamp. He held it aloft with one hand while he grabbed her face with the other. He turned it this way and that, his fingers vice-like against her skin. There was a splinter in her cheek from the wooden steps and blood on her face. He read fear in her eyes but something else, too. Something he recognised as easily as he recognised water; total and utter hatred. He released her and took a step backwards.

'You can drink the water from the sink. It tastes funny. It won't kill you, but it tastes funny. Do you understand me?'

Jessie nodded.

'Good, this is where we at. I'm going up top now. I'm tired and I need to rest up.'

'Please, oh please don't … don't leave me down here.'

'You need to rest up.' He narrowed his eyes and scratched at the bridge of his nose with his thumb. 'I want you fresh, no point running you like this. No point at all.'

She came off the bed at speed and grabbed the front of his shirt. 'If you let me go I swear I won't tell anyone, I swear to you I won't mention you to a soul.'

Caleb grabbed her hands and pushed her back, irritated. 'That's stupid. You got any idea how stupid that sounds? Do you think I'm stupid?'

'No, I–'

'So don't talk to me like I'm stupid.'

'I'm sorry. Please, I'm sorry. I … I don't think you're stupid.'

'Good, cause I ain't.'

'I'm sorry.'

'I reckon you'll be a pretty good one.'

Jessie blinked in confusion. 'I don't understand … a good one?'

But he was no longer interested in talking. He was tired and he needed to rest. He turned towards the door.

She was on him before he had laid his hand on the door, throwing her weight onto his back, trying to force her way past him. He shrugged her off, spun, grabbed her by the throat and smashed her into the wall as hard as he could. She grunted and scrabbled at his hand, trying to pry his fingers loose.

He squeezed until she slackened then released her. She slid down the wall with her eyes rolling every which way in her head. He was worried for a moment about her windpipe, but then she took a breath, and then another, and slowly her eyes refocused. She raised her hand to her throat, leaned over and coughed until she retched.

'You ain't damaged,' Caleb said and left the cell. He locked the door and left her alone, weeping in the darkness.

When Jessie had not made contact by dawn on Sunday, Mike phoned Fay to let her know what the situation was and then he called the law. Twenty-five minutes after he made the calls, Sheriff Earl Dubray and Fay arrived at his home, almost simultaneously. Mike was on the porch, waiting. He stood and invited both of them inside, offered fresh coffee, which they both accepted, and explained what was going on without interruption. When he was finished talking he lit a cigarette and leaned against the countertop, his face strained, his entire body tilted with exhaustion.

'Any chance she's gone to visit friends?' Earl said, adding three lumps of sugar to his coffee. 'Is that possible?'

'I don't think you understand me, Earl,' Mike said. 'Jessie wouldn't up and do something like that. Something has to have happened to her.'

'Look, Mike, I appreciate that you are concerned—'

'Damn right I'm concerned. It's Sunday morning and nobody has heard from Jessie since Friday. Wouldn't you be concerned?'

'You say she took the dog with her?'

'I said the dog is gone,' Mike corrected him.

'You reckon she's been gone since Friday, so how come you're only calling me in now?'

Mike glanced down at his boots for a second. 'I thought maybe she was mad at me.'

'For what?'

'For none of your damned business.'

'Mike,' Fay said.

'Things going okay between y'all?'

'You read the papers don't you, Earl?'

Earl blew on his coffee and took a sip. A strong-willed, capable man, his face took on a look Mike recognised from their school days, a look that said only Earl's professional courtesy kept him from saying whatever thought had flown through his mind.

'I read them, doesn't mean I believe every word printed in them.' Earl laid a thick brown forearm on the table. 'I need to ask questions, Mike, and I want you to answer them without acting like I'm trying to butt horns with you. I like Jessie, I always have. I understand your concerns, I truly do. But I got to do things by the book. You need to be straight with me now.'

Mike took another drag on his cigarette to calm himself. 'Okay.'

'How has Jessie been of late?'

Mike hooked his thumb into his pockets and glanced at Fay. 'I don't know. She was still recovering from the ... incident at the school.'

'I can understand that, after what she went through. But I suppose what I'm asking you is how has she been doing, in herself?'

'She *was* doing okay. Until that Levine woman took it upon herself to go snooping around looking to raise dirt.'

'Uh-huh.' Earl took a notebook from his breast pocket and flipped it open. He removed a pen from the spirals and began to write in small neat lines.

'Has she been sleeping okay?'

'What the hell kind of question is that?'

'The kind I'd like answered.'

'She's been sleeping, Earl. She sleeps.'

'She on pain meds still?'

'Yeah.'

'She take 'em?'

'So far as I know.'

'Any other kind of medication?'

Mike shrugged. 'Fraas has her on anti-anxiety tablets, and she's been taking sleeping tablets too.'

'So, you last saw Jessie on Thursday night. Not Friday.'

'Right.'

'So one of you didn't stay here Thursday night?'

'We were both here.'

'But you didn't actually see her on the Friday?'

'Correct.' Mike's shoulders slumped a little. 'We had a row, Earl, okay? She slept in the spare room that night. I left for work early before she got up.'

'So you don't know—'

'I saw her here on Friday,' Fay interrupted.

Earl turned his attention to her. 'What time was this?'

'About eleven in the morning.'

'How did she seem to you when you spoke to her?'

Fay coloured a little. 'She … she was upset.'

Earl tilted his head to the side. 'Ma'am?'

'I confronted her about her about that article in *The Gazette*.'

'I see,' Earl said steadily. 'So you, uh, exchanged views.'

'Well,' Fay twiddled with her glasses chain. 'I confess I did the majority of the talking.'

Earl made a note in his book. He looked at it for a moment. 'Would you say that the discussion ended well?'

'No, I would not.'

'And you didn't talk to her again after that?'

'No.'

Earl looked at Mike. 'You know Jessie went to see Ana Diaz a few days ago.'

'How do you know about that?' Mike asked.

'I know because it's my business to know what goes on in this town, Mike.'

'She wanted to see her. I told her it was a stupid thing to do but she went anyway.'

'She tell you the outcome of that visit?'

'What outcome?'

'Reports I have are that Ana's older boy hauled out and attacked Jessie.'

'He did what now?'

'She didn't talk to you about that?'

'No, she didn't.' Mike shook his head, looking down at his shoes. 'She never mentioned it at all.'

'What was the last thing you spoke about? Do you recall?'

'She wanted me to come home to talk; I told her I was going for a drink with Ace. She asked me to call her if I was going to be late back.'

'And did you? Call I mean?'

'No.'

'Would you say Jessie was in an emotional state?'

'An *emotional* state?'

'Yes.'

Mike thought for a moment, picturing Jessie standing by the counter, her eyes wide and unfocused. 'She asked me if I knew what dread was.'

'Dread?'

'That's what she said.'

Earl wrote that down and frowned at it, wrinkling his nose as though the word smelled bad.

'What about family?'

'Jessie doesn't have none, only us. Her folks are dead and she doesn't keep in contact with her remaining sibling. Hell, I didn't even know she had a sibling until recently.'

'She mention anything at all about–'

'She said nothing about going anywhere,' Mike's voice was beginning to rise in desperation. 'If she had said something I'd be there now.'

Earl closed his notebook and pocketed it. 'All right, I'll head into town and put out a missing person's report. If that's what you want. Could be, though, she might walk through that door any second. Like you say, she's had a hard time of it lately, sometimes folk need time alone to sort through their thoughts.'

Mike lowered his head. He couldn't bear looking at Earl Dubray's face. He had known the man most of his life and sure as hell knew him well enough to know Earl did not really believe what he was saying, even as the words left his mouth.

45

Jessie hammered on the door until her hands were raw and bleeding. She called and called for him to return, begged him not to leave her there. But he did not return and finally, through sheer exhaustion, she gave up trying.

She crawled across the floor and located the legs of the cot with her fingertips. Using the last of her strength, she pulled herself onto it, stripped off the clammy rain mac and curled on her side. She cried herself into a fitful sleep.

She dreamed of Rockville High. She saw Tracy Flowers walking down the hallways, the red stain spread over the back of her yellow sundress. Jessie called out to her friend and tried to reach her. She moved as though through treacle and by the time she reached her friend, Tracy had morphed into something rotten, a putrid gassy thing swollen and bruised. Jessie laid her hand on her shoulder and turned her around. Tracy's tongue protruded through her broken teeth, her face was a mass of shredded flesh and shattered bone.

Jessie whimpered in the dark. Her body twisted and stretched as another dream, older this time, came from the place she had long locked away.

Black as pitch and surrounded by flames and heat, a much younger

Jessie passed charred windows and soot-filled rooms, her skin blistering from contact with the red scorching heat. She was searching, blinded by tears, calling their names, knowing in her gut as she tore from room to room what she would find.

In a room to the rear of the house she found them laying upon a blackened bed, bodies cracked and furled tight against the agony of death, and as she reached for them she heard the howling begin outside the room, sounds of misery and fear, and deep in her sleep Jessie Conway knew that death was right on her shoulder. The sounds, the splintering wood … the howling was now in the room. This was death, this was where she would meet her nightmare in the flesh. She saw rotted fingers fold over her shoulder, smelled the fetid stench of the thing as it pulled her around to face–

Jessie screamed and in doing so, woke. She opened her eyes and reached out into the darkness. She blinked, completely disorientated. Eventually her eyes made out the faintest outline of a doorway close by and as the horrors of sleep left the horrors of her present situation flooded in their stead.

Jessie swung her feet over the side of the cot and stood up shakily. Her throat hurt from where he had grabbed her and she knew without looking she was covered in bruises. He was unbelievably strong; pushing him had been folly.

There was only the tiniest trace of light from the passage outside, but even so it heartened her some. She badly needed to urinate and did so, crouching over the hole in a deep squat. She washed her face and hands and neck and cupped some of the water to drink. He had not lied. The water tasted foul – earthy and metallic. She gagged but managed to force some of it down.

She paced the room, searching for any weakness or any possibility of escape. But the door was smooth metal with sunken hinges and the floor was compact earth. She dug under the door with her fingers, but gave up after a while: it was pointless. Claustrophobic and anxious, she climbed back onto the bed, pulled her legs to her chest and rested her forehead on her knees. She tried not to think of what lay in store for her. Speculating on that did nothing except make her panicky and fearful. She tried to distract herself from the situation, but despite her efforts, names came to mind: Jaycee, Natasha, women who had been living their lives one day, the next spirited away by men like the one who had taken her. Worse, she realised with a start, they were the lucky ones, if lucky they could be called. She knew their names because they had survived their ordeals. They had at least been able to return to some kind of life. What about the women who vanished and were never found again? What happened to them? How many of them were like her? Locked in a living grave, with only a madman as judge and jailor?

This brought fresh fears. What if something happened to him? Nobody would know where she was. She would most likely die here, rotting away in the darkness.

She pressed her fists against her temples. She thought of Mike's face, his wounded heart. She had not even kissed him goodbye. This upset her greatly and she began to weep. She vowed if she ever saw her husband again she would kiss him long and hard, she would tell him she loved him, she would never stop telling him she loved him.

She thought about the man who had taken her some more. She forced herself to remain calm and be as analytical as she could be. He was very strong. He had lifted her easily and she was shy of 130 pounds. His demeanour was calm, if oddly disconnected.

He had this place. This was not new to him.

A realisation made her tremble. How many more women had he taken? What had become of them?

She groaned, feeling gorge rise within her. She concentrated on her breathing, trying hard to remain as calm as possible. She did not know how much time had passed when she heard movement overhead and then footsteps on the stairs. She got to her feet.

He unlocked the door and opened it slowly, carefully. Sunlight flooded the chamber from above, forcing her to cover her eyes with her forearm.

'Sit down.'

She sat. He put something on the floor, pushed it inside and closed the door again.

'Wait!' Jessie leaped up and rushed across the room. 'Wait! Wait! I want to talk to you. *Come back.*' She hammered on the door with her fist; she kicked at it so hard her foot ached. 'What do you want with me? *You bastard, what do you want with me?*'

She heard the trap door slam and then she was alone again. She slid down along the door, unable to contain her tears.

After a while, she regained her composure and dried her face with the sleeve of her cotton top. Her eyes readjusted to the near darkness. She looked for what he had left for her. It was tray holding a bowl of rice and beans and a glass of milk. She picked the bowl up, then put it back down and pushed it away with her foot. Her stomach growled with hunger. She was disgusted by her needs and felt betrayed by them. She would not touch this food. Who knew what was in it.

She was still by the door when he returned after a short while.

'Move away from the door.'

She stayed utterly still. How did he know where she was?

'Move,' he said, with an edge to his voice she knew was genuine.

She got up and made her way to the cot. He unlocked the door and looked at the bowl.

'You need to eat.'

'Please, I want to go home.'

He slammed the door and locked it.

Jessie remained in the dark. She cried, she sang songs, she counted, anything to keep her mind occupied. When he returned hours later, he checked the bowl and grunted.

Jessie hung her head. She had eaten the food.

46

Mike was on his porch with a cup of coffee in one hand and the phone on his lap when his brother drove up.

Ace nodded to him as he climbed out. Mike watched him stretch, thinking his brother looked more haggard than ever, in faded jeans that hung from his hips by a tightly cinched belt and a thin red vest that only accentuated his skinny torso. He wore a red trucker's cap and once again he had forgone the pleasure of a shave.

'Who called you?'

'Karen.'

'There's fresh coffee made.'

Ace walked into the house and returned a moment later holding a steaming cup. He leaned against a support post and crossed his legs at the ankle.

'Any word?'

'Nope.'

'How you holding up?'

'Oh, just fine,' Mike said, wearily. 'I've got the world's finest police mind on the case.'

'Earl?'

'Yep.'

Ace did not reply. Over the years he and Earl had had many a run in. Though Ace had spent a number of years inside, Earl had yet to get the better of him on any score.

'I don't know what else I can do, 'cept wait. Don't know who else to call, or who else to talk with.'

Ace sipped his coffee and looked out across the yard. He watched a group of turkey buzzards fanning the air above the woods to the right of Mike's property. The birds circled the tops of the trees, riding easily on the morning thermals as they banked in spirals, flying in that jerky see-saw motion that made them so easy to recognise. Carrion birds, Ace thought.

'How long have *they* been out there?'

'What?'

'The birds.'

Mike followed his brother's gaze. 'I couldn't tell you. I hadn't noticed them.'

Ace drank more of his coffee and watched them, his unwavering expression betraying nothing. He put his cup down and straightened up.

'What's on your mind?' Mike asked.

'They're searching for something.'

'So?'

'So whatever it is ain't been there long enough for them to find it, but long enough for it to catch their attention.'

'What are you saying, Ace?'

'I'm saying maybe we ought to go take a look yonder and see what has those buzzards so excited.'

'You think she's up there,' Mike said, his voice made harsh with unease.

'I'm not thinking anything except taking a look. You can stay here if you want.'

Mike put his cup down and stood. 'Let's go.'

They hiked up through the woods, neither man talking. Ace chewed on an unlit cigarette and climbed the rising ground with long strides and surprising swiftness for a man who seemed as though he could barely keep himself upright. In no time at all he was quite a distance ahead of Mike.

Mike did not call for him to slow down. In truth, Mike was dragging his heels a little. Something was gnawing at him, warning him that his brother's instincts were probably correct. There was something up here, he knew that, but he couldn't bring himself to think of what it might be.

About thirty feet from the upper ridge, Ace stopped and then knelt down. He stayed like that for a while then rose again, slowly, and stood with his hands on his hips. Mike knew from his body language that he had found something and he felt his knees tremble as he pushed up the bank.

'What is it?' He began to run. '*What is it? Is it her? Is it Jessie?*'

Ace held up his hand and shouted down. 'It's not her.'

Mike gasped, feeling all the strength drain from him in relief. But as he drew closer to Ace he got a hit of decomposing flesh and knew whatever lay behind Ace, half hidden among the leaves and branches, was bad news.

And so it was.

'It's Rudy, Mike.' Ace said when he finally reached him. 'Look's like he's been shot through.'

Mike pushed past him and hunkered down. Rudy lay on his side, filthy and bloated. There was an ugly wound behind his left front leg, crawling with maggots. His lips were drawn back over his teeth, a last expression of the agony the old dog had endured. Mike ran a hand along his flank. Flies, disturbed by the intrusion, flew up and swarmed crazily around his head.

'Sons of bitches.'

Ace laid a hand on Mike's shoulder and patted twice. Mike balled his right hand into a fist and stood.

'Can you look after this? I need to go call Earl.'

Ace nodded and lit his cigarette. 'You got any tarp?'

'So let me see if I have this; you're saying your dog is dead.'

Mike stood with his hands on his hips inside Earl's office. It was a cramped space, with windows overlooking the court building across the street and an interior window facing the two of the five desks which were currently occupied by one fifth of Rockville's law enforcement. Earl had the air conditioner as high as it could possibly go, which was high enough to cause a chill.

'Shot up in the woods by my house. Been dead about a day or two.'

'I'm sorry to hear it.' Earl's expression remained neutral. His tone was calm and measured but there was a hint of condescending patience to it that shorted Mike's last nerve.

'Well?'

'Well what?'

'Aren't you going to look into it?'

'A dead dog?'

'Don't this prove Jessie is in some kind of trouble?'

'How? Plenty of hunters work those woods, Mike. Wouldn't be the first time someone's pet met with such an end. Might not even be hunters, kids acting the—'

'Are you shitting me?'

Earl leaned back in his chair and looked at him. 'You need to lower your voice, Mike.'

'No, what I need is for you to get off your ass and find out what happened to my wife.'

Earl's eyes grew flinty. 'I have an APB out on her.'

Mike threw up his hands and stormed out of the office. He was halfway to his car when his cell phone rang.

'Mike?'

'Yes.'

'Mike, uh, this is Dale Corrigan. I'm a friend of your brother.'

'Hey Dale.' Mike reached his truck and got in. He knew Dale a little: he owned a dive bar on Riverside, a rough-and-tumble place that made The Shack seem like a five-star hotel. 'What can I do for you?'

'Well Mike, thing of it is I found your wife's car.'

Mike gripped the steering wheel with his free hand and looked across the street to the station. He ought to return to Earl's office but decided against it.

'Where'd you find it?'

'I'm up here on Prospect Road. The car's parked on the old logging track under a bunch of saplings 'bout quarter of a mile down from the waterfall. You know where I'm talking about?'

'I know it.'

'Yeah, I already called Ace and he's on his way. I'll wait on y'all.'

'Appreciate it.'

Mike drove the distance to the Prospect Road in half the time it ought to have taken him by law. He knew the logging road Dale had mentioned. It was a long abandoned track that ran from the summit of Prospect Hill to the valley. No, abandoned was not right. It was still a popular spot for love-struck teenagers, drinkers, pot smokers and canoodlers of many stripes. Back in the early nineties it had also been the scene a bloody knife fight, the outcome of which had left two teenage boys dead and another seriously wounded. Mike had shown the place to Jessie not long after they had begun dating; they had kissed under the spray of the waterfall.

It was also the place where more than one resident of Rockville had taken leave of their problems.

Mike pulled onto the hard shoulder and parked behind Ace's pickup. Ace and Dale climbed out and as they walked towards him, Mike saw a look on his brother's face he could not read but did not like.

'Mike.' Dale Corrigan stuck out his hand and Mike shook it. Dale was shorter than him, but massively muscled. He wore his hair in a flattop and his right eyelid was puckered badly at the corner. It gave Dale the sleepy look of the mentally sluggish, a mistake folk only made once.

He was an ex-marine. He had been discharged for reasons unknown and which he did not discuss. Locally, it was rumoured he was a gun-runner and a dope peddler, a man who could get you what you needed when you needed it for a pre-agreed price. Mike knew Ace and Dale did some form of business together on occasion, though the nature of that business had never been discussed either. Mike guessed they liked each other well enough, though Dale Corrigan was not the sort of man to trick around with friendships for free.

'I came across the car up yonder.' Dale looked out at him from under eyebrows the colour of ripened corn.

'Any sign of Jessie?'

Dale shook his head. 'Nope, engine was cool when I found it and the keys were in the ignition. I left 'em there.'

'What time was this?'

'Just after eight,' Dale replied. 'Could have been here all night. I didn't know nothing about your wife bein' missing 'til got into town. That's when I called Ace.'

'Appreciate you calling, Dale.'

'What you want to do?' Ace asked.

'Start looking for her, I guess.'

Dale shrugged one shoulder. 'I came down this way from the western range. Didn't see no sign of no one.'

'Lot of land up there.'

'Road's closed off quarter a mile up. Some of the trees came down from the storms we had back in the spring. There ain't no way to drive it. Unless she walked, but why would she do that? There's nuthin' up there.' Dale produced a box of cigarettes from somewhere on his person. He shook two loose, offering first to Mike, who refused, and then to Ace, who did not. Dale lit them up and took a long drag.

'I know you've got to talk to the law about this.'

'Don't mean we have to mention you none,' Ace replied. 'Does it, Mike?'

'That be okay?' Dale addressed Mike directly.

'You have my say on it.'

'I hope you find your wife,' Dale said. 'She was always real nice whenever I spoke with her.'

Was, thought Mike, as Dale touched his fingers to his flattop and walked back to his Jeep.

Mike and Ace got into Mike's truck and were soon bouncing over rough rocks and dirt as the truck climbed a steep bank to the old logging roadway. Just as Dale had said, Jessie's Volvo was parked by the edge of the trail, under some spindly pine saplings. Mike parked behind her car, climbed out and approached it slowly. He rested his hand on the hood. Cool. The driver's door was unlocked, the keys in the ignition. He leaned inside and checked. There was no handbag or pocketbook inside. He pressed the horn three times in quick succession. He did it again, then a third time. If Jessie had been nearby she would surely hear him and return to the car.

Assuming she could.

Mike took the keys from the ignition and bounced them in the palm of his hand. Two keys. One was for the garage and one was for the car.

'These are the spare set, not the keys she normally uses.'

Mike popped the trunk; he found nothing unusual and nothing in the car to indicate where Jessie might have been or gone. Mike sat in behind the wheel and rested his head on it. As he did, he glanced down at the gearbox.

'This is in neutral.'

'So?'

'We don't leave our vehicles in neutral.'

'Maybe she—'

'Leg room feels wrong too.' Mike stretched his feet out.

Ace bent and looked. 'You sure?'

'I ought to be, I've driven it often enough. It's longer.'

Ace opened the passenger door, leaned across the seat and looked carefully at the sliding rims for the seat. 'Shorten it up.'

Mike did as he asked. Ace looked at the clean section that appeared where the detritus that naturally collected had been disturbed.

'Yep, it's been moved about two inches.'

Mike bounced the keys in his hand and peered through the windscreen at the surrounding trees. 'I don't think Jessie drove this car here. I think someone else did.'

'Who?'

'I don't know.'

Ace looked up the path and narrowed his eyes. 'Let's go take a gander.'

Ace and Mike followed the old logging road up as far as they could go by truck. Dale had not exaggerated about the mud-slide. The entire road was impassable, clogged as it was with rocks and broken trees and a steep bank of dried mud. Mike jumped out and scrambled his way to the top of the obstruction. He cupped his hands around his mouth and bellowed, 'Jessie!'

Deep within the woods, birds fluttered and took flight; Mike heard the frantic beating of wings before silence descended again.

'Jess!'

Mike turned in one direction and then another, calling his wife's name into the surrounding trees. After a while, he climbed back down to the road where Ace stood waiting in the shade.

'We need to round up some folk and get these woods searched.'

'I guess we do.'

'She could be lying hurt somewhere.'

Ace hooked his thumbs into the waistband of his jeans. 'What would she be doing up here?'

'I don't know.'

They made their way back towards the vehicle, but as they rounded the corner Mike suddenly stopped walking and turned his head.

'What is it?' Ace asked.

Mike did not reply. He was listening to the sound of the water as it crashed over the rocks near by. He glanced to his left and peered through the tiny section of evergreens that separated the logging path from the waterfall. These days a single chain hung from the cliff to the metal post with a yellow sign, picturing a man falling over a cliff, warning people not to go out onto the rocks.

'Mike?'

Mike stood looking at the chain as though he'd never seen one in all his born days. He had been up this way many a time as a kid, exploring and hiking. His old man had always warned him to keep off the rocks. More than one 'explorer' and sightseer had miscalculated how treacherous they were. Naturally, all that advice had made this place irresistible to kids and teenagers alike.

Mike stepped off the road and over the chain. He walked through the trees and towards the water. Ace called after him but Mike kept walking. The soil retreated as he reached the first of the shallow water pools. He stepped over one, then another. He cleared the final tree and stepped out into rock made smooth by the elements and thousands of curious footsteps. Spray from the waterfall splattered his boots and make the surface under his feet slippery.

He was almost to the ledge when he saw it. He picked it up and stood looking at the rushing water. His gaze drifted to the whitewater rapid below. Despite the heat, his skin prickled with goose bumps.

When he walked back towards the logging track, Ace was at the chain, watching him.

'What is it? What's wrong?'

Mike stepped over the chain and pressed what he had found into his brother's hand. Ace looked down. It was an old leather collar, scuffed and shaped from a lifetime of wearing. From it hung a silver identity disk shaped like a cartoon bone. And on that, he saw now, a name.

Rudy.

'We used to come up here when we were courting,' Mike said, his voice hollow and unnatural. 'She liked it here, she liked the water.'

'This might not mean what you think it means.'

'Why else would this be here, Ace?'

'I don't know why.'

Mike looked waxy and unwell. He stared at his brother with a broken finality.

'I got a bad feeling about this. Oh God, Ace, what did she do?'

Ace spat to the side and jerked his head towards the truck. 'We need to get us a search party. So come on, we're burning daylight.'

'I'm going to die here,' Jessie whispered into the darkness. 'I'm going to die in this place.'

As soon as she had spoken the words she wished she could take them back, but like so many other things in her life, once it was out there it was out forever.

She got off the cot and paced the tiny cell. Time was a mystery to her. Was it morning? Noon? How long had she been down there? Would he come back? The heat was overwhelming so she moved to the doorway and tried to lean her head against the crack. Was that any better? She couldn't tell.

What if this was it? What if this was her life now; endless days pacing like a caged animal in the dark? If that was it she would end it, she would find a way and end it.

She turned and leaned her shoulder against the door. She hummed a little, but the sound was forced and eerie. She tried to remember old ditties her maternal grandmother, Gamma G, used to sing to comfort her when she was a child. Memories of her grandmother made her feel less afraid, so she focused her efforts on that, bringing to mind her grandmother's voice, her clothing, her endless cheerful stories about the old days. Even in her later years, when ulcers ate through the flesh in her legs, Gamma's indomitable spirit and stoic acceptance of her place in the world made her a pleasure to be near.

Jessie rested her head on her knees and sang softly. Somehow this allowed her a moment of clarity. If this man wanted her dead she would be dead already. Leading from that, it was clear he had another purpose in mind, one that required her to have some measure of rest and energy.

But what could he want?

'No point running you like this,' he had said. What had he meant by 'running' her?

She sang another song, and then another. She felt herself settle.

He was strong, so fighting with him was pointless and would only get her injured. She needed to keep her strength and her wits about her. He had an intention, if he hadn't she'd be dead already.

Running her.

Why had he said that? Did he mean that in a literal sense? He wanted to make her run?

She closed her eyes and sang a little more. She thought of him outside her house, the casual way he had tricked her into approaching him.

Oh, poor Rudy.

No, she snapped, not *those* thoughts.

She thought about what little she had glimpsed when she had been pulled from the trunk. It seemed they were in the countryside … lots of trees … possibly a farm of some kind perhaps.

She might only get one chance, assuming she got one at all. If she did, Jessie thought, humming a song Gamma used to hum as she peeled vegetables by the sink in Jessie's parents' home, she would make that chance count.

Some time later she heard noises overhead and footsteps on the stairs. Jessie moved away from the door and stood by the cot. He opened the cell door and slid another tray of food to her. He stood in the doorway, looking at her in a dispassionate way. Jessie looked back at him. Despite her fear, this time she did not plead with him to let her go; she had accepted that that was a fruitless waste of time.

'What's your average?'

'Excuse me?'

'You got dirt in your ears? You're a track runner; I saw it in the papers. What was your average?'

Jessie blinked, confused by the question. 'I – I don't know what you mean.'

He looked irritated. 'What was the longest you ever ran?'

'Oh, um, a half marathon.'

'How far's that?'

'Thirteen miles.'

He leaned against the doorframe, thinking.

'What speed?'

'What?'

'How fast'd you run it?'

'One hour twenty-five.'

'That's pretty fast. Them kids you shot, at the school. How far away was you?'

'Why are you asking me these *stupid* questions? I don't know, okay, I don't know.'

'You know. How far?'

Jessie closed her eyes and took a number of deep breaths. She saw Hector, his wispy moustache, the widening of his eyes.

'I don't know. Not far, only a few feet.'

'And you was under fire?'

'Yes.'

When she opened her eyes again he had closed the door and locked it. She waited until she was sure he was gone before she located the tray and brought it up to the cot. She ate, thinking dark thoughts of a kind she had long forgotten, or rather thoughts she had convinced herself no longer inhabited any quarter of her mind.

Mike called the Sheriff's department and told Earl what had been found. Earl said he would send a tow truck and that he himself would be by as soon as he could.

'Don't bother. I'm coming back into town.'

'Say what?'

'I need to organise some people to start a search.'

'I don't want a whole mess of people up there tramping around.'

'There's nothing to see here any road, Earl.'

'That's for me to decide, I'll call you when I make my preliminary investigation.'

Mike and Ace waited for the tow to arrive and followed it into town. They drank a cup of coffee while they waited for the Sheriff to return their call and tell them to come by the station, by which time it was past noon and Mike Conway was close to boiling point.

'So it was parked up with the keys in the ignition?' Earl said, writing in his notebook.

'Parked, yeah, but I already told you I don't think Jessie did the parking?'

'How's that?'

'It was left in neutral, we don't do that, and the seat was pushed too far back for Jessie too.'

'The seat?'

'Yeah, *the seat*,' Mike said, exasperated. 'It was pushed back further than normal. I told you all this when I called you!'

'That all?'

Mike hesitated.

'If you're keeping something from me, Mike, I can't help you.'

Mike took Rudy's collar from his pocket and laid it on the desk. Earl lifted it and turned it over in his hand, reading the name printed on the silver bone.

'Ain't this the name of the dead dog?'

'Yes.'

'Where'd you find it?'

'Out on the rocks by the waterfall.'

Earl's expression did not change, but his eyes gave his thoughts away. 'She wouldn't do that, Earl.'

'What made you think to go up that way, Mike?'

'He didn't. I found the car,' Ace spoke for the first time since they had entered in the office.

'Did you now?' Earl looked at him. 'How come you happened to be up that way?'

'I need a reason to be places, Earl?'

'I'm just a little curious I guess.'

'What difference does it make who found the car?' Mike said, irritated by the line Earl was taking. 'Fact is it was *there*. And we're wasting time standing around here yammering about it.'

'I thought the dog was found over in the woods by your house.'

'He was.'

Earl looked down at the collar for a long moment. Mike shifted his weight from one foot to another. 'Earl, it's gone noon, we're wasting time.'

'I've sent Martins up to take a look around.'

'And?'

'And what?'

'How about a search party?'

'I don't have the manpower to organise a search party based on nothing more than a parked car. You said yourself there was no sign of a struggle and the car had a key in the ignition. Now I'm not dismissing your concerns, Mike, but I need you to understand me here when I say I can't do a whole lot more than give a man or two to this at the moment. I don't know if you heard about the shooting over in Sioqua Valley – there's two dead with another two wounded. I've got cases coming out of my ears.'

'Goddamn it Earl, I need your help here,' Mike snapped, his expression murderous.

'You need to dial it down a notch.'

'Dial my ass. She could be up there hurt; she could be laying injured out in those damned woods someplace. I can't just sit around and wait, Earl. I need to be doing something.'

'Mike, listen to me. I've put an APB on her and I've called the hospitals and anyone I can think of, but there is not much more I can do at this point.'

'Jessie was not driving that car and Jessie did not kill our dog.'

'Up until a few days ago you didn't even know your wife was married before.'

Mike darted forward but Ace grabbed him and hauled him back to his heels.

Mike shook his brother off and held out a shaking finger. 'I won't forget this, Earl, you better remember that.'

'And you better remember who you're taking to.'

Mike grabbed his cap from where it had fallen and left, slamming the door.

Ace stood for a moment, eyeballing Earl.

'What are you looking at?' Earl said, smoothing his hair.

'Not a whole lot,' Ace said. 'And that is the truth of it.'

'You need to prepare him, Ace; you need to do that for your brother. Only two reasons folk go up there these days. I doubt Jessie was courting.'

'You don't worry about what I need to do.'

Ace exited, ignoring the slack-jawed Vonda Kelp at reception. He found Mike standing by the truck. His brother's face was the colour and texture of tallow.

'You okay?'

'That's one useless son of a bitch back there.'

Ace lit a cigarette and blew a stream of smoke out of the corner of his mouth. 'I'll make a few calls, call in a few favours.'

'She could be anywhere.'

'You really think she's up there?'

'She wouldn't do what he thinks she did, Ace. She wouldn't do that.'

'You sure?'

Mike looked across the street to the Sheriff's office; his eyes were bright with tears and muscles jumped in his jaw.

'Quitting's not her style, Ace.'

Ace rested a hand on this shoulder and gave it a squeeze.

'Then we won't quit on her neither.'

51

Mike went back to his house, gathered some gear and returned to the logging road. As promised – and despite the short notice – Ace had managed to rustle up a large group of men and women and had assembled them by where Jessie's car had been located.

Mike was gratified and a little humbled by the turnout. As well as Ace's friends, there was Lou-Ann Granger and her brother Todd, and Ray from the diner near where Jessie worked. Mingled among the people, hunting dogs of every stripe and breed strained at their leashes, keening and barking up a storm.

'How are you holding up?'

Mike turned and found himself face to face with Walter Hynes. Walter wore a snow-white vest, khaki shorts and trainers with coloured gel heels.

'Walt, what are you doing here?'

'Karen called and told me what had happened. I'm here to lend a pair of feet.'

'I appreciate that, Walt.'

While they shook hands, Ace wandered up with his dog Captain on a retractable line. He looked at Walter for a moment, his mouth twitching softly.

'Hello, Ace.'

'Walt. Nice duds.'

Walter stiffened a touch. 'These are trail shoes, designed for this kind of terrain.'

'They designed for snake bite?'

'What?'

'Plenty of 'em up this way. Mosquitos too, I reckon you're gonna end up a buffet in that get up. I got a spray in the truck, you need it.'

'I'll be fine.'

'Suit yourself.' Ace turned his attention to Mike. 'Just got a call. Dale's on his way with a number of fellows to help with the search.'

'Decent of him.'

'Yeah,' Ace said, cutting his eyes at Walter. 'Might not be a bad thing if you leave him to search the western slope of the range.'

Mike knew there was more to the request than Ace was saying but he didn't really give a damn at that point. 'If that's where he wants to search he can do so, long as he searches.'

'All right then.' Ace crushed his cigarette butt under his heel. 'I'll take Captain and head up–'

'Mike!'

'What's she doing here,' Mike said.

Ace shrugged. 'Search me. I didn't call her.'

Fay walked up the dirt road towards them carrying a long walking stick in her right hand. She wore beige three-quarter-length linen pants, a cream shirt and sturdy boots. A large floppy hat adorned her head. She stopped before the men, she nodded a greeting to Walter and pulled herself to her full height. She had a determined set to her jaw that Mike recognised. 'Where do you need me?'

'I don't. It's hotter than hell out here. Go on back to the house and I'll call you the minute I know anything.'

'I am not going to sit around that house a minute longer. You should have told me you had organised a search. I could have called people.'

'Who did tell you?'

'Karen.'

'Karen sent you?' Ace said with a twisted smile, 'Where's *she* at?'

Fay ignored her oldest son. 'I assume you have a course of action in mind.'

'I do, and it don't involve you.'

That hurt her feelings, Mike could see that, but all that served to do was make her tilt her jaw a little more skyward. 'That's too bad because I'm here.'

'It's going to be a lot of walking. I'm not going to have time to wait for stragglers.'

'I am aware of that.' She glanced at Walter, then back to Mike, her features softening. 'I want to help. Please, Mike.'

Mike sighed. 'Fine, Lou-Ann's here, maybe you can go with her.' He glanced at his watch. 'How many are we?'

Ace did a rapid head count. 'Thirty – no wait, here comes Dale.'

Dale Corrigan drove his Jeep along the path as far as he could and parked up. He got out, followed by three other large men Mike knew from around but did not socialise with. One of them, Danny Winston, had recently been released from a long spell inside. Despite his other concerns Mike wondered about Danny's sudden civic-minded spirit.

Dale opened the back of the Jeep and a large red-nosed pit-bull jumped down. It was held firm by one of the other men until Dale attached a long lead to his leather breastplate. The other dogs huffed and cried at the newcomer as it approached. Dale stopped a few feet away. The pit stood up on his hind legs, leaning his full weight on the harness, his cropped ears tilted forward. His muscles rippled in the sunlight.

'Better make that thirty-four,' Ace said, 'and dog.'

'I hope he keeps that thing on the leash,' Walter said to no one in particular.

Mike acknowledged Dale with a nod before turning to the assembled crowd. 'Folks,' he said, lifting his voice so that everyone could hear him. 'First off I want to thank you all for coming…'

52

Jessie slept on and off in a fashion until she heard his footsteps again. He opened the door and stood there for a moment, watching her. The light from the lantern he held aloft hurt her eyes, and she folded her forearm across her face until she became accustomed to it.

'You listen good.'

Jessie said nothing, but she nodded.

'I'm aiming to take you out of here. I don't want any trouble with you. If you look for trouble you will surely get it.' He pulled the door closed and locked it again.

Jessie lowered her arms and sat on the side of the cot. She wondered what time it was, now that the door had been opened the air in the cell felt cooler by a few degrees. She got up, peed, drank as much of the disgusting water as she could stomach and paced the tiny room until he returned.

'Let's go.'

Jessie slid past him and climbed the wooden steps that led to the ground floor. As she climbed she wondered how she could get away from him, what she might be able to accomplish if only her nerve would hold her?

In the end, he didn't give her much of a chance to do anything. As soon as they cleared the door he bound her wrists behind her and said, 'Walk where I show you.'

They exited the barn. Jessie took a long inhalation of fresh pine-scented air. She knew dawn was not far away, although the shadows remained deep. Her eyes followed the pale tinges of light splintering the sky behind the purple-hued mountains to the east.

'Move.'

He struck her between the shoulder blades and forced her to walk over the uneven ground to an old pick-up truck. He made her climb up onto the flatbed and when she did as he asked he tied her feet together.

Jessie finally managed to get a good look at him and was shocked by what she saw. He wore full camouflage gear and the skin above his beard had been smeared with dark greasepaint. She flinched when he put his hand on her. This seemed to amuse him. He pulled a spare wheel away, then lifted a wooden panel set in the floor. Jessie saw that there was narrow space barely big enough for an adult human built into the bed of the cab.

'Get in.'

Jessie looked at the tiny space and hopped back.

'I can't go in there. Please, I'm claustrophobic, I–'

The blow was unexpected and so rapid she had not even seen him move his hand. One minute she was standing, the next her face slammed against the cold metal of the bed.

'I told you there was to be no trouble.'

He dragged Jessie to the lip of the space and kicked her inside. He put more tape over her mouth and leaned across her.

'Ain't nobody out these ways, but make sounds and I will kill you. Understand?' He did not wait to see if she understood. He replaced the wood panel and Jessie was once again in darkness. She felt the truck's springs sag, heard the engine turn over and a door slam.

They were on the move.

She tried to manoeuvre her body into a more comfortable position, but there was little room to do anything. She gritted her teeth as the vehicle bounced over rocks and stones. She tried to keep calm, to figure out a plan.

She focused on the man who had her. Whatever she was dealing with here, she knew she was wasting any time looking for pity. There had been nothing in his eyes, no expression, no anger or excitement. Even when he struck her nothing changed. He had wanted her to do something and she had resisted so he had struck her. She had seen that calmness before. Her first husband Doug had worn it often. She knew she was nothing to him, only a human source for his sick amusement.

She turned her attention to the journey, trying to list the turns and stops. She heard the rumble of wood again and tried to gauge the distance he had travelled from the cabin to there, and from there to the next turn. She felt the truck slow and turn. Wherever he was taking her, they were now on a poor surface and climbing. She heard him drop down through the gears.

She thought of the landscape when he had led her out of the cell. What she had managed to view was not encouraging. No one could help her.

Stop thinking that way.

The truck drove over a large pothole so hard she smacked her face against the wooden cover and was forced to clench her teeth against the pain. Whatever he was planning, she was not going to go down easy. She was scared but she would not make it easy for him.

After a while, the truck slowed, then reversed and stopped. She felt it rock gently and she waited, holding her breath. She heard the sound of something being pulled back. Seconds later she was breathing clean air and blinking up at a brightening sky.

His face appeared above her. He reached in and hauled her to her feet. He stood her up on the flatbed, studying her closely. He raised his right hand to her face. Jessie shrank back from his touch and looked around. They were in a clearing of a wood. The air was cooler than it had been back at the cabin and there was a slight mist rising through the trees.

Without warning, he grabbed her and pushed her over the side. Jessie landed on the dirt hard enough to knock the wind out of her. He jumped down and pulled a large hunting knife from a sheath by his hip.

Jessie's eyes widened when she saw the knife. She screamed behind the gag and tried to dig her heels into the dirt to scrabble away. He grabbed her and cut the plastic binds from her wrists and feet.

'Get up.'

Jessie got shakily to her feet. She rolled her shoulders and flexed the muscles in her back. There was blood on her sleeve from where he had earlier struck her and she had cut one knee in the fall from the flatbed. He ripped the tape from her mouth.

'You hear a bridge a while back?'

'Yes.'

He pointed across the clearing with the knife. 'Yonder through the trees is a trail; you find that you can go follow it down to a creek. Find the creek and it will lead you on down to the bridge.'

'You're letting me go?' Jessie looked at him disbelievingly. 'Are you letting me go?'

He shrugged one shoulder. 'You got five minutes.'

'Five minutes what?'

'Head start.'

Suddenly Jessie understood.

She didn't hesitate.

She ran.

Caleb watched her go, a little surprised at the suddenness of her run, but pleased nonetheless. It confirmed what he had hoped. This one worked off her instincts and she did not second-guess herself. She was fleet of foot too. She made it to the trees and disappeared from view within seconds.

Caleb looked at his watch, humming tunelessly under his breath. When five minutes had elapsed he gathered this equipment and started after her.

53

They searched high and low all over the hill and the surrounding valley until evening began to fall, keeping in touch by cell phone as each section of land was covered. But it was to no avail. Close to dusk, tired and dirty, they regrouped by their vehicles, the earlier energy and spirit long gone. Quietly, people said their good-byes to Mike. Some patted his back, others let their eyes do all the talking before they loaded their animals into cabs and trailers and headed back down the mountain to shower and grab some much-needed food.

Mike sat on the fender of Ace's truck, his head hanging low, dejected. In his heart he had not really expected to find Jessie that day, but hope had lingered long after logic had departed.

Fay walked down to him, her arm linked through Walter's. The knees of her pants were covered in dirt and grass stains from where she had earlier in the day slipped on a slope. She looked old and worn out.

'Mike?' Fay said. 'Son? Why don't you come on over to the house, let me fix you something to eat. You're done in.'

Mike slapped at a mosquito chewing his neck and shook his head. He did not make eye contact with her. 'I need to go home in case there's been any calls.'

Fay's lower lip quivered. She looked towards Ace for a sign that he might intervene, but he acted like he didn't notice her trying to catch his eye.

'Mike–'

Mike turned his back on her and lit a cigarette.

'Tell you what, Walter, why don't you run Mom on home?' Ace said, lifting Captain into the trailer of his truck. He offered the dog water from his own water bottle.

'Come on, Fay,' Walter said softly. He said his goodbyes to Ace and Mike and tried to lead her away. She hesitated for a moment.

'I don't believe harm will come to Jessie, Mike. I don't believe God would let her come to harm.'

'No?' Mike said bitterly. 'What are you basing that on? The bang-up job he's been doing so far?'

'I know you're angry, son, but please don't be angry with Him.'

'Right now anger is all I got.'

Fay stared at her son's back. Her eyes glistened in the twilight.

'Fay, come on now.'

She allowed Walter to lead her away.

Ace finished watering his dog and walked to the front of the truck towards Mike. He heard an engine, turned his head and stared as a black Escalade made its way slowly up the road towards them.

'We've got company.'

Mike bent and looked around the fender. His eyes widened.

'That goddamned bitch.'

He snapped upright. Ace caught him by his bicep, but Mike shook him off as Darla Levine stepped out of the passenger side of the Escalade. Darla took a step forward. She wore a long silver dress with matching silver pumps, her highlights shone, despite the encroaching darkness.

'Mr Conway, I–'

Mike did not stop moving. He grabbed her by both shoulders, lifted her off her feet and slammed her against the side of the Jeep. Darla yelped in surprise.

'What the hell are you doing here?'

'I … I heard you found your wife's car. I'm here to offer my assistance.'

'Your *what?*' Mike could not keep the fury from his voice. 'You wouldn't know assistance if it came up and bit you on the shrunken ass.'

Darla's driver, the skinny Mexican Mike had sent sprawling on his ass at Harry's, opened the door and looked over the roof at him. 'Yo man, get your fucking hands offa her.'

'You best hold your tongue if you want to keep it.' Ace said with flat menace, strolling down the rutted road.

'I understand that you are angry with me,' Darla was saying, her words spilling over her lipstick too fast to carry her normal airs and graces with them. 'Please, I came here to tell you I'll help. I'll write a story asking for people to look out for her, I'll–'

Mike released her and stepped back. He looked past her to the driver.

'You best be on your way and take this piece of shit with you. I'm done being polite.'

'Mr Conway, if you'd just let me–'

Mike smashed his fist into the side of the Jeep, inches from Darla's head, denting the panel with the force of the blow. He jabbed a bloodied set of knuckles into Darla's face.

'I said I am done.'

Darla scrambled into the passenger seat. She looked terrified.

Mike didn't care. He walked past Ace and back to this truck without saying another word.

'What you waitin' for?' Ace said to the driver. 'Get.'

Chippy did not need to be told twice. He got.

Ace watched silently as the Escalade backed down the dirt road, and waited until it passed from view before he followed his brother.

54

Jessie ran as though the hounds of hell were hot on her heels. She broke through the tree line and plunged headlong into the gloom. Panic stricken and half blinded by the sudden change in light, she blundered on, convinced he was right behind her.

She fought to stay upright as she leaped over roots and rocks. Spiny branches tore at her skin and low-lying creepers snarled her feet. She zigzagged, certain she would hear a shot then feel a bullet punch through her skin. She stumbled onto a kind of track, righted herself and set off running again.

Terror put wind to her back and for the first mile or so she sprinted as hard as she could. But near the end of her second she was forced to pull up, completely winded. She leaned her hand against a tree trunk and gasped for air. Lactic acid flooded her muscles; her lungs felt as though they were burning and as hard as she fought against it, she had no choice but to vomit into the ferns by the base of the tree.

Clearing her stomach helped a little. She wiped her mouth with the back of her hand, glanced over her shoulder and tried to guess how much of a start she really had and how much she was holding.

The woods were cool and dark. A thought occurred to Jessie. The t-shirt she was wearing, though grubby from being worn for a number of days, would be easy to spot among the green and olive surrounds. Jessie stripped it off and rubbed it vigorously on the ground, smearing it with dirt and moss and grass until it was absolutely filthy. When she had dirtied it up as much as possible she put it back on and began to run again, slower this time, aiming for distance as much as speed.

A few miles on, she stopped to catch her breath and cock her head to listen. Apart from a few twittering birds and the blood rushing though her ears she heard nothing.

She ran on again, thinking, trying to make sense of his decision. She didn't for one second buy that he had released her out of the goodness of his heart. Which meant he planned to recapture her, but how? He knew she had pace. Was he going to try out run her? She pictured what he had been wearing: cargo pants, thick-soled boots. No, he would not outrun her in those. He had an alternative plan.

She had no idea where she was going and no idea where he was, but if he had been telling her the truth she had at least five minutes on him. As along as she kept moving she could stay ahead of him, maybe even extend the lead.

But why the head start?

He was going to outflank her.

How?

Jessie skidded to a halt.

What a fool she was! Her natural instincts had told her to go down and she had followed them. She could conserve more of her energy and maybe keep her lead for a little longer. She had known this instinctively.

And he would have also known this.

'Down' to the creek, 'down' to the bridge', those had been his words, his directions, and like a stupid sheep she had followed them to the letter.

She twirled around and stood with her hands on her hips, her body heaving.

Or maybe he wanted her to think that? Could it be a double bluff?

She wiped the sweat from her face and looked back the way she had come. They had been climbing the whole time they were in the truck, she was certain of it. The roads were below somewhere. Down was freedom.

Maybe it was, maybe it wasn't.

If she chose different it meant a climb into the mountains. Even assuming she made it over whatever ridges were above her, what then? She had no idea where she was and could easily wind up lost in the wilderness.

Lost or recaptured. What a choice.

She chewed on her lip in despair, starting to feel frustrated. Maybe she ought to try and hide? Double back?

The creek had to lead down. She knew there had to be a road not far from where he had released her. By her reckoning, they had been driving for half an hour, so maybe fifteen miles, maybe less. She could run that. She could make it if she really put everything she had into it. A road had to mean traffic and people.

Salvation.

No, *think!* Why would he have told her to find the creek? Why would he want her to go down?

Jessie rocked her head back between her shoulder blades. Above her, the trees whispered their secrets to a disinterested sky.

Another thirty seconds went by; more of her lead wasted.

Move. Make a goddamned decision and *move.*

She retraced her footsteps for about five hundred feet and leaped off the track into thick undergrowth. She landed on a section of bark-strewn bank and began to climb.

55

The road was in deep shadow when Ace drove off of his brother's property; the remainder of the day's light gently retreated in bursts of red cloud over the western sky.

Ace had told Mike he was heading home, but he pulled in a little way up the road and parked again. He climbed out and stretched, feeling muscles pop in his back. It had been a gruelling day, but he was used to running on next to nothing, and as bad he felt physically, he would rather feel that way a thousand times over than how Mike had to be feeling right at that moment. He was worried about his younger brother and had offered to stay with him. Mike had refused him, saying he did not feel much like company.

Ace knew what was weighing heavy on his brother's heart. Ever since they had found Jessie's car up on the logging road, Mike had been battling to tamp down the unspoken, gut-wrenching idea that Jessie was dead, done in by her own hand. Ace could see the guilt and fear written all over him.

But Ace wasn't sure he believed suicide to be the case. That was not to say it wasn't possible, but his sister-in-law had never struck him as a cruel woman and to do what Mike feared would have been the cruellest thing she could possibly have done to him. Jessie was, Ace thought with genuine affection, someone he admired for her ability to see past the shit and dirt of life and was happy to add a little grace to her surroundings. The Jessie he knew would not inflict a deliberate agony on those who loved her.

He lit a cigarette and inhaled deeply. Behind him, Captain hung his head out through the driver's door and gave a soft huff, reminding Ace that where he went, Captain would be happy to follow. Ace let the dog out and Captain sat by his feet, gazing up at him. Even though the dog had to be as weary as he, Captain was ready and willing to do his master's bidding. Ace scratched the top of his head, the trace of a smile on his lips. Most dogs could be trained to hunt, Ace had done so many a time before, but with Captain the instinct was in his DNA, passed down from long blood lines of brave, diligent animals who would rather die of exhaustion than let their master down.

Ace fetched a torch from the glove compartment, then tied a long thin line to Captain's collar and walked down the road. The night was silent, apart from the chirp of crickets and the click of Captain's nails on asphalt.

They entered the woods where they had done so two days before and walked half a mile along a trail line before Ace stopped and located the exact bank where he had found Rudy. He bent down and held Rudy's collar under Captain's nose, letting the dog sniff it carefully.

'Seek, seek.'

Captain trotted to the front, crisscrossing the path. Ace left enough give on the line for him to work comfortably.

They worked left to right along the trail. Captain's demeanour was different now, as he was focused on his task. Every so often he pulled the lead line taut as he collected scents of interest and siphoned them through his remarkable nose. When he found one of these, he would pause and retrace his step, but he did not indicate to Ace.

A half a mile in, Captain picked up the pace, leaped off the track and began to climb the left embankment. Ace let him have as much head as possible and dug his boots deep into the compact soil to follow. At the top of the ridge, Captain hung a sharp right and began to tug, moving along the tree line. Ace's grip on his torch tightened as he recognised the same slopes he and Mike had climbed; he knew where they were headed.

Captain led him exactly to the spot he had located Rudy's corpse.

'Good boy,' Ace said, but Captain was not finished. He snuffed around the flattened ferns and plants and pulled hard on his tie to a section deeper into the undergrowth. Ace allowed him lead on.

A couple of yards in, Captain signed and gave a deep cry. 'Barru,' he called. 'Barru.'

Ace pushed him to one side with his knee. He shone the torch on what Captain was so interested in. It was an arrow. He picked it up and examined it. There was dried blood on the shaft; blood which, he suspected, belonged to Rudy. Half a foot long, with unusual fletching and paint design, it had a hand-tooled obsidian flathead, and some-one with considerable skill had created it.

Ace bounced the arrow in the palm of his hand and looked behind him. He calculated the distance from where Rudy had lain to here: twenty feet. Yep, this was the weapon.

Which brought him to his next thought. It took skill to make and use a traditional arrow like this one, and skill to shoot a moving target.

This was no accident.

Someone had wanted the dog dead, out of the way.

He walked Captain back to where he had found Rudy and searched around the area a little more thoroughly. He found impressions in the grass that had not yet sprung back. Ace calculated the distance from Rudy's body. He could not be certain, but he did not think he or Mike had been this far up the slope. He directed Captain's attention to the area and ordered him to seek once again.

Captain put his nose to the ground and lifted it once or twice, unsure. He circled back to the original site, then returned to where Ace stood. This time he moved past Ace and climbed a shorter, rockier ridge, pausing every few feet to check a tuft of grass or seemingly innocuous stone. At the crest of the ridge, Captain sniffed around in a circle, wagged his tail and sat.

Ace reined him in and climbed to the ridge. The ridge was covered in crab grass and weeds, most of which had been flattened and trodden into the ground. Someone had been up here, for a while too.

Ace stood and looked around. A slow breath left his chest as he realised that from where he stood, he was looking directly down into the front yard of his brother's home. The lights were on inside the house and he watched Mike come out on to the porch in his bare feet, a bottle of beer in one hand and his phone in the other.

'Son of a bitch.'

Caleb tightened the leather strap that held the quiver to his hip. He crossed the rocky open ground and followed her line, moving quietly and confidently through the thick rhododendrons before the trees and into the woods. Once there, he allowed time for his eyes to acclimatise to the gloom, after which he began to search for her signature track, a mark that belonged to Jessie and Jessie alone. He found it in less than thirty seconds – the herringbone imprint of her tennis shoes.

It was easy to follow her progress. She had been moving with haste and one of the reasons he chose this point of release was the abundance of undergrowth. Everywhere he looked he found traces of Jessie's passing, broken twigs, freshly bruised vegetation, leaves bent or torn. This was the 'shine' and it was as obvious to him as a runway.

He trailed her out until the track. From here, as he had predicted, Jessie had not strayed, although judging from the length of her strides she was running hard.

He followed her trail for over a mile, taking note of the changes in her stride length and the depth of her footsteps as she slowed. He stopped by the tree where Jessie had rested. He squatted and studied the dirt by the root system of the tree. The ground had been much disturbed and he wondered what she had been doing. He knew not, but he picked her footprints up once again and followed them.

As he followed, he felt a prickle of disappointment. He had not expected her to be quite as predictable as the others. But, he supposed, life had long taught him that people, by and large, were stupid and unimaginative.

He carried on tracking her until he reached a section where the path veered steeply downhill and out of view. Here he stopped. Once they hit this section they were well and truly set in their direction. If he was right, and she kept running to the creek at the same pace, he would be there about eight minutes before her. It was time for him to play his trump card. The mines.

Caleb dropped down from the track into the undergrowth and picked his way carefully over the briars and rocks. The mines had been there for hundreds of years and had been long abandoned. They didn't even show up on maps any longer; he had checked. Caleb had discovered them by accident one morning while out hunting white-tails. He had slipped on a bank slick from one of the many sudden thunder squalls that passed by this section of the mountain, and tumbled over the lip of an embankment. He fell twenty feet into a shallow ravine, the fall broken, somewhat painfully, by a host of poison oak.

Whilst lying amongst the wretched plant, trying to draw air into his body, Caleb had noticed gaps in the ivy overhanging the rocks and assumed he had ripped it free in his fall. Closer inspection revealed it to be the collapsed and near invisible entrance of an old mine. Caleb had marked the spot with a green inverted branch and returned the next day with a flashlight, rope, chalk, water and a pickaxe.

It had taken him six weekends to clear the first passage and shore up the rotting timbers below the earth. Once he was finished, the shaft allowed him access to deeper areas that were less damaged. The shaft beyond was narrower, with barely room for his shoulders to pass through, but pass through they did until he reached a cavern that spanned a fast-moving river which he guessed was part of the Black Water Creek.

The next time Caleb returned to the cavern, he carried with him in his knapsack a small orange buoy and a spool of heavy-duty twine. He tied the end of the twine to a clump of rock inside the cave, testing it carefully for purchase. Satisfied it would not snap or come loose, he looped the spool through the ties on the buoy and set it into the fast moving water. It was snagged by the current immediately and vanished in seconds.

Caleb made his way back to the surface and hiked across the mountain to where the creek came flowing from the rocks. He found a stony outcrop near an old trail and sure enough, there the buoy twirled and dipped on the surface of the calmer water about a hundred feet clear of the cave opening.

Caleb sat down and stared at the buoy, thinking. The line itself was about one hundred and ten feet long. That meant the opposite side of the underground cave was about five feet from the rock face. If he could cross the underwater cavern and widen the exit he would have a perfect – and unknown – way to move through the mountain.

He had done exactly that.

He thought of Jessie Conway's expression when she made it to the water and realised he was there before her. Most times, the sight of him alone was enough to make them give up. They fell to their knees on the bank, exhausted, broken by the realisation that despite their best efforts, their fate was sealed.

Caleb heard the water up ahead. He wondered what her reaction would be. Would she be different from the others?

He hoped so.

It was why he had chosen her.

57

Mike sat on the porch and sipped his beer. He was tired. No, more than that, he felt destroyed. He wondered how he was going to face another day without Jessie. The idea that he should carry on without her sickened and frightened him. He couldn't see how it would be possible to continue without her smile, her love.

The phone on his lap bleeped. He glanced down, but it was another reminder that his voicemail was full. He wished people would leave him be, then thought of the number who had turned out that day to support him and he felt like a heel. These people were his friends; simple folk, like him, with jobs and children and lives that demanded their participation. They had come at short notice and stood to be counted when he had needed them.

Of course the rumour mill was already in full swing, too. Word had already reached him that some folk thought was Jessie dead, having flung herself from the waterfall, others muttered that she had skipped town in shame.

Where was she?

Mike closed his eyes. He had never felt so afraid before, so helpless.

'You don't need to go hitching yourself to someone like me,' she told him once, when he had made it clear he was interested in more that a casual fling. They had been walking across the town square to his truck, after an evening at the cinema.

'Need?' he had stopped walking and caught her hand in his. 'No, I guess I don't *need* to do anything.'

'I'm not the woman for you, Mike. I have–'

'This is not about need,' he had interjected, resting one hand on her shoulder. 'I *want* to marry you.'

Jessie had looked at him startled. 'We're only seeing each other a few weeks.'

'I don't care about that.'

'You don't even *know* me.'

'I know what I know and that's good enough for me.'

She had grown serious then, her eyes drifting left as they often did when her mind left the present and went elsewhere. After a few moments she looked up at him again.

'Mike,' she said it so sadly he felt his breath catch in his chest, and he knew then, immediately, that he loved her, and if she said no she would break his heart.

'No harm in food, is there?' he said, trying hard to keep the pleading from his voice. 'Let's go grab a bite to eat.'

They had gone for food. What had transpired lay unspoken between them. Mike had known, then and there, that whatever secrets she had, whatever pain they caused her, he could stand up to them. He would let her tell them in her own time and in her own way. As long as she was with him, he figured, he would be the rock she could cling to in whatever storm came their way.

He had tried. As had she, he knew that, and maybe it had been easy to pretend there was nothing to question. Jessie had never ventured much by way of information, and over the months and years he had simply stopped asking. He knew whatever she carried had hurt her deeply. He had learned to read the signals, to pre-empt the sudden depressions, to leave her be when she struggled with her private battle. To wait until she emerged, exhausted and wan, but victorious, on the other side. In return, she had loved him with a ferocity that never wavered and her passion for him seemed to grow with every ounce of freedom he granted.

So, it made not a lick of sense to him that Jessie, the woman he knew and loved, would go up onto a ridge, drop a dog collar and toss her self into the raging waters. No matter how dense the clouds around her, no matter how sharp the agony, the woman he knew and loved would not do that. Not to herself and not to him.

He had to get out of the house. He had to get out of there before he went crazy. He went inside, grabbed the keys for his truck and drove into town, winding up at Ray's Diner. Feeling fully defeated, he got out of the truck. He went inside and heard the fleeting hush as heads turned his way. Ray looked up from his crossword at the end of the bar, put his pen down and said, 'Good to see you, Mike.'

Mike nodded and took a seat at the counter. He took his cap off and wiped his hand over his head, feeling older than he had ever felt in his life.

'What can I get you?'

Mike yanked a menu from the counter and flipped it over, with little or not interest.

'You got any food left? I know it's late, but—'

'You can have whatever you like.'

'I'll take a steak sandwich, Ray, and give me a beer.'

'Sure thing.'

As Ray went to see about his food, Connie Vale, a short, ruddy-cheeked woman with a dimpled smile that belied a tough life, approached him and laid her hand on his forearm.

'How you doing, Mike?'

'I'm okay, Connie. Hanging in there.'

'Me and Bob are real sorry we couldn't come today, but we can come tomorrow, if you need us.'

'I appreciate it Connie, but I think today was plenty. I thank you for your offer.'

Her fingers tightened on his arm. 'I'm sorry, Mike. She was a real nice lady. I don't care what that paper has to say 'bout any of that other business. I can tell you I won't be buying it again neither.'

'I appreciate you saying that.'

'You need anything you call, okay?'

Mike thanked her again, feeling eyes on him from every angle. This had been a mistake. When Connie returned to her table he tried Ace's number. It went directly to his answering machine.

His food arrived. Mike picked at it with little enthusiasm, drank his drink, and ordered another. He traded a few words with Ray, drained the last of his beer and paid the cheque, despite Ray's protests. As he walked to the door, a second woman rose from a booth and made her way towards him. Mike recognised her as Louisa Winters. He could see she was well into her cups. Her eyes were red and small, her skin flushed with an alcoholic bloom.

'Mr Conway?'

'Ma'am.'

'I knew it was you. Do you remember me? Your father used to come over to my Jimmy's place regular back in the day.'

'I remember, Miss Winters. How are you?'

'I am fine. Just fine.' She smiled, and leaned into closer to him. He could smell the alcohol and not just from her breath. It seemed to ooze from her pores. 'I'm real sorry to hear about your wife.'

'Thank you.'

'She seemed like a real nice person. Real nice.'

'Thank you.' He tried to ease past her and get the hell out before another person mentioned how nice Jessie *had* been, using the past tense. But when he tried to step away she gripped his arm and held him in place.

'I was telling a man all about her just the other day; she sure knew how to treat people. You can't be taught that, it has to come natural. Your daddy was the same. A real gentleman.'

Mike removed his arm from her grip. 'I'm glad you think so.'

'I do, I surely do. Hope he found your place okay,' Louisa said. She turned and weaved her way over to the bar.

Mike, almost at the door, paused and glanced over his shoulder. 'What do you mean?'

'The fella … the fella who was asking how to get to your place.'

'Which fella was this?'

'Beardy guy,' she shrugged. 'He was here asking after y'all. Yeah, real nice he was.'

Mike followed her to the bar. 'When was this, Louisa?'

'I don't know exactly. A few days ago?'

'Think.'

'Ray will know. *Hey, Ray.*'

Ray looked up from lowering a tray of steaming glasses into a dishwasher. 'What?"

'When was that fella in here?'

'What fella?'

'The one I was talking to.'

Ray slammed the door and pressed a button. 'Want to narrow that down a bit, Louisa?'

'He was generous, that ought to narrow it enough round these parts.'

Ray flicked a dish towel over his shoulder and walked to the end of the bar. 'The Maker's Mark guy?'

'That's him.'

'Thursday.'

'Thursday,' Louisa repeated to Mike.

'You see this guy, Ray?'

'He was here a while, sitting two seats from where you were having your food.'

'He was asking about us? About Jessie?'

'Couldn't be sure. He shut his yap anytime I came near him. Probably trying to hide that accent of his.'

'Accent?'

'He didn't have no accent,' Louisa said.

Ray snorted. 'I'm knocking around long enough to know an accent when I hear one.'

He wiped a glass with the dish towel, smearing it from clean to dirty. 'Come on Louisa, you must have noticed that hill twang.'

She shrugged one shoulder and plopped down onto a stool, exhausted from thinking.

'What was he asking about? 'Mike asked.

'I dunno. He talked about a lot of things. He spoke about … uh … his sick mother and the school and uh, things of that nature.'

'What about Jessie? What was he asking about my wife?'

'I didn't really like to talk about that none.'

'Louisa.'

'Well, he was real keen on knowing about her, he said she was … uh …' she scrunched her features tightly together, 'uh, I guess a hero or something. He wanted to send her flowers. Like I told you, he was nice.'

'You gave him our home address?'

Louisa shot Mike a guilty look and then turned to the barman. 'Ray you saw him, right? He was nice, right?'

'I couldn't say, Louisa. I didn't talk to him.'

Mike said, 'Ray, I need you to tell me everything you remember about this guy. You still got the camera outside?'

'I do.'

'I'm going to need to see Thursday's footage.'

'Well sure, Mike. What's going on?'

Before Mike could answer, the door opened and Ace walked in, looking wired and as grimy as hell. He headed directly to Mike and leaned into his ear, turning his back to Ray and Louisa. 'We need to talk.'

'What is it?'

'It's Jessie. I think she is in a world of trouble.'

58

The first part of the ascent seemed easy. So much so that Jessie felt a ridiculously giddy surge of triumph about her decision. That didn't last: half a mile up, the incline grew steeper and the loose and sliding surface began to take its toll on her already exhausted limbs. She kept going though, and finally scrambled over the lip of a ridge, coming to rest by a pile of crumbling branches that had washed down the slope and collided with the base of a broken tree. She sank to her knees and rested for a moment, sucking air into her lungs in great gasping drags.

Her mouth was dry and thick with mucus. She was extremely thirsty and the rising heat did not help. She wasn't sure how long she could keep up this pace unless she found water.

She wiped her brow with the hem of her filthy shirt and rose to her feet. Soon Jessie began to climb again, a little slower than before but no less determined.

The second climb was tougher than the first. In some places, the undergrowth was so dense she could not force her way though and had little option but to skirt the trees until she found a lighter patch of vegetation. Being slowed this way frustrated her and sapped at her strength and all the while she felt sure he would appear behind her.

The sun was high in the sky when she managed to scramble a final bank and reach a platform allowing her to see, at last, the summit of what she had been climbing. She shielded her eyes with her hand and tried to gauge the distance. Three miles? Maybe four? She could do that, couldn't she?

She pressed on, but heat and thirst were slowing her down and she began to make simple yet clumsy mistakes. She slipped on a loose rock and fell, scraping her shin badly, leaving a smear of her blood behind. Insects plagued her, biting and stinging until she gave up trying to defend herself against them. She had no more thoughts about the summit or what might lie on the other side of the mountain; her only thought was to put one foot in front of the other, to keep moving.

After another long and arduous rise, she broke through the trees once more. Her heart sank a little when she studied the next section of the mountain. It wasn't that it was steep, although it was. What worried her was that the ridge above the next bank of trees seemed to be mostly rock and shale. The slopes above it were dotted with bushes and a number of spindly trees, but the rock section was alarmingly bare, with only a number of wispy roots jutting out like the bleached limbs of the dead through the few pockets of pinking earth.

Open ground.

Worse than being open, the slope was staggered. From where she stood, she could not tell if what was beyond the outcrop was climbable or not. She could see a belt of trees about three hundred or so yards further up. It was likely that the ground evened up where they grew, so maybe, *maybe*, it was not as impossible as she feared.

She had to get across the open ground first. Immediately, doubt and fear accosted her. What was she expecting to find, assuming she made it this far anyway? She licked her dry lips, thinking. What if, after all this effort, there were only more mountains?

God, she was so thirsty.

He had all the advantages. He knew the terrain, the lay of the land. He had equipment, probably water too.

Climbing that would be hard and slow.

She shook her head, viciously chasing the doubting voice from within. What choice did she have? Stumble around in the trees until it was dark and she was lost and too exhausted to take another step? Wait to be found and slaughtered like a wounded deer? No more whingeing. No more self-pity. She had outrun him; now she had to out-think him.

Jessie took a deep breath and began to climb again. In no time at all she had left the relative shade of the trees and faced the bluff. She calculated the distance; a couple of hundred feet, give or take.

'You can do this,' she said aloud before she began the next ascent. She pitched herself forward, grabbing at scrub catclaw and sharp-edged embedded rocks, anything that might help her gain height. Halfway up the first bank she slipped. Jessie grabbed on to a root and looked behind her. She had slipped only a few inches, but it was enough to scare her. She needed to concentrate and pay attention to where she put her feet. If she fell or broke her leg here she was dead. If he didn't find and kill her himself, the elements alone would take care of her.

Jessie dug the toes of her tennis shoes into the hard crumbly soil and hauled herself on. The sun overhead was relentless, it burned her skin and made her head ache but still she climbed.

It took her another forty minutes to clear the bald face of the incline and slip into the trees. Utterly exhausted, Jessie Conway began to lope forwards in an ungainly run, heading deeper into the shade. There was only one thing on her mind now, only one single thought.

Survival.

'Settle down,' Earl Dubray said, tightening the belt of his dressing gown around his waist, sounding anything but settled himself. He ushered Mike inside and closed over the door to his living room, pretending not to notice the curious looks of his teenage sons, who had been playing a video game when Mike arrived and nearly hammered the door clean off its hinges.

'I will not settle down.' Mike Conway shoved the cassette he had taken from Ray's Diner onto Earl's hands. 'I'm telling you what I have been telling you from the start – somebody is behind Jessie's disappearance.'

Earl looked down at the tape. 'What is this?'

'It's the CCTV tape from the car park at Ray's Diner. There's something on it I want you to see.'

'Start from the beginning again: you say a man was asking questions?'

'Yeah, he was in Ray's Diner on Thursday asking Louisa Winters all kinds of questions about us.'

'What kind of questions?'

'How the hell should I know? All I do know is that he was asking, and he got information about where we live.'

'And?'

'And? *And?*'

'And I'm saying this town has been inundated with people from all over the country asking about Jessie for weeks. Why have you got a bee in your bonnet about this guy?'

'Ace reckons someone has been watching the house.'

'Oh? How'd he come by this notion?'

'He says there's trampled grass up on the ridge near where we found Rudy. He says you can see right onto the property from there.'

Earl looked at him sharply. '*Trampled grass?*'

'That's what I said.'

'Ace back on that wacky backy or something?'

Mike glowered at him.

'Come on Mike, trampled grass? Be serious. You want me to go take a look at flattened grass.'

'I want you to take on board somebody might have been watching our house.'

'Could have been any critter done that.'

'You think a critter shot Rudy? I don't know of any critters that shoot arrows into old dogs.'

'What makes you think it was an arrow?'

'Or whatever the hell it was then,' Mike said quickly, forgetting his word to Ace. 'Look, to hell with the grass, you need to look at that tape.'

'Now? At this hour?'

'I think this is the guy who was asking questions about Jessie. Right before she went missing.'

Earl sighed. 'Mike, look. I know you're going through a tough time–'

'He had our address, said he wanted to send flowers. Look at this tape, Earl, he made sure he was as off camera much as possible – even the way he shields his face is messed up.'

'Mike—'

'*I'm asking you just to look at it.*'

'All, right, come on through into the kitchen, we got a little portable in there will play it'.

Mike followed Earl down a corridor crowded with photos of a growing family. Earl had become a grandfather during the winter for the second time. Mike sometimes forgot there was only two years between Earl and him.

'I spoke with your Momma again,' Earl said, not looking at him directly, as he pushed open a swing door and led them into a spacious kitchen with a marble-topped island dead centre. 'She said Jessie was real low in her spirits the days leading up to her disappearance.'

'She says a lot of things.'

The television was bolted to the wall to the side of a double-door fridge opposite a breakfast counter. Mike could picture Earl seated there watching the news over his cereal of a morning.

Earl plugged the TV in and slipped the tape into the little slot below the screen.

'Fast forward to around eight-thirty.'

In silence, they watched patrons of Ray's pull in and pull out of the car park. A few minutes before nine, a car pulled in and parked in the far end of the lot, on the blind side of a rig.

'That's him,' Mike said, moving closer to the television. The man – and they could only really assume that it was a man – appeared at the right-hand corner of the screen and walked along a low walk that divided the lot from the pavement. He skirted the entire car park before he came to the main door.

'You see that?'

'I see a man walking into a bar.'

'Ask yourself why would he walk like that, less he don't want to be seen?'

'If he didn't want to be seen why the hell go to a bar?'

'Just play the damn tape, Earl.'

Earl fast-forwarded for a while, and together they watched the same curious performance as the man exited Ray's and drove away.

'Well?' Mike demanded when they had viewed it a second time.

'Well what?'

'I reckon that's a Taurus. Can't tell colour on the tape but I reckon it's light coloured.'

'Could be.'

'He wasn't local so chances are he was staying in the area. We need to find this man.'

'And ask him what? Why he walks funny or why he was asking after a woman who has been all over the news and television for weeks?'

'Are you going to sit there and tell me you're not going to do nothing? Jessie deserves more than that, Earl.'

'Mike, I think you and I both know what happened to Jessie. I'm sorry for it, you have no idea how much, but you need to start facing up to some facts. Your home was not broken into, Jessie's car was not broken into; it was parked neatly in an area well known for … well, where people go. It's possible your wife found your dog dead and snapped. Probably she removed the collar herself. She's been under immense pressure, Mike. I think you know Jessie is not coming back. In your heart, I think you already know it.'

Mike stared Earl for a long moment. It looked he was going to say something more, but instead he walked past him, pressed eject and retrieved the tape.

'Mike.'

'We're done, Earl.'

'Mike, come on now, sit down. Let me make you a drink.'

Mike left Earl's home and walked down the drive to where Ace waited in his truck, with the window down, smoking a cigarette. He got in and slammed the door.

'Well?'

'You were right. A stick of dynamite wouldn't make a lick of difference.'

'We done wasting time with this shit then?' By 'this' Ace was talking about 'the law'.

Mike threw the tape on the dashboard.

'We're done.'

60

Caleb climbed through the cavern and emerged, blinking, into the sunlight. He jumped up onto the rocks facing over the path and positioned himself high enough so that he would be able to watch her as she made the final approach towards the creek. This was his favourite spot; the penultimate zone before the real fun could begin.

He got comfortable and glanced down towards the creek. There were a number of old rotten trees bent across the water. They were too slippery and feeble to climb on, but she might try to use them to help herself wade across. It could work, if she was prepared to get cold and wet. It had worked once or twice before. One of his earlier Category As had made it to the far bank, slipping and sinking and gasping before falling heavily into the rushes and weeds. He smiled. What a fighter *she* had been.

But most of them did not attempt to cross. Most of them gave up as soon as they realised that the current running through the freezing water was treacherous. Faced with a daunting uphill climb over rocks, they all turned and followed the creek south. He liked to watch their expressions before he whistled from his vantage point. The shift, when they saw him and realised how hopeless their plight, was glorious.

The temperature was beginning to rise. Caleb took a sip from his canteen, shifted his weight from one hip to another and waited.

Before long, a young white-tail buck dropped off the bank near-est him and skittered down the rocks towards the water. Caleb stayed completely still, watching the animal's graceful movements. Halfway to the riverbank the buck stopped and stood stock-still, listening. Its ears twitched back and forth, trying to locate the source of its unease. After a few moments, it moved on and disappeared into the trees. Caleb watched it go, perplexed at its fearless and casual movements. While he had not expected it to exhibit any sign that it had noticed him, he had fully expected it to be able to hear Jessie's imminent arrival. That it did not do so indicated to Caleb that something was wrong.

He checked his watch. From the length of Jessie's stride she ought to have been almost upon him by now. Yet he heard nothing, saw nothing, and neither had the buck. He looked up along the path.

He waited another few minutes, trying to keep his irritation in check. Maybe she'd fallen or twisted an ankle. That had happened before and he'd had to trot back to despatch his game where she lay. That had annoyed him, he recalled. It always annoyed him when a hunt ended early.

He looked at his watch again. Another minute went by.

Then another.

He slipped the Winchester over his shoulder and began to climb down from the rocks. As soon as his feet hit the dirt he broke into a jog and trotted back up the path, half expecting her to come around a corner any second. But the woods remained silent as the sun beat down on him. Caleb Switch began to have doubts.

He began to run faster, scanning the ground for indentations. He found nothing for over a mile, then closer to two.

What the hell was going on?

He had gone almost two and a half miles before he spotted a scuffed herringbone print. He tracked it back a short way. She had been running, but then she had walked and stopped against a tree for a spell. He looked back in the direction he had come. From this angle, the path curved ahead and dipped from view. It was exactly the sort of route a person might hope for if they were fleeing. So something had either stopped her or she had changed her mind.

He moved to the right-hand side of the track and let his eyes drift over the leaf piles and plants growing down the steep slope. He narrowed his eyes, but could find no sign of unnatural disturbance anywhere. He crossed and studied the ground leading steeply up away from the track. Within seconds, he spotted a freshly snapped fern and beyond that, further up the incline, a branch with lichen that had been turned.

She had gone up.

Caleb stared at the ridge in amazement. They never went up.

He glanced at his watch and calculated. At this stage, she had more than a thirty-five-minute head start on him.

This would be quite a challenge.

Caleb slung his bow over his shoulder and began to forge his way uphill. He moved fast, choosing his line carefully, making sure to conserve as much energy as he could. He would need that for when he caught up to her.

Mike woke up in the passenger seat of Ace's truck and rubbed his eyes. He squinted through the windscreen. It was dark, though dawn was approaching. The headlights illuminated a secondary road surrounded on both sides by endless trees.

'Where the hell are we?'

'Carter County,' Ace replied.

'Tennessee?'

'Yup.'

'You've been driving all night? Hell, what time is it?'

'Close on five.'

'Want me to drive for a while?' Mike asked.

'I'm all right.'

Ace reached between their seats and grabbed a can of cola from a cooler. He passed it to Mike and opened another for himself. He threw back his head and tipped half of it down his throat in one go. They drove on in silence for a while. The sun rose, its fresh light making everything seem faint and inconsequential. Mike checked his cell phone, but there was nothing new about Jessie.

'Maybe I ought to have stayed in Rockville. In case there's word.'

'You'd rather sit around and wait for Earl to find an idea?'

'I should maybe have given him the arrow.'

'Wouldn't make no difference. That man's cogs only spin one way.'

Mike sighed and settled back in his seat.

'Where are we going again?'

'Place called Swallow Ridge.'

'Never heard of it.'

'Not surprised.'

'Why are we going there?'

'I told you already. To talk with a man who might be able to help us some.'

'Who?'

'His name is Nathanial.'

'Nathanial? Who is he?'

'He's a friend of mine.'

'From where?'

The tip of Ace's mouth curled slightly. 'Back in the day.'

'Why we going to see this guy? Why don't we just call him?'

'Don't think he's got a phone.'

'Who doesn't have a phone in this day and age?'

'The guy we're going to see.'

'Goddamn it, Ace.'

'What?'

'I hate your cryptic shit, I really do.'

They drove another while in silence.

'You asked me at The Shack why I didn't ask Coraline out?'

Mike glanced at Ace, surprised at this sudden change in direction. 'I did?'

'I told you to quit digging.'

'Sounds like you offered good advice.'

'I've been thinking about what you said. That got me thinking about other things. I ain't never been one for the ladies. The type I run with ain't exactly into rings and all that jazz. But I wanted you to know that you and Jessie,' he changed into a lower gear as they rounded a tight bend, 'you and Jessie made me think how things could be different. I thought you ought to know that.'

'Me and Jess, huh?'

'Yep. That's right.'

He said no more on the subject and they drove on, climbing higher, tighter roads, cresting hills and finding nothing but more hills beyond them. Finally, Ace pulled off the road and drove down a narrow lane leading to small blue house. Either side of the lane was flanked by tomato and pepper plants, shoulder height and weighed down with fruit; small speckled chickens pecked and scratched in the yard and a long limbed dog of mixed origin loped out to greet them, barking with plenty of noise but little menace.

Ace opened the glove compartment and removed the arrow, which he had wrapped in cloth. He cracked his neck from side to side. 'Let's go.'

Together they walked past the still barking dog and climbed the steps onto the porch. Ace gave the door three sharp raps. A small woman, past the first flush of youth by a country mile, opened the door and peered out.

'Well I'll be durn,' she said. 'But you're a sight for sore eyes, Ace.'

'Hey, Lucy.'

'Thought you'd forgotten we knew each other.'

'Naw,' Ace looked surprisingly sheepish. 'I've been busy is all. This here is my brother Mike.'

'I can see *that*,' she said, looking past him to where Mike hung back shyly. 'He favours you.'

'I'm looking for Nathanial. He about?'

'Where d'ya think?' She jerked her head left. 'He's out in the work-room. Seeing as you're calling you can save me a trip. Tell him I don't much mind one way or the other if his breakfast goes cold but I won't be fixin' another.'

'Yes Ma'am.'

'Can I fix you something? You look like you could do with a good meal.'

'No thank you Lucy, but I appreciate the offer.'

She nodded curtly and went back indoors. Ace led Mike around the side of the house to where a stone barn with wooden doors sat nestled amongst a number of azalea bushes bursting with blooms. The doors were open and Mike could see a figure within, bent over a small wooden table upon which lay various tools.

'How do, Ace,' the figure called out without looking up.

'Doin' well, Nathanial. You?'

'Oh, tolerable.'

'Lucy says your breakfast is ready.'

The man waved a dismissive hand at this news. Looked like breakfast was going to get a whole lot colder.

'This is my brother Mike.'

The figure straightened slowly and turned. Mike placed him at close to eighty. He had a shock of white hair and matching eyebrows. He was well over six feet tall, but frail with it, though it was clear he had once been an imposing figure of a man.

'You must be the fella that fixes the vehicles.'

'Yes sir, that's me.'

'Your brother here talks highly of you.'

'Glad to hear it.'

Nathanial searched Mike's face closely before turning his attention back to Ace. 'Bein' as it's so early I can't hardly think is a social call Ace, though that would be welcome. It's been a while.'

'Yes sir, it has.' Ace spoke with such sadness Mike glanced at him in surprise.

'How's the life treatin' you?'

'I can't complain.'

'Stayin' on the straight and narrow?'

'For the most part.'

'Good to hear. So what can I do for you?'

'I spoke to a man last night called Willie Scarsdale, showed him something and he said I ought to come talk to you.'

'Old Willie still beatin' brush?'

'Not so much these days; glaucoma.'

'Shame.' Nathanial shook his head.

'Would you look at something, give me your thoughts on it?'

Ace unwrapped the arrow from the cloth and held it out to Nathanial. Nathanial took it and studied it for a moment.

'Where did you get this?'

'I found this near to where my brother's dog lay dead.'

'A dog?'

'Yes sir.'

'Well, that's an unfortunate end for the animal, but I don't see—' Nathanial raised the arrow to the light and frowned. 'Obsidian, don't see much of these traditional heads no more.'

'Willie said you might recognise it.'

'Maybe. I'd have to check some. You boys want to leave it with me and I'll see what I can find out?'

'Sir.' Mike stepped forward. 'My wife Jessie is missing, She's been gone since last Friday and I am nearly out of my mind sick with worry. Tell the truth, I thought she had left me and taken the animal with her. I know now her car remained in town and our dog was killed around the time she went missing. If there's anything you can tell us about that arrow, Sir, I would really appreciate hearing it.'

'You think this has something to do with your wife?'

'I do,' Ace said. 'I think it has a lot to do with it.'

Another expression crossed Nathanial's noble face. Mike felt gut sick watching the transformation.

'Sir?'

'Come on inside,' Nathanial said finally, 'let me see what I can stir up.'

It was moss; dark and green and growing on a shaded section of rock. Jessie stared at it. From somewhere, a faint trickle of water had surfaced and fed it.

She licked her lips: they were dry and parched and her throat ached. She ripped a piece of moss from the rock and smelled it. Damp and earthy; she squeezed it between her fingers until her hand shook, trying to extract a bead of moisture.

Nothing, not a single drop.

She flung the moss aside with a snarl of impotent rage. This was not fair, this was not *right*.

After a moment, she managed to regain composure. She ripped another piece of moss from the rock and examined it. She cleaned the roots off and, after a moment of hesitation, popped it into her mouth and began to chew.

It was cool, cool but disgusting. She gagged, but kept on chewing. What little moisture the plant held soothed and cooled her mouth and she chewed until it had dissolved into mush and then spat it out. Before her stomach turned, she grabbed another handful, stuffed it in to her mouth and chewed again. This time she did gag, but not until she had extracted every last single drop of moisture and lessened her ferocious thirst. It was not much, but it was something. She stuffed some of the moss into her pockets and began to climb again.

Halfway up the next embankment she stepped on a loose rock, lost her footing and fell. Before she could catch something, she tumbled back down the slope, rolling and bouncing until she slammed into the dirt at the bottom of the scree.

Jessie lay amongst the rocks and weeds, facing skywards, winded and bleeding from a number of cuts. Her shoulder was on fire and when she turned her head she saw that the skin above her left bicep had split open and was bleeding profusely.

She tried to get to her feet. The air shimmered; she put out her hands but the earth tilted beneath her and she fell down again. This time she stayed down until she was sure she had enough strength to remain upright. When she finally stood, she found she was cut and bleeding from various places and she was minus a shoe. She spotted it a few feet away and limped over to get it.

When she had reclaimed her tennis shoe, Jessie faced the embankment again and searched out a shallower line to climb. Her head throbbed and when she blinked the ground before her sometimes wavered.

She knew the fall had cost her time and energy she did not have. With growing despair, she drifted wearily along the base of the scree, seeking a new route. The vegetation this high up the mountain was sparse; thin spindly pines grew at awkward angles through the poor soil. There were more rocks and stones, lying in wait for the unsuspecting ankle.

Finally she found a less steep incline. She wiped her forehead and looked at the baked surface. Was this really the right thing to do? Crossing the rocks left her exposed, and she knew he had a gun. If she went out there and he saw her he could easily pick her off.

What if she stayed in the woods? Maybe she could hide somewhere.

She dismissed that idea almost immediately. He had to know these woods and she did not. He would find her there without question.

She looked down, blood was running down her arm and pooling by her shoe. She scuffed at it to hide it. Her body felt like sitting down. She was utterly exhausted, depleted of all energy. It scared her how much she wanted to stop. She turned and scanned the valley below, peering towards the dense foliage below, listening for any sound that betrayed him. Birds sang and a lone white butterfly bobbed past. He could be anywhere out there.

Fact time.

There were no options open to her. If she stayed put or tried to hide he would find her and he would kill her.

Game over.

She smeared the blood on her arm and wiped her hands against her trousers before pressing on.

The heat was relentless. Despite the lesser angle, rocks and pebbles skittered down and away from her with every step, bouncing over the hardened soil, gathering speed as they fell. At times, Jessie was almost pressed level against the hill face as she dug her aching toes into the compact earth, frantically searching for traction. It was not long before her hands began to bleed, torn ragged from snagging brush and rough stone. She tried to keep to the cover of the stubby bushes that sprouted here and there through the soil, but more and more she found herself exposed and vulnerable on bald sections. She did not stop and she did not look down.

She no longer cared about below; all her energy was focused on up.

Close to the top of the scree she paused, clung to a dried, half-buried root and squinted upwards. Above her lay a short stubby band of scrubland, after that she could see another rocky outcrop, and then she was almost in the mountain proper. There would be shelter there, caves, shade, perhaps water. The thought of water made her double her efforts. She dug her toes in and pushed off. She was almost at the top when the crack of a rifle filled the air and she heard the ricochet of a round to her left and saw a kick of dirt.

Oh my God, he's shooting at me.

She pressed herself flat into the dirt, then realised that was pointless. She needed to get to cover. Jessie began to climb faster, trying to reach the small band of scrub trees and bushes growing above the scree.

She was only feet away when the second shot rang out.

Mike sat beside Ace on a scarred leather sofa and waited impatiently as Nathanial shuffled around a small room off the cluttered living room. He came in and out of the room many times, retrieving photos from various boxes and folders, blowing dust from lids and frowning at contents that seemed to surprise him. A number of times, Mike heard him grunt and mutter, but finally he laid his hand on what he had been searching for.

'Here you go.'

Nathanial came out and handed a number of pictures to Ace. 'I thought I might have a few others but I guess over the years I musta misplaced them. Don't think I threw 'em out, but you never do know. Things have a way of walking out the door in this house.' He raised his head and aimed the last line towards the kitchen.

Ace spread the three photos on the coffee table before him and Mike. The photos were aged, faded yellow and curled at the edges. In the first one, a number of men stood by the rear of a pickup carrying deer carcasses. Mike recognised Nathanial, though he was considerably younger, and a younger man wearing a blue cap with fold-down earflaps.

'Nate sure did like the cap,' Ace said softly, touching his hand against the photo.

Mike glanced at his brother.

'He did,' Nathanial said, his voice tinged with sadness. 'Said it was good luck.' He leaned over the table. 'Other fellow there is Aldo Switch, he's the fellow used to make these arrowheads. Sharp as a boar's tusk they were, hard as flint.'

Ace shifted onto the second photo.

Two men stood over dead animals in each, one young, one older.

'That's Aldo Switch there,' Nathanial said, nodding to the photo. 'See the equipment?'

Mike raised the photo to the light and studied the picture. Between the men lay a massive Kodiak bear, his paws outstretched, with blood trickling from his nostrils. The older man squatted beside its head, his chin raised, his dark eyes arrogant and the lines around his mouth set in a haughty cruel manner. Both men carried longbows and quivers. The fletching on the bows was identical to the one that lay on the table before Ace and Mike.

Mike passed the photo to Ace for closer inspection. His hand trembled a little as he did so. Ace took it and nodded, then added. 'Kodiak, taken in spring by the looks of it.'

'Aldo never did pay no heed to laws and customs,' Nathanial said with a snort. 'He'd tell you flat out he'd hunt when he wanted and to hell with anyone who thought different.'

'Where can we find this man?' Mike asked.

'Sorry son, you're barking up the wrong tree with that one. Aldo went out hunting winter of '98, up the mountains somewhere, never came back. Not that too many mourned his passing. He was a mean son of a bitch, even on his good days.'

Ace tapped the photo. 'Who's that with him?'

'That's his boy.'

'What's his name?'

'Tell the truth I don't know.'

'You don't know?'

'I never heard Aldo call him by his Christian name. Kid didn't talk much. Some folk reckoned he was not right in the head, but me, I reckon he had a hard row to hoe, that one.'

Mike stared at the photo. The younger Switch was tall and thin to the point of skeletal. He wore dark hair shaved close to his head and a livid scar ran from his mouth to under his jaw line. His eyes were dark like his father's; he stared into the camera with little or no expression.

Nathanial opened a different box and found another photo; this one was of the younger Switch standing over a bighorn sheep. Again, he faced the camera, unsmiling and seemingly uninterested in his game or having his photo taken. Something else stuck Mike: there was snow on the ground yet the kid wore a thin jacket and wore no hat or gloves.

'Kid was a natural,' Nathanial was saying. 'Saw him take down turkeys on the wing, and the Lord knows those stupid creatures don't give much by way of second chance if you miss. He could shoot the ticks off a squirrel with barely a breath taken to aim. Aldo used to bet on him against out-of-towners with crossbows and rifles. Kid used a homemade stick bow, long as he was tall.' Nathanial shook his head. 'People used to bet against him, but only the once. The boy was one track. He got a bead on something he'd track it until he had it. Aldo liked to brag about his skill, saying could have made a real professional go of it with him if he'd a mind. Even talked about entering him in a few of the competitions. Never did follow through. Aldo was an intemperate man, and too jealous to put the boy forward. Put drink in him and the combination was lethal.'

'Where were they from?'

'Little Fork. You know it?'

Mike and Ace shook their heads.

'Scut of a place about thirty miles east a here. Up beyond the pine range. I can give you directions.'

'That would be appreciated.'

'Not much left of it now, I suppose … not much back then neither.'

'You mind if we take these, Nathanial?' Mike asked.

'Take 'em. They're no use to me.'

Mike gathered the photos and put them in the breast pocket of his shirt.

'That boy,' Nathanial said, musing through his memory. 'He really was a strange one.'

'What age would he be now?'

'In his late twenties I expect.'

'Might he still have family up around those parts?'

'Could not hardly say; it's been a long time since I heard tell the name Switch. After Aldo went missing, the boy didn't show for no more shoots. I figured he'd drifted on with himself. Might have sold on his father's gear. Can't hurt to ask.'

Ace and Mike exchanged a look that Nathanial noticed.

'You think this Switch fella has something to do with your wife?'

'I don't know, but I'd sure like to talk with him one way or another.'

'I don't recall him being much of a talker.'

'He'll talk to me,' Mike said firmly, as he got to his feet. 'Yes sir he will.'

64

Caleb stopped and took a long drink from his carry on. He gulped the water down, recapped the plastic bottle and strapped it back to his waist. He cocked his head and listened; he heard nothing but birdsong. He looked at the ground closely, searching out her trail. He found a section of soil that had been disturbed by her tennis shoe and pressed his fingers to it. Only the deepest part held a trace of cooler, damper soil. She was moving much slower now than she had been, exhausted, no doubt, by the incline and the heat. He was gaining on her rapidly.

Caleb climbed on, moving a little faster now that he knew she was slowing. His earlier displeasure was gone. It was good that she had turned out to be a worthy adversary. It had been a long time since one had made him work this hard, and he appreciated that. He wondered if he might tell her how close she had come. Once over the mountain, there were a number of homes scattered about the valley. They were folk like him, mostly, pure country and careful to mind their own and turn an eye. So far this remote area had remained relatively free from the infestation of blow-ins, the city slickers buying up tracts of unyielding land to build sprawling mod-con cabins in a futile attempt to get in touch with their inner woodsman.

Caleb's lip curled with contempt even thinking about them. Half the mountains he had once roamed freely were destroyed by pop-up towns festooned with antique stores and shops filled with hiking gear and 'authentic' rural junk. Turn a road now you could find Dairy Queens and twee, overpriced restaurants named after long-dead or non-existent 'Grandmas', populated by flavourless Yankees, resting their spotless Timberlands on highly polished stools and sipping frothy lattes, waxing lyrical about the great outdoors they were half afraid to venture into lest they lose the signal on their cell phones. It sickened him. *They* sickened him.

Caleb stepped over another cluster of rocks and skirted a sheer rock fall covered with lichen and moss. He bent down and picked up a little soil with his fingers, allowing it to crumble between them. He could see she had passed here and had stopped to search for water. The slime-coated rocks would not have offered much by way of comfort, though he was not surprised to find pieces of chewed moss.

He hiked to a section of the next ridge and stopped. Caleb wiped the sweat from his forehead and braced his shoulder against a fir. He searched the mountain above him, moving his eyes left to right, then right to left again. He chewed his inner cheek. If she was up there she had to be hiding, or she had changed direction, but that didn't seem likely.

He scanned again and on the next sweep detected movement.

Bingo.

He climbed the rocks to get a better view. Yep, there was no doubt, and she was climbing hard. He was impressed by how far she had managed to get. He unhooked his rifle and raised it to his shoulder. He closed one eye and slipped his finger through the guard and rested it against the trigger gently.

He waited, breathing slowly and easily, ignoring the heat and the sweat that ran down his back. She stopped climbing for some reason.

He waited.

From this distance he could probably hit her, but that did not interest him. That would be a waste. But he could certainly have a little fun.

On the slope Jessie began to move again. Caleb fired and watched as his prey froze, and then began climbing with speed towards cover. He grinned, raised the rifle and fired again, this time aiming for the ground above Jessie's head. Amazingly, she did not stop, and as he watched she made it to the tree line and disappeared from view.

Caleb shook his head. She was brave but she was a fool after all. She was trapped now in that small pocket of cover. Above her was naked rock, below was the scree. There was no place to hide. She had taken her gamble to go up.

And she had lost.

Caleb climbed down from the rock and began the last ascent to collect his prize.

65

Mike and Ace said their goodbyes to Nathanial and following his directions drove directly towards Little Fork. Not long after leaving, Mike looked over at his brother, his curiosity getting the better of him.

'How do you know that man?'

Ace glanced in the rear-view mirror and repositioned his cap. 'His son Nate and me used to be tight.'

'I never head you talk about no Nate.'

'Yeah well, you didn't know him so no point talkin' about him with you.'

'Where is he now?'

'Dead. Probably.'

'Probably? You don't know?'

'No, not for sure.'

'But how–'

'Leave it alone, Mike.'

Neither brother spoke much after that, except to consult a road map now and then as they drove deeper and deeper into the countryside.

Little Fork was not much more than a crossroads with some surrounding houses. Ace pulled in to a two-pump gas station and filled the truck, yawning and scratching the stubble on his face. Mike got out and looked around.

'What do you think?'

'I think I might let you drive for a bit.'

Captain hung his head over the side of the trailer and wagged his tail at Ace's voice.

'Let's go inside and ask.'

The elderly proprietor eyeballed them hard for a long moment upon hearing the name they asked after.

'Switch?'

'Yes sir,' Mike replied.

'They're all gone, far as I know.'

The door behind them dinged as another man came into the store. He was young but brawny and walked with the cocky swagger of a man used to getting his way.

'Howdy, Ed.'

'Buddy,' the old man nodded, leaning both hands on the counter. 'That be all fellas?'

Mike stepped to the side to let the younger man pass, but he stood near them instead, glancing out through the dirty glass of the door towards Ace's truck.

'That your dog?'

'Yep.'

'What kind is he?'

'Part Plott, part Catahoula.'

'Nice-looking animal. How much he go for?'

Ace threw down the money for his smokes and the gas. 'Where'd they used to be?' he asked the storeowner. 'Before they were gone?'

'Mister, I don't know how many ways I can tell you the nothing I know.'

Ace looked at him for a long moment.

'Problem, Ed?' The younger man said.

'None that needs be.'

Mike shuffled from one foot to the other. 'Come on, let's go.'

Ace tipped his cap with his index finger and pocketed his smokes. Outside, he lit one and wiped the back of his neck with his hand.

'Now what?' Mike said.

'I need to give Captain a drink. Go in the truck, I'll be but a minute. I need to buy some water.'

'There's water in the truck.'

'It's warm. I want to get him some cold water.'

Mike glanced back at the shop. 'Ace, come on.'

'I'll be but a minute.'

Mike dragged his heels slowly towards the truck. Ace waited for him to reach it before he pitched his cigarette away and re-entered the store.

Minutes ticked by. Mike fidgeted and kept his eyes on the door. He wished there were not so many old signs and stickers on the glass. He thought he could see movement within but could not ascertain who was doing the moving. After what seemed like an age, Ace reappeared and strolled across the forecourt.

He climbed into the truck and slammed the door.

'Where's the water?'

'Huh?'

'The cold water.'

'Ah, the freezer was busted, no colder than what we already have.'

The younger man came out and hurried directly to his truck, head straight and his eyes fixed on the ground. He got to his vehicle and left tracks on the forecourt in his haste to get going.

'Got an address on the Switch family.'

'Huh?'

'I was asking about the water when the old man suddenly remembered where the Switch family lived. Aldo's daughter, Grace, is still there.'

'He remembered names and all, just like that?'

'Just like that,' Ace said. 'Memory is funny that way.'

For the first time in days Mike laughed.

Half an hour later, they pulled up outside a wooden house sur-rounded by husks of long-abandoned, rusting machinery. An old Pontiac with a busted tail light sat in the main drive and a chained sandy-coloured dog came out from under the porch and barked at them. The dog was old and stiff legged; its bark was high and fearful.

'You sure this is the right place?'

'This is it.'

They peered through the windscreen and as they did a woman came out onto the porch, carrying an infant on her hip, and stared at them. Mike could not tell if the child was male or female. The woman was probably only in her mid-twenties but she looked worn down. She wore her hair long with thick bangs. She had on a yellow jumper of a type even Mike knew had never been in fashion and a denim skirt buttoned down the front. Despite the heat, her legs disappeared into a pair of tasselled suede boots. Her expression was wary, hostile even, and she remained close to the door as they approached. Mike and Ace stopped before the steps to the porch.

'Ma'am, my name is Mike Conway. This is my brother, Ace.'

'I ain't interested in your names,' the woman said. Her voice was soft and heavily accented, almost singsong, '*ah ain inturrestad n yr naymes*'.

'Are you Grace Switch?'

'Why you askin'?'

'Ma'am, we wanted to ask you about some arrows your daddy had.'

'My daddy's dead.'

'Yes Ma'am, we did hear so, but we were hoping you might be able to recollect if he sold them on to anyone? Or if maybe your brother might still have them.'

Mike passed her one of the photos Nathanial had given them.

Her reaction was immediate. It was as though Mike had thrown a bucket of ice water in her face. Every muscle stiffened for a beat, then softened. She could control her features, Mike thought, but she could not disguise the fear in her eyes.

'I don't know nothin' about him. I don't know where he's at so don't ask me.'

'Ma'am?'

'What did I just say?' She looked around her, 'I don't know nothin' about his business, so don't ask me.'

Mike walked to the edge of the porch steps. The dog growled at him, putting a bit more energy into his warning than he had his greeting.

'Please, Ma'am. I really need your help.'

'I don't *need* to be involved in any of his business.'

'Yes, you do, you need to know my name and you need to know my face. My name is Mike Conway; my wife's name is Jessie Conway. She's been missing since Friday.'

He jumped down from the step and went back to the Jeep to get the arrow, which he then carried back to the porch. 'This here was found close to my dog; he was shot.' He held it out for her to see. She glanced at it and swallowed a number of times rapidly. The skin around her eyes was pinched and white. She actually looked sick with fear.

'My wife is missing.'

'I can't help you.'

'Can't or won't.'

'Please mister, you need to go.'

'I don't understand any of this,' Mike said, her fear rubbing off on him. 'If you know something you need to talk to me. What do you mean your brother's business? Does he have these arrows?'

'Didn't you hear me? I can't help you, I am heartily sorry.'

Ace approached the steps. The dog backed up at his approach. 'I understand your reluctance to talk to us Ma'am, but this is real important.'

'You don't understand,' she said, her head whipping around so fast the child she carried whimpered. 'I can't talk to y'all … if he finds out … you need to leave.'

Mike lunged and grabbed her by her free hand. The dog flung itself against the chain, snapping and snarling, practically strangling itself to reach him. The child began to howl in terror.

'If you know something you need to tell me.'

'Let go a me.'

'Mike!'

Ace grabbed him and hauled him back off the step.

'You know something!' Mike yelled. 'I know you know something; I can see it in your face. You know what it is – you tell me what's happened to my wife! Goddamn you!'

She stood rigid for a moment, white as a sheet. The child was screaming, clinging to her with its face squeezed tight and red. Suddenly she bolted for the door and slammed it shut behind her.

Ace shoved Mike, hard. 'Get in the truck.'

'Get the hell off me. It's all right for you to strong arm some old coot but I can't shake the one person who knows where Jessie might be?'

'Shut the hell up and get in the damn truck. I ain't asking again.'

Mike glanced once at the door and muttered a curse. He stalked around to the passenger side, got in and slammed the door hard enough to make the half-ton truck shake. Ace removed his cap and wiped the sweat from his head with the back of his arm. He spat, shook his head and walked back onto the porch. He leaned his head against the door and tapped it gently.

'Ma'am, I don't know if you can hear me. I want to apologise for my brother scaring you like that. He's pretty upset about his wife.' He waited for a beat. 'I know you're a good person, I know you're scared. But Grace, you can, right here, you can help us and in doing so we might be able to help you some. If your brother is connected with Jessie's disappearance and I catch up to him you best believe he's not going to be bothering you about it. You understand what I'm telling you?'

Ace stuck a cigarette in his mouth, struck a match against the wood frame and lit it. He stood there for almost a full two minutes before the door opened to a slit.

Her eyes searched his face and her voice when she spoke was soft and resigned. 'You bein' straight with me? His wife is gone?'

'Yes, Ma'am.'

'What you say is real tight?'

'Tighter than a drum. If he has Jessie then he ain't got no wiggle room with me.'

She sighed and leaned against the doorframe. Ace could smell the sweat coming from her body; the skin around her hairline was prickled with droplets of moisture. She looked past him to the truck. Ace did not push her. He knew she was struggling with a decision of magnitude.

'He won't go easy. You need to understand that. Caleb ain't going to quit.'

'Okay.'

'No, now you need to understand what *I* am sayin' to *you*. You think you're gonna go up there and take him to the law, make him talk. But you don't know him. You don't know nuthin' *like* him. He's not like other folk. He don't think like folk and he don't act like them. You need to remember that.'

'I will, Ma'am. I won't hurt your brother, if I can help it.'

She looked up at him, her eyes widening.

'Then my God that is the rock you will perish on.'

'Ma'am?'

'My brother is like a rabid dog. You can't reason with him, you can't figure him out. You get a chance to take him down, mister, you better not waste it, because he won't.'

66

Jessie scrabbled her way under a scrub bush and pressed her body into the dust, panting and in agony. She felt weak and nauseous. Her arm hurt so badly it was agony to move it.

She wiped the sweat from her brow with her good hand and tried to squint through the dappled light and the spindly trees. She visualised him on her trail, seeing him drawing closer as she dithered and dilly-dallied on the edge of sanity, with only her heart racing in her ears for company.

She was trapped and she knew it, as it had taken her no time at all to run the length of the cover and realise it was scant. With him below somewhere, her chances of climbing into the rocks and finding water or shade were completely blown. But if she remained where she was he would be on her in no time.

She closed her eyes for a moment, wishing she could think straight. Up, she needed to go up, and to do that she needed to climb without being shot. Inexplicably she thought of Kyle Saunders, of his face when she had rushed him in the school. With that, another thought came to her. A thought so ridiculous she momentarily forgot her pain.

I must be delirious.

So what?

Crazy.

What choice did she have?

Jessie crawled out from under the bush and took another look at the overhanging rocks. She knew that if she ever was to reach them there was only one thing she could do. At that moment crazy was all she had.

She got up and began to run. She broke cover and bolted for the huge boulders that marked the beginning of the rock climb.

Caleb saw her break cover and disappear into the rocks. He gave a satisfied grunt as he cleared the top of the scree and stood sucking air.

It was time to finish this.

He took off after her, keeping his eye on the sections of rock around which she had vanished. He saw blood on the ground and knew from the way she was running she was injured. Part of him was glad. It was hot and he was tired from the climb. There was nowhere from here but up, and even if she did attempt it, at this stage he would, despite his earlier reluctance, simply shoot her down if he had to.

Caleb reached the rocks, noticed another large smear of blood on two of them and pressed on. It was ridiculously easy. The blood drop- lets were as obvious as wet footprints in sand. He squeezed his body between two massive boulders towards a ledge that led to a wider shelf. He was adjusting his quiver when something struck him on the head.

Caleb staggered backwards. He raised his hands, but something looped around his arms and stuck him a second unmerciful blow.

He tried to remain upright, but dropped onto one knee. Dazed from the blow, he fumbled the Winchester from his shoulder just as Jessie Conway dropped into the gap from the rock above, swung her foot and kicked him square in the chest.

Caleb tumbled backward, the Winchester gone from his hands. He saw it land by the ledge and grunted as he and Jessie Conway lunged towards it. Jessie reached it first. In desperation, Caleb ripped his knife free from its scabbard and struck out wildly.

The knife caught Jessie. She screamed and Caleb felt blood spray across the back of his hand. He tried to stab her again, but she rolled and swung something towards his head. This time Caleb snatched at it, locked his fingers around it and hauled. Jessie let go and dived for the Winchester, but Caleb was too quick, and in the tussle the gun tipped over the ledge and was gone. Jessie twisted her body away and kicked him, catching him in the hip. She climbed to her feet. Caleb saw that he had wounded her in the thigh and that she was bleeding badly. She was pretty torn up everywhere else too, he noticed, blinking hard as his vision flickered and blurred. Jessie glanced at him, her eyes wild.

Then Caleb was alone.

He tried to get up, but could not. The buzzing sound filled his head. He leaned all his weight on one hand and tilted his head back, careful to breathe through his mouth. He tasted copper. There was blood and dust in his mouth and nostrils and blood on his hands – some hers, some his. He blinked and focused on what he had taken from her.

It was a bra; a lacy bra filled with rocks, the material tied in a knot around them.

Despite his pain, Caleb began to laugh. He looked at the sky above and howled with laughter, ignoring the lightning in his brain, the blood, the broken tooth clacking against its neighbours. He might never have stopped had he not needed to lean forward and spit blood from his mouth.

After a while he rose shakily to his feet and wiped his eyes. He picked up his bow and checked it over to make sure it was undamaged. No matter about the gun, he thought, sliding his quiver onto his hip. By the time he was finished with this bitch she be would be sorry that shooting was no longer an option.

67

It was late afternoon, rolling into early evening, by the time Mike and Ace reached the area Caleb's sister had said to check, and a further hour before Ace managed to find the road with the little wooden bridge. 'Quiet round here, ain't it?' he said as they drove across.

'We haven't met a single vehicle in over an hour.' Mike squinted through the open window at the dense woodland on either side of the road. 'Or a house for that matter.'

'She said this guy won't come easy,' Ace said, leaning one arm out the window.

'I don't give a shit about that. I don't give a shit about *him*. I just want to know where Jessie is.'

'He might take some persuading.'

Mike glanced at his brother. 'We need him *alive* to talk.'

'I know that.'

'We on the same page here, right Ace? My only priority is to find Jessie.'

'There might be bloodshed.'

'Then so be it.'

Muscles jumped in Ace's jaw. A few miles further on, they came to a fork in the road. Ace slowed the truck to a crawl.

'We do this there's no going back, Mike.'

'There's no going anywhere without her. Drive.'

Ace released the clutch and took the right road. They drove for another half mile, before turning off onto a lane barely wide enough for the truck to pass. Finally they pulled off the track into a small homestead, the front yard thick with weeds and grass.

The cabin was old, but they could see it had been maintained. The roof looked relatively new, but it was the steel door, incongruously fixed to the front of the property, that stood out most. Ace crawled the truck in, his eyes watchful. To the rear of the cabin stood an ancient barn; its roof sagged like a sway-backed horse.

Ace backed the truck under some trees and faced it towards the road. When he got out, Ace took his rifle from the rack and carried it loose in his hand. He quieted Captain with a soft word and looked towards the cabin.

'No sign of action.'

'I see that.' Mike lifted his own rifle. 'Let's go.'

They walked around the cabin to be sure there was no one home. All the windows and doors were locked.

'What do you want to do?' Ace asked.

Mike stepped up onto the porch, turned his rifle and smashed one of the windows with the stock. He knocked out the remaining glass, handed Ace his weapon to hold and climbed through the window. He returned the favour and Ace climbed in after him.

Ace stood on the bare boards and looked around at the animal heads hanging from the walls and the old weapons that adorned the beams. 'Looks like a hunter's lodge.'

Mike tore through the cabin in minutes but there was no trace that Jessie had ever been there. He cursed and ran his hands through his hair. 'She's not here. Jesus, Ace, there's no sign of her. What if this is a wild fucking goose chase, huh? What then? We've been wasting our time? We're what? What? She's been gone for days, she could be any-where. She could be … *anywhere.*' Mike dropped to his haunches and hid his face behind his hand, his rifle cradled in the crook of his arm.

Ace let him be. The pain ripping through his brother was not going to be eased by some pithy remark or gesture. He opened the fridge door and closed it again; he studied a map on the wall for a moment then looked around the rest of the room. He fingered a locked metal tool case and ran his hands along the workbench. Neat, meticulous even. The shelf over the bench contained a number of plain cardboard boxes. Ace took one down and opened it. It was filled with feathers. Ace sifted through them and lifted one out.

'Take a look at this.'

He held out so Mike could inspect it. 'Eagle, same as the one that killed Rudy.'

Mike took it in his trembling hand. He lifted his tear-soaked face.

'Let's go check out that barn.'

They climbed back out the window and crossed the yard, keeping their ears open and their eyes peeled, staying real close to one another. Unsurprisingly, the barn was locked by a thick chain and a padlock.

Ace went back to the truck and returned with a lump hammer. Three strikes later and the lock lay smashed open in the dirt. Ace and Mike grabbed the doors and hauled them open.

'Taurus,' Ace said, nodding his head to the gold car parked inside the door.

'It's the car from Ray's Diner, I'm sure of it.'

'You okay?'

'Yeah,' Mike said, his expression grim. 'Peachy.'

Ace tried the door handle and found that is was unlocked. He popped the trunk, and pretended he didn't notice Mike's expression of agonised relief when it was found to be empty. Next he checked the glove compartment.

'Got something.' He lifted out some paperwork and read through it. 'Says here this is owned by a Maryanne Weils.'

Mike tapped the roof with his finger. 'I don't care what it *says*, Ace, this is the car he drove. I *know* it.'

They searched the rest of the barn. It was Ace who spotted the trap door. He pulled it open and descended the wooden steps into the cellar below. After carefully pushing open the cell door with the nose of his rifle, he squatted on his hunkers and sniffed the food dishes and a drink container. He was still there when his brother stepped into the doorway behind him.

'Aw,' Mike's eyes widened when he saw the cot and toilet. 'Aw, Jesus Lord.'

Ace lifted the beaker. 'Milk, ain't full spoiled yet.'

Mike ignored him. He walked to the cot and lifted the pillow. He tilted it towards the light. There was a dark red hair caught in the piping, a colour the envy of all the bottle-red women in Rockville. He began to tremble and could not stop. When he looked around the tiny space he imagined her here, felt her terror, her claustrophobia. He buried his face in the pillow, inhaling as deeply as he could, trying to capture her scent.

Jessie.

He wept.

'Listen to me Mike. There's food inside the cabin, right? Maybe enough for a day,' Ace said softly, 'Clothing too. We have the key for the Taurus, so I'm guessing he's still around the area, meaning he's on foot or he has another vehicle. Either way, looks to me like he's coming back. Mike, Mike come on now.'

Mike managed to compose himself enough to speak. 'What do we do?'

'We can go looking for him, but if we miss him we don't know when he might surface again. We knocked out the man's window, he's gonna know straight out the gate he's got visitors.'

'I don't understand,' Mike choked back a sob. 'You want us to sit around and *wait?*'

Ace jerked his thumb to the steps. 'We can talk topside.'

'You think she's already dead, don't you?'

Ace put a cigarette in his mouth and lit it while he looked around the tiny cell. His face was in shadow, his thoughts hidden from view. 'I am not making that pronouncement.'

'*Then what?* What is it you're not saying? I saw a look on your face when we crossed the yard up there. You tried to hide it, but I know you Ace, I know you as you know yourself.'

Without a word, Ace turned and walked up the stairs. Mike rushed after him.

'Goddamn it, Ace! You talk to me now.'

As soon as Mike cleared the steps, Ace kicked the door closed and yanked Mike closer to him by the front of his shirt.

'Keep yelling, maybe you can let folk over the next county know our location. Quit it and help me with these doors.'

'What was it?'

Ace moved his cigarette to the corner of his mouth without touching it. His eyeballs were streaked pink with temper. Without a word he jerked his head for Mike to follow him outside.

'What do ya see?'

'Grass? Weeds?' Mike looked around the decrepit yard. 'What am I supposed to be looking at?'

'Mounds and depressions.'

'De–' Mike frowned. Then it hit him what Ace was talking about. He walked to the nearest mound, it was not new and the grass grew freely on it, but there were more, many more. He looked at Ace aghast.

'Dear Lord, how many are there?'

Ace closed the barn doors and joined him. 'Dunno, let's take a look.'

'I don't know if I can do this.'

'Stay here then, I'll go.'

Ace walked off, smoke drifting over his shoulder as he moved around the property. He retuned to Mike.

'Few recent enough, but none of 'em brand new.'

Mike literally sagged with relief. He was pale and sweating. Ace wondered how much more his little brother could take in one day.

'You want we should call someone 'bout this place?'

Mike raised his gaze skywards and let out a long shaky breath.

'Dear Jesus Lord.'

Ace blew out streams of smoke through his nostrils. 'Let's move the truck out of sight.'

An explosive stitch ripped through Jessie's side, causing her so much pain she was almost bent double. She stumbled on, each step more agonising than the one that had come before it. She managed to shuffle on another few hundred feet before she crashed to a halt against a small outcrop of rock.

She lay where she fell, desperately trying to suck air into her burning lungs. Her throat was raw and she barely had the strength to lift her head. All the adrenaline was gone now; she was exhausted, beyond exhausted.

You fool, she berated herself, you should have tried to finish him off. You had a chance; you had a *chance*.

She looked down, the wound on her thigh was bleeding heavily and she was weak from shock and blood loss – the leg of her pants was stiff and stained dark from it. She opened her pants and eased them down her leg to examine the wound. As soon as she put her fingers to it, blood began to run afresh. It was deep, maybe to the bone, she guessed, and the flow so heavy she was scared he might have nicked an artery. She doubted it could hold her for much longer.

No time to worry about it now, you need to keep moving.

She pulled her pants up, refastened them and leaned hard onto her hands. Stopping had been a mistake. Already she was beginning to stiffen, her aching muscles completely spent. She knew if she rested too long she might not get up again. This was it. There was no gimmick to any of it: she either rose now or she was done.

Jessie got to her feet, but the ground was shaky beneath her. She clung to the rock to steady herself, took a deep breath, then another. Finally she eased upright into a standing position. She let her good leg bear as much of the weight as it could.

The next section was technically difficult and took everything she had. She climbed over rock and hard soil. The ground rose sharply though, so she had no choice but to pause for rest every few hundred feet, glancing over her shoulder as she did, waiting to see some sign of her pursuer.

Finally she pushed her way through a bunch of scrub bushes and found herself standing out on a rocky cliff face overlooking a gorge. In disbelief, Jessie stepped gingerly to the ledge and peered over. There was nothing but a long sheer drop down into bushes and trees several hundred feet below.

No other way down.

Jessie reeled back, stunned. Her legs trembled from exhaustion and a sudden wave of vertigo.

'Oh no, no. No.'

She peered up at the vast expanse of rock rising above her. It was limestone, mostly smooth in places, but there might be enough crevices to use if she had the strength to climb. She inched back from the edge of the ledge and stood looking up. She chewed on her lip.

It had been a mistake coming this way. She should have known better; she should have gone to ground or hidden in amongst the trees. She had messed up.

You're wasting time.

Jessie shielded her eyes with her hand. There was a ledge far above. It looked high and her legs had nothing left.

She looked down again. Why had she come this way? Why?

She wiped her hands on her pants and went to the foot of the rock face. After a moment, she took a deep breath, grabbed a handful of rock and hoisted herself upwards. She swung her injured leg left but missed the crevice she was aiming for and slid to the ground again.

'Shit.'

She slammed her hand against the unforgiving stone, gritted her teeth and stepped close again. With steely determination, she braced herself against the ground and pushed off with her good foot. This time when she swung her arm up, her fingers found a crevice. She clung to it with all her might, waited for her feet to find whatever purchase they could, and swung up again.

Do not look down, she warned herself, don't you dare look down.

Jessie Conway did not look down. If she had, she might have seen Caleb Switch moving onto the rocks, his eyes fixed on her every move.

Confident now, but still wary, Caleb rested with his back against a boulder and took a long drink from his water canister. He wiped his mouth and spilled some over the back of his neck. The sun sat lower in the sky and the heat had dissipated a little. His head ached badly but he no longer had any problems with his vision. Despite her attack, he was feeling pretty damned good about himself.

He looked down and noticed a small pool of blood beneath his boots. She had stopped here and rested for a spell. Good. He hoped she was hurting, he hoped she was feeling pain. He hoped she realised whatever she was feeling now would be nothing to what he would make her feel as soon as he caught up to her.

He took another drink. He was amazed at her audacity, doubling back like that. It went against every human instinct, so much so he would never have believed it possible. He might even have to come up with a new category for prey like her.

His old man used to say a wounded beast was one of the most deadly creatures on earth. Didn't matter if it was a bear or a possum, Aldo used to say, you injure or corner one then you best be prepared to kill it or suffer the consequences. Course, the old man had said a lot of things over the years, and kept on saying things right up until the day Caleb had put a bullet in his back and another in his head.

How the old bastard would have laughed at his son being taken out by a bra.

The thought of his father dredged up memories that Caleb has long shelved in a dusty portion of his brain. Aldo Switch had been a trapper and a hunter of some note. He was unfriendly to the point of feral and considered himself a man's man, content to terrorise his wife and children and abscond at the turn of a breeze. In those absences, Caleb's mother, sometimes swollen with child and beaten down by responsibility, would spend her evenings drinking cheap, foul-smelling alcohol, before falling asleep on the sofa, sobbing over the feckless no-good mean son of a bitch she had been fool enough to marry.

Caleb had never understood her sadness when Aldo was gone; for him it was the only time he could let his guard down a little. For those few precious times, he was free of the man with the eyes of a snake and the fuse that was liable to blow over a perceived notion as easily as a genuine one. Caleb could eat his cereal in peace, look in whatever direction he pleased and rest in his bed without fear of being awoken to a flurry of fists.

On the day he had killed his father, Caleb had left their home with no such thought on his mind. They had travelled eighty miles north in Aldo's beat-up truck, heading deep into the wilderness. Caleb remembered Aldo had been in a strange mood, cheery even, bouncing with a nervous energy that Caleb knew could just as easily spell trouble.

'It's just sitting there. Can't believe it was abandoned. Got me a *friend*' – Aldo had flicked his eyes slyly at Caleb – 'to look up the deeds and yup, owned by a batshit old fuck with shit in his drawers and shit for brains. Didn't even remember he owned it, ain't that something? Didn't even *know*! He's sitting there in some home with shit for brains and shit leaking outa his ass and he's worth gold.'

Caleb had leaned his head against the cracked glass of the passenger window and tried not to think about the image his father was creating. Normally his silence allowed him to slip under the radar, but on that particular day, the radar was monumentally messed up.

'You listenin' to me, boy?'

Caleb, then only two months shy of fifteen, was almost full height, but still sinew and bone. The question was a shot over his bow. The rest of his day depended on how he answered that question.

'Hey, I'm talkin' to you.'

'I'm listening.' But he had not been listening. Instead he had been thinking; he had been thinking that this was how it would be. He thought of Aldo's rages, his unpredictable force ripping to pieces Caleb's fragile life. He thought of the nature of Aldo. He thought of him as a black tunnel, stretching on with no light at the end, no end at all.

'You better pay me heed, boy.'

And there it was, that note he knew so well, the familiar black thread that Aldo tightened around them.

That day something else occurred to Caleb Switch, as they had parked the truck and walked the ancient trails. That day a thought took bloom in Caleb Switch's young mind and as he allowed it room, the thought that was unbelievable at first was then strangely … sensible.

There would be no respite as long as Aldo lived.

No respite. No end to his cruelty, to his endless rages.

Not as long as Aldo lived.

Aldo marched ahead at a blistering pace wearing a dark green jacket with many pockets. It was grimy with dirt and he had worn it for as long as Caleb could remember. Caleb watched his father's broad shoulders and whispered his intent on the frigid air. He waited to see how it sat with him.

It sat fine. It sat better than fine.

They located the hides and Aldo sent Caleb up the trees to repair them. Caleb worked fast, replacing the rotten board and line hooks, his fingers numb with cold. As he worked, he repeated his intent under his breath, over and over like a mantra.

When he was finished, Caleb climbed down slowly and carefully. Aldo offered no word of thanks. He jerked his head and they returned to the Jeep.

Caleb had to admit he was a touch curious about Aldo's 'secret'. Aldo was the kind of man who preferred his left hand know nothing about what the right might be doing. Certainly his father never took Caleb into confidence about anything.

They turned left at a fork in the road. Aldo leaned so far forward over the steering wheel his nose almost touched the glass.

'Deers round here ain't used to people. Y'can practically walk up to one, pop it on the nose and it's yours,' Aldo said, his voice giddy. 'Saw bald eagles t'other time, know 'bout a nest up near the bluff, heard tell of a fella looks to buy eggs for real money. Bit of a climb but nothing you can't handle when the time's right.' He glanced at Caleb, his eyes glittered like spark plugs. 'This is prime land, dummy, prime!'

Suddenly he swung off the road, through what looked like nothing but ditch. Caleb threw his arms across his face, expecting the truck to crash, but instead it jumped and ground over a mound of soil and shot out into an overgrown yard.

'Ayeh!' Aldo said, slamming the truck to halt. Caleb lowered his arms slowly and peered through the windscreen at a small cabin. His eyes moved over it, making note of the collapsed chimneystack, the rotten loose boards, the badly patched tin roof. He could just about make out the pitch of a roof behind the cabin and guessed what ever was back there was in much the same state.

'What is this place?'

Aldo took a piece of paper from an inside pocket, opened it and shoved it under Caleb's nose. 'This is mine is what it is.'

Caleb read the deed of sale, flicking his eyes across the words, allowing his brain to digest the wording.

'Prime,' Aldo said again, refolding the paper and putting it back in his pocket. 'Woods is full a game, and no fucking John Law making demands on tag anywhere near here. Come on, boy.'

They got out. Caleb whispered the words again; they danced like smoke on the air before his face, but Aldo's attention had drifted.

'Fix it up we can rent this shit easy. Ain't no reason to quit on the seasons neither.' Aldo walked off with his hands on his hips, squinting up at the roof.

Caleb walked slowly back to the truck and removed his father's Winchester from the rack. He closed over the door and stood with the freezing wind nipping at his cheeks, his eyes watering. The gun felt light in his hands and as he lifted it to his shoulder and slid his finger through the trigger guard he whispered the mantra once more.

Aldo Switch never saw it coming.

Caleb would later think about that, and decide that it didn't matter a curse. Aldo Switch had had it coming his whole life. And now, Caleb thought, moving off again, finding more of Jessie Conway's blood trail, she had it coming too.

Jessie's hands ached and were too slippery from blood to keep going. She slumped onto a narrow ledge halfway up the bluff and rubbed them against the surface of the rock, smearing them with dirt, desperately hoping it might help her grip.

She was exhausted, too weak to carry on, too frightened not to do so. Exposed here, with the wind picking up, she could not help but wonder if this was it, if this was her day to die. She had vowed not to look down, but now allowed herself a glimpse to the western horizon. Sunset was approaching, and with it her efforts and crazy ambitious hope seemed utterly laughable.

She rested her forehead against the rock face and tried to muster her reserves for the final climb. Her limbs were stiff and heavy and she no longer trusted her sight. She leaned out and looked up. Twenty feet. She tried not to think further than that.

A strong gust unsettled her and forced her to think about moving. She licked her lips and opened and closed her hands to loosen them. The slope here was not as steep, but that did not mean it was any less tricky to negotiate. There was very little to grab hold of if she slipped, and if she slipped it was a long way down to the rocks below.

She straightened, leaning into the wind again. Her muscles refused to engage for a moment and her initial grappling scared her senseless. Finally, her fingers dug deep into the soil and she hoisted herself up another foot towards the summit.

At ten feet from the top, she had to stop and rest. She looked over her shoulder and now the entire valley was visible to her. In the distance, she could make out the headlights of vehicles cruising down a road, a cruel reminder of the macabre pantomime of life. Her death would be nothing more than a footnote in history. Out there, people were heading home from work, thinking about food and what show to watch on television. They were talking to each other about trivial things, or vital things, or maybe not talking at all. They knew nothing about her.

But he knew. He was back there somewhere, in the dark, searching for her.

He knew.

Jessie swung her feet out behind her and dug her toes deep into the scree, ignoring the pain in her fingers, pressing on. She could see a small line of scrub bushes now, jutting prickled branches from the thin soil. Her lungs burned, her back ached, her bloody hands were in agony, but still she pulled and reached, driving her body closer and closer to the summit.

Finally she managed to crawl over the final ledge. She was so exhausted she could not pull herself any further and lay there prone, with her feet dangling over the edge. She pressed her cheek into the dirt, feeling her heart knocking against her ribs. The wind dried the sweat on her body to salt. She knew she had to keep moving, she knew she was not yet safe. But knowing all these things as she did, it was almost unbearable when she hauled her legs under her and pushed herself up.

The sun was almost set behind the mountains and the sky was streaked with bands of purple and indigo; they seemed so close she could reach up and touch them. She turned her head, facing across the deeply shadowed trees. She thought she heard water somewhere. Far below, she saw in the valley the twinkling lights of a house – more than one. She tried to guess the distance; eight, maybe nine miles? Vast tracts of deep forest lay between her and them. She would be travelling in pitch dark for the most part. She clenched her bloody hands into fists. First she needed to get down from this damned mountain without breaking a leg, and then she could worry about her next move.

She took a step forward and as she did something punched her hard in the shoulder. She fell onto her knees. She felt pain and heat. She looked down and was shocked to see the tip of an arrowhead jutting through her clavicle, glistening red in the fading light.

Dazed and shocked, Jessie tried to crawl away from the ledge, but her arms would not support her weight. She managed to get her feet under her somehow, but on rising stumbled and pitched into nothing; free falling now, hitting rock and shrubs, gaining speed, flailing. She was launched into air and then came another crushing bone-shattering collision.

Jessie lay still, with one leg bent double beneath her. It took a while before she could breathe again. She tried to move, but could manage only to turn one leg out. She rolled her eyes so that she could watch the horizon line far above her. She waited.

Nothing.

She managed to move her head slowly. The arrow was still protruded through her skin and now her left arm lay twisted at an angle at which it ought not to be. She guessed it was broken, though strangely she felt no pain.

Wasn't that funny?

She managed to roll over a little and lifted her arm the right way around. She tried to sit up, but could not. She wondered if her back was broken.

Water. She heard water running somewhere, loud and fast.

She used her heel to shove her way backwards along the dirt and discovered she had fallen onto a shelf of soil and rock. Below where she rested a river rushed hard down the hill, white foam still visible in the fading light. She turned her head and looked back up to the ridge from which she had fallen.

It took a while, but she made out the shape of a man silhouetted against the skyline. She felt his gaze pass over her as he scanned the area, then return to where she lay, broken in the dirt.

Jessie knew her race was run. Even now the blood pooled beneath her and what was left of her vision became speckled and black around the edges. She took a number of shallow breaths and tried to focus on him, trying to pinpoint where he was, but she could not stay fully conscious.

Far above her a plane went by. She watched twin lines of soft fluffy white trailing behind it in the pale purple sky. She breathed out and breathed in again. She touched the arrowhead with the fingers of her working hand. Sharp. She understood that: sharp, but only a word, nothing more.

For the first time since he had taken her, Jessie felt a sense of calm. She searched the sky above, locating one faint star and then another. It was so beautiful, she thought, majestic in its simplicity. A tear leaked from the corner of her eye, rolled down her cheek and entered her bloodied ear. She heard him land with a thump somewhere nearby.

She felt no fear.

'I am sorry if I offended thee. I am in your hands,' she said, softly as a second tear joined the first. 'I am in your hands now.'

With tremendous effort of will she dug her heel into the ground and pushed her body closer to the ledge. She rested there and thought about Mike. She thought about his smile, about the way the skin crinkled around the corners of his eyes when he laughed. She wished more than anything she had kissed him goodbye that last morning. She wished so badly their last words together had not been wasteful ones.

Twigs snapped nearby. She concentrated on her breathing. She felt the heat in the soil beneath her and tried to not to tremble.

She felt his presence before she saw him. He was there when she rolled her eyes left, standing in the shadows, watching her.

Be strong now, she thought, be strong. Don't beg.

Carefully he approached, his step light. When he drew closer she saw that he had a bow in his hands, with an arrow nocked, ready to fly. He lowered it when he saw how mangled she was.

'You sure worked me good.'

Jessie did not respond. What was there to say to this thing? What special pleading would he enjoy?

'Never had a one like you before, you better believe it.'

Jessie spoke softly, her words barely audible even to her.

He walked to her, bent down on one knee and placed his bow on the ground. He looked at her crooked foot, then raised his hand and pressed his fingers against the arrowhead as Jessie had done moments before, twisting it a little to gauge her reactions.

'You don't feel it, huh? Most likely you're in shock.'

Jessie's lips kept moving.

'You praying?'

He leaned his head closer to hers.

'What're you saying? Hands? What hands?'

Jessie grabbed the front of his jacket with her good hand, swung her good leg up up and hooked it around the small of his back. Before Caleb could stop her, she threw all her weight to one side and pitched both of their bodies over the edge.

Locked together, they fell into darkness, into nothing.

Everett Wilson was glad of the Thermos his wife had given him for his previous birthday. His coffee was almost as hot now as when he had left camp shortly before dawn. At the time, he had figured Lizzie had been a little unimaginative in her choice of gift, not that he had said so. But now, well, he could see the logic of her ways. Not that he would say so. The woman already held the deeds on being right.

He sipped the black liquid and leaned back against the rocks, savouring the morning light as it filtered through the branches and made the creek sparkle and shimmer. He turned his head slightly to watch his son. E.J. was standing waist deep near the opposite bank with his broad back to his father. Everett liked to watch his son fish; hell, he liked any time he had with the boy these days. Boy, he shook his head. No, not any more; E.J. was twenty-five years old. He was no boy. Where did the time go?

'How you doin', son?'

'I know he's in there.' E.J. leaned back and cast his line under the trees overhanging the bank. There was a trout in shadows as big as his arm and by God E.J. was planning to nab that sucker before the day was out.

Everett grinned at his determination. There would be no real shortage of good fish if they were patient. These waters were rich with fish, the woods teeming with wildlife. It was rare indeed to find too many folk around these valleys. It took time to get to the main campsites by road, another day to hike all the way up through the woods to the last official camp, and the best part of the morning to reach the site where Everett and his son had bivouacked the night before.

Still, it was worth the trek, Everett thought, feeling the contented glow of a man at peace with his surroundings. He had four days stretching before him with his son – four days of peace and quiet, of tranquil fishing and hiking. It almost made up for the rest of the year he was stuck behind the counter at the second-hand electrical store he ran with his wife, Lizzie.

Almost.

E.J. drew back his line and cast again.

'He still not biting?'

'Nope,' E.J. said, glancing back over his shoulder, 'he's pretty stubborn.'

'He's plenty full is all.'

'Think I ought to change the lure?'

Everett shook his head. 'Nope, he'll come up for it, you wait and see.'

'If you say so.'

Everett was pleased his son still sought advice from him. He finished his coffee and threw the dregs onto the grass. He packed the Thermos into the rucksack he carried and retied that to the branches nearest where they fished. 'I got to take a leak. Be back in a second.'

E.J. grunted, keeping his gaze on the shadows where he figured the big trout was resting.

Everett crossed the pebbly bank and stepped through the trees. Though still early, the heat was cloying and he could feel the sweat trickle down his spine to the light cotton pants he wore beneath his waders. Gnats buzzed and zinged about his head, but they did not bite. Lizzie had provided him with an excellent repellent, better than the stuff he had used the year before and that was for darned sure. Another thing he would be keeping to himself.

He unhooked the straps and lowered the waders to below his knees. He peed onto a patch of poison ivy and sighed with relief.

He was shaking the last drops off when he caught a glimpse of something in the undergrowth. He leaned forward and squinted, not entirely trusting his eyes. He pulled up his straps and forced his way through the thicket. He stopped and squatted, still trying to make sense of what he was seeing, for before him was a body, small, covered in dirt and leaves and bits of grass.

'E.J.!' he called. 'Come here quick!' He knelt down and carefully removed some of the debris. He heard his son come crashing through the undergrowth.

'*Dad?*'

'Over here, I found a body. I think it's a woman.'

E.J. slammed to a halt next to him. '*What?*'

'A woman's body, look.'

'What's she doing out here?'

'I don't know.'

E.J. reached for her, but Everett caught his hand.

'Maybe we ought not to touch her.'

'Is she dead?'

Everett's head snapped back. He hadn't even checked. He gingerly laid his hands on the woman and rolled her over onto her back.

'She's been shot with an arrow,' Everett said, shocked despite himself. He'd seen many a hunting accident over the years, but nothing like this.

'She's not stiff,' E.J. said.

'She's been in the water I reckon, might have worn off.'

'If she was in the water how'd she come to be up here on the bank?'

335

'Well I don't know.'

Everett moved her arm, pulled a handkerchief from his shirt pocket and used it to clean some of the dirt and mulch from the woman's face. He bent his face and listened. After a moment he jerked upright. 'I think she's still alive.'

Everett took the woman's hand in his and searched for a pulse. Her skin felt cold and clammy. Unbelievably, he felt it; it was faint and unsteady, but a pulse nonetheless. 'She's got a pulse. She's alive.'

E.J. got up and ran back to their bags. He returned moments later carrying the towel they used to dry their equipment and his mobile phone.

'I thought you wasn't going to bring that thing fishing?' Everett said, before he could stop himself.

E.J. took no notice of his disappointed expression. 'Hello? Emergency Services?'

Everett turned his attention back to the woman and folded his fingers over her wrist. 'Hold on honey, you're safe now.'

72

Mike and Ace waited at the cabin all night, taking turns sleeping, but Caleb Switch made no appearance. The following morning when Ace opened his eyes, he saw Mike seated at the workbench, crestfallen.

'He's not coming back.'

'No,' Ace said, stretching, 'it ain't looking likely.'

'We've wasted so much time here.'

'We did what we had to.'

'At least we can let the cops know about this place now.' Mike stood and walked to the busted-out window. He stood for a moment, looking out over the yard. 'How many bodies do you reckon are out there?'

'Hard to say. More than fifteen though.'

'Think their people wonder about them still?'

'I imagine so.'

'I don't understand why anyone would do something like this. Why her? Why Jessie?'

Ace moved an unlit cigarette around his mouth. His tattoos glowed blue in the light of the rising sun. 'You won't ever understand the kind of person, Mike, and you ought to be glad about that.'

Mike turned to look as his brother. He looked scared and angry and tormented. 'You saying you understand him?'

'Him? No. But I've known men like him; men who can kill and maim as easy as breathe, men who don't hold with mercy. They don't even understand the concept.'

'Did you learn this when you were inside?'

Ace shrugged. 'Inside, outside – there's no wall that can hold evil.'

'There's got to be some reason.'

'There probably is, but not one we're gonna know. These people ain't like us, his own sister said the same and she–'

Captain raised his head and cocked it.

Ace stopped talking and pressed his finger to his lips.

Captain stood and tilted his head this way and that. His tail started to twitch. After a moment, he threw back his head and released a long mournful howl. Mike stared at him, feeling the hairs rising on his arms at the sound.

'What the hell is he doing?'

Ace stood and walked to the broken window, he looked out and cocked his own head.

'Sirens,' he said.

'Huh?'

'Sirens.'

'I don't hear nothing.'

'Me neither, but got to be, that's what sets him off.'

Mike's shoulder slumped. 'Let's go, we need to find the nearest town and put in a report on this place.'

'You sure you want to do that?'

'Yeah.'

'Once the cops are involved that's it, this place will be done. This link to him will be cut.'

'Don't you get it, Ace?' Mike asked, his voice steeped in misery.

'What?'

'It's already done. She's gone.'

338

Mike climbed out through the window and walked around back to where they had hidden the truck from view.

Ace looked around the silent room, with Captain awaiting his instructions. He gathered his weapon and one or two items that did not belong to him and followed after his younger brother.

They drove back down the mountain in silence. The nearest town was Rhee, so Ace aimed the truck in that direction, his foot to the floor most of the way.

Outside the police station, Ace sat in the truck with the engine running, watching the comings and going through the door.

'Well, might as well be done what needs to be done.'

'Them other people he buried. They got family somewhere, people wondering where they are and what happened to them. They deserve an answer. They deserve peace of mind.'

Ace nodded and turned his head to watch the street.

'You coming in?'

'No, I never did like this kind of place.'

Mike climbed out. He hitched his jeans up on his waist and climbed the steps to the station like the condemned climbing the steps of the gallows.

Ace turned on the radio and listened to a local station playing some god-awful crap. He did not change the station; for some reason the music seemed fitting. He drank a lukewarm coke and let his arm dangle from the window thinking of Jessie and the man he now had to try to find. If Mike was right and was Jessie gone, Ace swore a silent pledge that he would do everything in his power to make that wrong right again.

He drained the last of his coke as Mike came flying through the door, his face wild. He ran towards the truck so fast he slammed against it with his hip. Ace jerked upright.

'What is it?'

'There was a woman found earlier this morning, up in the woods! They took her to the county hospital.'

'Alive?'

'I think so.'

'Jessie?'

'I don't know, she'd no ID on her, but initial reports reckon she's in her thirties.'

'Where's this hospital?'

'Next town over.'

'Well, get in.'

A large woman in a police uniform came out onto the steps.

'Mr Conway? Mr Conway sir, I'm going to need you to come back here and give a proper statement. Sir?'

Mike jumped into the passenger seat.

'*Mr Conway!*' the officer called.

'Ma'am, I'll be at the hospital,' Mike yelled out of the window. 'You send someone that way and I'll write out and sign any damn thing you like!' He turned to Ace. 'What the hell are you waiting for? Drive. *Drive!*'

Ace slammed the truck into reverse, braked, spun the wheel and tore out of there, leaving a cloud of dust in his wake.

At first the pain was intense and shocking. She felt movements, or thought she did but could not be 100 per cent sure. Only the pain was real, but after a while even that dulled.

Jessie floated, swimming in and out of the world. She had many dreams and heard voices, some close, others distant and fading. She thought she heard her own name being called, but when she tried to locate the caller she drifted through space and time until she was more lost than before.

Pain entered and left as if on a whim. Between the jolts she saw faces, people she knew, talking over her. She saw her parents in the distance, standing hip to hip under a chestnut tree, sunlight dazzling behind them. She walked towards them but never gained an inch and then they too began to shimmer and fade.

'I want to come with you,' she said, beginning to cry softly. 'I'm here, I'm here.'

When Jessie opened her eyes Mike was the first person she saw. He was seated ramrod straight by a window, staring out into space. Her tongue was so swollen it scrapped against her teeth when she tried to say his name. She swallowed painfully and tried again.

'Mike.'

She had barely whispered it, but he turned to her and broke into a smile. He looked exhausted and gaunt. The skin seemed to hang from his cheekbones like felt.

'Hello there.'

She tried to make sense of her thoughts; they jumbled about too freely to catch. Finally she managed to snag one.

'You're here.'

'Yep,' Mike said. 'I'm here. I am right here and I am going nowhere.'

She tried to understand how this was possible. But thinking made her head hurt and after a while she drifted back to sleep again.

The next time she woke she was a little more lucid. Mike was still there.

'Hey lady,' he said.

She began to cry and could not stop. She felt Mike's hands on her forehead.

'It's okay, it's okay.'

'I ... how are you here?'

'We were here when you were found, next town over. Ace figured out who had you.'

Jessie furrowed her brow. The faint sound she thought she heard when she opened her eyes first returned.

'You were found in the woods, by a river. Don't you remember any of it?'

'I ... remember climbing. There was a man ... he had a beard.'

'His name is Caleb Switch.'

She digested this news, or tried to do so. Knowing what he was called made little or no impact. So he had a name. What did that change? She wondered why she felt so light headed. Before she could figure it out she was gone again.

She woke up a while later hearing muffled voices. Something told her to keep still. She listened. She identified Mike's voice even through he was speaking very softly. His tone, however, was furious.

'I already told you I don't know where he is, I *already* told you. He drove off out of here and didn't tell me where he was going.'

'He's a witness. He can't just drive off when it suits him.'

'He's gone, that's it.'

She couldn't make out the next part of the conversation, then she heard a male voice she didn't recognise say, 'You need to make a formal statement, and to do that you've got to go back to the station…'

'I am going nowhere. You hear me?'

'Sir—'

'Keep your voice down.'

More mumbling, fierce and protracted, then … 'I don't give a shit. If it weren't for Ace, they wouldn't even know where to start looking. He has enough information to find this guy if he'd get off his ass and look.'

'She can give us an eye-witness description.'

'Are you deaf? Don't you think she's been through enough?'

Jessie shifted and managed to raise her head. Mike and a man in uniform were standing at the door to her room.

'Mike?'

Mike turned in her direction. 'Jessie?'

'Please … let him in.'

'You don't have to talk to anyone. I told them everything I know about where you were held.' Mike came to her and took her hand in his. At his touch Jessie began to weep. She did not know why, only that she could not stop.

'I will not let anything happen to you,' Mike said, speaking with such fierceness his voice broke. 'I promise you.'

Jessie felt his hand tighten on hers. She opened her eyes again, her vision blurred from tears. 'Get the Sheriff.'

'Sweetheart, all of that can wait.'

'You don't understand.'

'What?'

'If he's out there, I'm not safe. None of us are.'

74

Ace left the hospital car park and used the directions given to him by a shaken Everett Wilson, whom he had spoken with in the waiting room of the hospital. He drove directly to the camping ground where the Wilsons had stayed on their fishing trip.

He unloaded Captain from the back of the truck and filled a small rucksack with water and provisions. He collected his rifle from the rack and set off, following the river upstream.

He hiked fast and efficiently, making sure to keep his ears and eyes open for any sign of activity. By the time he reached where Everett and his son had been fishing, it was late afternoon and the river looked silver in the light. He allowed Captain to drink river water and rest a little while he scouted the banks near where Jessie was found and he thought about how this expedition was likely to end.

Satisfied with his direction, he tied a long line to Captain. He opened the rucksack and removed the item of clothing he had taken from Caleb Switch's cabin and held it out for Captain to scent. 'Seek,' he said.

It took less time than he had expected. At exactly five past four Captain signed and Ace located a badly wounded man dragging his broken body behind him through the undergrowth about two miles east of the river.

The crawling man stopped moving when Captain barked behind him. He leaned on his elbows and rolled over onto his side.

Ace reined Captain back and stood staring at the man. His face was black and blue, with scratches all over. One of his eyes was bloodied and torn, sightless in a broken socket.

'You Caleb Switch?' Ace asked, sticking a cigarette into his mouth and lighting it.

The man hissed air through his cracked lips.

'You Switch or ain't you?'

'How did you find me?'

'Captain here never misses.'

'A *dog*.' Caleb managed to inject as much venom into two words as brevity would allow.

'Yeah,' said Ace, 'a dog.'

Caleb coughed, turned his head and stared at the sky through the canopy of leaves. 'I don't care for dogs.'

'I don't care for sickos.'

'That what you think I am?'

'Don't matter what I think.'

'So what now,' he rolled his eye in Ace's direction. 'You going to bring me in, dogman?'

Ace walked away from him a safe distance and tied Captain to the base of a tree. When he returned he lifted his rifle and pointed it at the broken man.

'You goin' to shoot an unarmed man?' Caleb asked. He had a tinge of incredulity to his voice, but no fear, Ace noticed, nothing remotely like fear. He probably didn't even know what fear was. Ace knew then, without a shadow of a doubt, what he was dealing with.

'Seems the humane thing to do,' Ace said, and fired.

Jessie drank a cup of coffee and watched her husband work through the window of the kitchen. He was bare of chest and the sheen of sweat on his skin emphasised his muscles as he worked, repairing the roof of the barn that had been damaged by high winds during a sudden summer storm. She thought of how lucky it was that she could be here at this moment, present. In small private moments like this she marvelled at the grace she had been given.

It had been a tough few months for her as she recovered from her ordeal. Her arm, finally out of the cast, was still sore and weak and ached when she overdid it. Some nights she had nightmares so bad she shook until her teeth rattled. Yet somehow, despite her ordeal, or maybe because of it, she had found an inner peace again, a little place she could retreat to and take solace in being alive.

Caleb Switch had not been found. At first, this news had terrified her and she feared him coming to finish the job he had started. That was until Ace had come early to the hospital for a visit one day and told her that she was to no longer worry about such a possibility.

'I don't understand,' Jessie had replied.

'He won't be troubling you.'

'Have they found him?'

'No, and they most likely won't.'

She searched his thin face. The realisation of what he was telling her was a little time coming but when it did she began to cry; great wracking sobs that choked her.

'Oh Ace, no.'

'It's done.'

Ace made no move to comfort her. He sat with his head bowed, his hands dangling between his legs.

When she finally got a hold of herself he said, 'I know everything is on you now. You decide to tell the police, I want you to know that I'm okay with that.'

Jessie looked at his bowed head. 'Ace look at me.'

He lifted his head.

'I had this moment once,' Jessie paused, trying to find her voice, trying to find a way to convey to him her emotional state. 'A long time ago I had a chance to rid this world of a man who … who was like this man you found. I had a choice and I chose the one I chose. I'm not sorry, I wasn't then and I'm not sorry now.'

Ace stared at her, saying nothing.

'I wanted him to die, Ace.'

'It ain't nobody's business what you wanted.'

Jessie stared at him, feeling fresh tears prickling behind her eyes.

'Truth of it is,' Ace continued, 'not every piece of shit deserves to live.'

'You don't believe that.'

He smiled then, an unusual rare thing for Ace.

'Ain't nobody's business what I *believe* neither.'

That night, Jessie wrapped her good arm around Mike's waist and slid over onto his body in the dark. Without either of them saying a word, they made love and afterwards lay naked, holding each other tight in the darkness.

'I thought I had lost you,' Mike said.

'I think I was lost.'

'Are you home now?'

'I'm home,' Jessie said, laying her head on his shoulder, 'I'm home.'

ACKNOWLEDGEMENTS

Well now, this could take a while. Thank you to my readers; without you the whole writing malarkey would seem rather pointless. I appreciate your mails and chats throughout the year and it is always illuminating. Thank you to my friends who keep me sane while I ponder, scribble and wax lyrical, especially Anna, Antonia, Bryan, Billy, Ciara C., Corrina, Jennie, Madeleine, Megan, Sam, Sarah and Tara, Sinéad G.; you guys rock and I'd be a bit lost without you. Thank you to Crossfit Ireland for keeping me fit all year; sitting at a computer all day does not lend itself to a lithe physique, believe me. Thank you also to Declan Burke for keeping Irish crime fiction vibrant with Crime Always Pays (crimealwayspays.blogspot.com).

A huge thank you to Tana French for taking the time to read this novel when it was in poorly printed form. You're a gem, lady. I owe an enormous debt of gratitude to Kriss Kuss, who kindly let me crash at LYH and who drove through a storm with only a rat on her shoulder and German technology to deliver us safely. Thank you to Dave Kriebel for taking the time to explain various weapons to me in a calm and patient manner. A massive thank you to Mr Mike Treadway and his good lady wife for graciously taking the time to explain stickbows and how to make them, and for teaching me to shoot a foam deer in a single afternoon. Mike is a master craftsman and the visit to his workplace in North Carolina is something I will remember forever.

Thanks also to Maeve and Stephanie of Saltwater Publishing, to John and all at Gill & Macmillan, to David Rudnick for his artistic genius and the quite brilliant Annie Atkins for her photography. Thanks as always to my agent Faith O'Grady for putting up with me.

And, as always, thank you and much love to my family, to Terry and Tim, and to Jordan. There is only one last person to thank and that's my husband, Andrew. Without his unwavering support this book might never have seen the light of day. I know no finer person.

Arlene Hunt
August 2011